The Persolus Race

Voyages into the Unknown

Alex O'Neill
with
M.M. Dixon

Cover art courtesy: Amasja Kooljen
Cover text: C. C. Forshee & Alex O'Neill
Editors: M. M. Dixon, George O'Neill

Find out more about this anthology at **thepersolusrace.com**

ISBN: 9781737468325 (Print)
9781737468332 (Ebook)

Contents

Introduction

Around the time my first book, *The Persolus Race: Volume One*, was published, in September 2021, the world began to return to normal following the COVID-19 crisis. While in many ways that was fantastic news, it also meant I no longer had the time to write in the way that I would have liked, and work on Volume Two fizzled out.

Despite this, I still had a few ideas for stories set in the Persolus Race universe floating around in my head and in notebooks. In a conversation with M. M. Dixon in April 2022, I explained that I might try to release one smaller Persolus Race anthology entirely made of my own work. She suggested I try to find a common theme within all these stories to tie it together, and hence the title *Voyages into the Unknown* was born. Three and a half years later, here we are: Six short stories with connecting themes, all set in the Persolus Race universe.

Each story originated from a slightly different place. *The Woman who climbed Olympus Mons* came late the anthology, only being added just before release. It is a story entirely of my own creation, as I wanted to combine my two passions of science-fiction, and adventure sports, into one story. Each story within the anthology is placed due to its chronological order, *The Woman who Climbed Olympus Mons* coming first.

The Man in the Mountain is a drastic re-write of a story of the same name which appeared in *Volume One,* based on a time-travel concept initially suggested by my father, George O'Neill. With that story, I had felt that I rushed the time working on it to manage the project, and that there was far more 'story' to be told with it, introducing new characters and expanding existing plotlines to make it more of a science-fiction romance. The new version of *The Man in the Mountain* is nearly twice the length of its *Volume One* counterpart, a very different story now.

Omniscience is the original idea of Ted Marois, a writer who was involved in *Volume One* during the early stages but had to pull out of the project due to personal reasons. His story, *Malevolence*, later retitled to *Omniscience*, was a dark science-fiction horror story that I felt fit the Persolus Race universe perfectly. It follows the story of a team of scientists testing out a new model of FTL engine on what should be a routine voyage. I finished the story with his permission, releasing it as a booklet in 2023, which I have sold at comic conventions. The version of *Omniscience* that appears in this book is again extended with a different ending to before.

Nomads of the Light was an idea put forward by M. M. Dixon, who had worked on *Volume One* with me. It followed the story of a downed ship, stuck on a planet where the survivors could only live at dusk and pre-dawn due to the extreme temperature swings on the planet. We agreed to tell it using only diary entries written by the main two survivors, collaborating over video calls to ensure that the entirety of the story was told across the two narrative viewpoints.

Timezones is another story in this anthology that is entirely mine. It came from a vision of a town where the rich and self-important in the future could live in a different time period as their holiday. I envisaged a Roman encampment, next to a Viking one, next to a Tudor-era town with houses made of wattle and daub. Initially, the story felt like a potential Doctor Who episode, but I eventually found a narrative around the idea with a set of characters that could fit the Persolus Race universe.

The final story, *The Great Gamble*, is also an original of mine. I had been toying with the idea of a 'great space epic' where several deep-space adventurers set out to try and find aliens in a universe where in theory there were none before I even had the full outline of *Volume One*. That would be a full-length novel of its own, and I started to think about the central characters, themes, and plot to that novel. However, I did start to think that it would be useful to introduce the central characters of that novel in a short story, perhaps covering how they procured their ship and crew for that adventure. And that was how *The Great Gamble* was born.

When considering *Volume Two*, I thought that writing my own anthology would be easier than managing and co-writing one with other people. *Volume One* took sixteen months to finish, whilst this book took forty-two months. Let the numbers tell you which project was easier.

In summary, *Voyages into the Unknown* represents a collection of six stories, all loosely tied together by theme.

I hope you enjoy them,
Alex O'Neill

Prologue: We are Alone

By Alex O'Neill

In 1969, the human race, found on Earth, sent a man to the moon.

In 2029, they landed on Mars.

In 2036, they built great geoengineering projects to slow the effects of climate change, allowing the economy and, therefore, scientific research to grow without further worry.

In 2040, the Integrated Space Agency, or ISA, was created by the space agencies of countries within the United Nations.

The human race advanced and reached into the stars, developing the first hyperspeed engine. Earth's best scientists set about understanding atmospheric science, botany, and soils. They put together terraforming engines, known as Edens.

By the end of the 26th century, most of the Milky Way had been explored, and many planets in nearby systems had been terraformed for humans. Despite hopes, no alien life had been found.

In 2949, the human race developed its first faster-than-light (FTL) speed engine.

By 3462, the human race had travelled to the edge of the Virgo Supercluster.

They did not stop there. The human race carried on expanding, landing on planets, using up their resources—water, fuel, and air— to power their ships; to power their Edens; to run experiments.

In 3999, the ISA made an announcement. Despite the expansion, despite searches, despite attempts to make contact, no intelligent life had been found anywhere within the Virgo Supercluster.

The human race must face the very real possibility that they are alone in the universe.

The Woman Who Climbed Olympus Mons

By Alex O'Neill

Chapter One

24th June 2085

Renea Bessant reached for the ledge. Her rope was tight, pulling between in the gap to the right of her head, down in front of body, avoiding chafing due to the space suit. She raised her head to look up at the ledge above, where Jacques stood, setting a new quickdraw into the soft red stone. She took a deep breath, and looked down, initially at the three-mile immediate drop below the cliff that they were climbing. A lifetime of climbing and mountaineering at an elite level still did not prepare her or that sight; thousands of meters of sheer cliff almost straight down, like a great red wall littered with nooks and crannies. They could just about make out the distant dim lights of huge camera crews far below like the blinking of impossibly small stars to mirror those above them. Around them hummed teams of drones and self-driving helicopters, capturing every moment of the team's ascent, and cutting through the still Martian air.

Renea then focused in on the third member of their climbing party, Adher, who moved gracefully up below them, moving his hands and feet softly and swiftly from hold to hold. Adher, wearing a space suit like the other two of them, carried most of their equipment, and was their most experienced medic. A guide by trade, Adher had led Renea on her first climb in 2069 when she had summited Toubkal in Morocco. Her two companions were near opposites: Adher's tall height was a stark contrast to his quiet persona, whilst Jac resembled a small dog in his stature and noisiness. Both were very strong climbers, and their familiar presence reassured her.

Renea paused for a moment; this next move was tricky. Her right hand was high, her left low, and to move up, she switched feet nimbly despite the size of the boots she had to wear. She then put her left hand up to a clear hold, and her feet followed closely behind, moving her person up towards the quickdraw that Jac had set.

"Jac to Renea, come in," The distorted voice came from a small comm link inside her helmet.

"Receiving," she replied, as she steadied herself across both of her feet.

"We have a small ledge area within sight, I recommend we stop here." he stated.

"Got it,." Renea replied, and began to haul herself up, and Adher following close behind.

As they settled down onto the ledge, Renea put her arm around the back of her spacesuit, allowing the water tank to filter through a tube to her the mouthpiece. As Adher arrived on the ledge, she leaned over and pressed his water tank button too, allowing him to take a drink.

After a moment, Adher took a seat next Jac, who was already sat down, back up against the red rock wall. Renea remained standing.

"I'm thinking about the schematics" Jac stated as Adher started to drink the protein feed that was next to his water tank "there should be no ledge at this point. We must be moving slower than originally planned."

Renea paused for a moment.

"We're not," Renea said, "We made a turn at the base of that overhang, about two hundred meters down, we went left, not right."

"You knew this?" Jac asked "You did not say."

"It does not matter" Renea stated, shaking her head "We go straight up this next cliff, arrive at another ledge that takes us right and then it ascends towards the top of the cliff face. It's potentially gentler than our original route."

"Are you sure? How is it possible?" Jac asked.

"I memorised the entire mountain, not just this route." Renea responded, "It's useful to be safe".

"That is fantastic" Jac said "and terrifying. Is there nothing you cannot do?"

Renea laughed aloud at this question, but then the conversation went quiet when she could not find anything to follow up.

"What are our bets for the competition?" Jac asked.

"Well" Renea stated "I am certain that the British team will have gone on their original route. They are a larger team. I did not speak to them about it, as you can imagine. The Nepalese team's medic, Mingma, spoke to me briefly. They have maps built into their helmets they are using at each stopping point. A little old school, but it worked for them on Ascraeus Mons last year."

Jac shuddered at the mention of this event. The professional Nepalese team who they were now up against them had crossed the Tharsis Montes peaks in an incredible time, leaving all the European and American teams for dust. Although neither Renea nor Jac had been mentally at their best during that time, it certainly put both them and the British team on the back foot straight out of the gate, even if they had higher profile climbers.

After a few more minutes of rest, with Adher saying almost nothing, Renea moved over to where he was sat, and chose to tap his foot with her own.

"Time to go." Renea said

"Do we have to," Adher responded, his head drooped forward a little "I would like longer."

"I'm sorry," Renea responded, "We have no choice." She gave Adher a hand up, and he dusted himself down – while he had been drinking a smoothie, in his head clearly, he imagined something nicer, some Makouda from home perhaps. *What she would give herself for some pastries, maybe some fries, right now. A nice large glass of red wine, or even a beer. But for now, they had the protein smoothies, and water. That would have to do.*

Renea grimaced, and pulled herself up onto the wall, her carabiner now clipped into the rope. She began to ascend, and placed a quickdraw into the rock, only about three metres up, allowing it run through. Once her feet were above that quickdraw, she called out "One," and looked down to see Jac started to ascend too. He made even the most difficult movements in their thick padded spacesuits look smooth. *With Mars only having around forty percent of Earth's gravity, their movements felt swifter, and less difficult. There was no chance on Earth any team could manage a five-mile cliff face.*

Then, when she had ascended some more, she placed in a second quickdraw and called out "two", giving Adher the initiative to start climbing too, more of a natural trekker than a climber, he made more movements per section than either her or Jac.

The continued on up the wall, in a section that Renea hoped would be over quickly, so that they could rest and start the trek section of the ascension soon.

Ten Hours earlier

"For many years, there has been serious contention about the land usage of Mars' neutral zone, with a push towards an Antarctic Treaty-style peace agreement which eventually was published in 2075 as 'The Olympus Accord'. This accord bans the use of drones, shuttles, or aircraft in certain contested areas to prevent open warfare between Earth-based factions. However, budding climbing countries have found a loophole: Olympus Mons is considered neutral territory, but the first nation to plant a flag at the peak gets political prestige or territorial rights to a key resource." The newsreader explained, individuals in spacesuits jostling about all around him, reporters and camera staff everywhere that could be seen, the reddish dusty ground being turned up by officials, press, climbers and observers jostling around in the background.

"And here we are, what we are seeing now will be talked about for hundreds of years. Many have called this climb 'impossible', with Olympus Mons garnering the nickname 'The Impossible Mountain'. That isn't the case for the leader of the French climbing team out on Olympus Mons over the next few days. If you don't know the name of Renea Bessant by now, then maybe you've been living on a different planet. First coming to the world's attention in the 2078 youth world speed climbing trials, she has been aptly named the 'French Superwoman'. With her are her long-time climbing partner and friend Jac Greene, and their support man, Adher Akhannouch, originally a mountain guide from the Atlas Mountains. The smallest of the three teams going out this weekend, we will be speaking to them later." he continued.

The team of five British climbers could be still seen and a tall lean man with bleach-blonde hair, their leader, could be made out amongst them. The reporter made their way over to him.

"Second of all, the British team and their leader Tom Libretti. Libretti is a serious rising star in the world of speed ascents, breaking the speed record on K2 just last year. A little bit of a potential dark horse in this competition, this is his first extra-terrestrial climb. We're able to join him now."

As the reporter headed over, Tom Libretti waved at him. As the reporter joined in next to the tall climber, Tom placed a hand on his shoulder.

"So, Tom, how are you feeling?"

"Oh I'm a little nervous, I suppose, I'm only human." Tom replied, "But we've got a good team and an excellent understanding of the route. You know, we've had the training, we've got the support back home, I just think we're all looking forward to the win."

"And what about the competition?"

"Oh, I don't think it's going to be easy; we're going to have to move fast."

"Anyone in particular to look out for?" the reporter asked.

"I think the Nepalese team are strong. They set the speed record on Tharsis Montes and that was impressive, I must admit. David is a well-respected leader in the Sherpa community, and I think his team are going to follow him up this mountain very efficiently."

"And what do you think this win would mean for your country?"

"I mean, it could mean a lot, but it's not up to me how things change. I'm just glad we've had the funding and support to do this climb."

"I was wondering if you wanted to comment on the history between yourself and Renea Bessant?"

If the question phased Tom, he did not show it. "Well, Renea's a very strong climber herself. Technically speaking, she's the most impressive female climber on the planet."

"So you're not going to address the rivalry between you and her over the last ten years?" the reporter pushed.

"Listen" Tom responded, smiling slightly and retracting his hand from the reporter's shoulder "She's very competent, yes. Has she got what it takes mentally? I don't know. All I can say is I'm going to do what I do best with my team, and let the results speak for themselves."

***

The reporter moved on from Tom Libretti and his team, and made his way over to the Nepalese team. Their team leader, David Sherpa, was the opposite of Tom in almost every way; short, with a thick handlebar moustache, finely combed black hair, with piercing dark green eyes. He looked more like a shop owner than he did one of the finest climbers in the world. The reporter cosied up to him in the same way he had with Tom, but David kept his distance, standing almost two foot away from the reporter.

"So, David, how are you feeling?"

"Oh, good man." David Sherpa responded it stilted English.

"After the time set on Tharsis Montes, you must be feeling confident. Do you think that good luck is blowing in your direction?" the reporter asked.

"It's not about luck brother, we work hardest, we win." David responded. The reporter looked at David as if he was to say something else, but he just smiled at the camera.

"Well," the reporter said after a few seconds had best, now turning back to the camera in front of them "A man of confidence, and seemingly few words, David Sherpa. Thank you."

"Thank you, brother." David responded swiftly.

With that, the reporter turned back to the camera fully, and he began to walk; the camera following him away from the Nepalese team.

"Well," he stated, his face beaming with excitement "That was the last time we speak directly to our climbers before the competition starts. From there, coverage switches over to our extensive drone network will take over control of your viewing experience. Now, you might not be able to tell at home, but I am not underselling it when I say that the atmosphere here is electric". As the reporter spoke, the camera he was speaking to panned out, cutting over the enormous crowd that had gathered in the breathable dome around the base of the huge mountain. A sea of dots going back for hundreds of meters, the event having gathered anyone who could afford to make the trip. Slowly, the camera swung back round the panoramic view of the crowd, and back to the reporter, the enormous shape of Olympus Mons looming in the near distance behind him.

"So" the reporter continued "The start of this massive event is only minutes away. Soon, our climbers will leave the confines of this breathable habitation zone, and using their spacesuits and oxygen packs to head upwards out of Mars' thin atmosphere and towards the summit. We all appreciate that the gravity on Mars is only about a third of that on Earth, this is still going to require two full days of ascent. We at International Western Sports wish them all the very best of luck!"

As she chose to move away from the crowds, Renea felt the atmosphere of energy around them become colder as Jac moved in next to her, already dressed in his spacesuit.

"Time to move boss" he said "the other teams are in their positions. We are falling behind already."

"I know" Renea responded. But her actions said otherwise – she remained still, facing towards the crowds and the reporter in the distance "Something feels off, I'm not sure why."

"Renea" Jac said as Adheer walked past, now completely in his spacesuit too "Stop fighting your destiny. Get on the rock and prove yourself."

Renea took a deep breath, and turned towards the mountain, pulling up the zips on the spacesuit. She began to put one foot in front of the other towards Olympus Mons, her body sweating already, but due to nerves, not the strain of the climb.

Present time

The French climbing team followed the ridge up to their left, continuing to ascend upwards in a diagonal line up the mountain's southern face. Renea led, followed by Jac, and Adher took the rear. As they walked up the ridge, it began to widen out, and at the same time it became gentler. Renea's hope was swiftly quashed when she felt the wind around them begin to pick up. Renea knew that deep down, it was not the wind which would damage their suits, but the red dust – and that they would have to take shelter as quickly as possible so that their suits would remain intact.

She knew there was somewhere where they could took into the rock, to get some shelter, but it was still thirty metres above their position. A sudden gust smacked her into the rock, and then they head a crash – Jac and Renea turned to see Adher down on all fours.

"Quick!" Renea claimed, "We need to move to higher ground!" and turned, putting one foot in front of the other. Whilst moving as cleanly and quickly as she could, she still felt cumbersome. She was, of course, wearing a large space suit with three tanks attached to it, for water, air and nutrients. Still, she felt her body receive the adrenaline it needed for her legs to start pushing her up the mountain, her feet tapping ever so efficiently on the rock floor as she headed up the ridge, and found herself in the alcove she had hoped to stop at. The wind howled round the bowl of her helmet, and in her excitement, she tripped, one foot over the other, and fell against the cliff wall.

Luckily, her hands were like lightning, coming out to catch herself. As soon as she readied herself, Jac joined her. They both turned together, and looked down the ridge they had walked up – and in the distance, behind the sea of misty red dust filling the air from the wind they saw the shape of Adher get slightly larger. He lumbered up the path, carrying the lion's share of their kit, eventually joining them in the alcove, almost as if he didn't notice the howling winds around them.

"This weather," he stated, making eye contact with both of them "Is awful," and despite the tension of their situation, Jac and Renea found themselves laughing. "It is just terrible." Adher continued, oblivious to how humorous the other two found his deadpan delivery. They spread their arms out, the three of them huddling like spacesuit-donning penguins, hiding from the harsh winds of the planet Mars until the worst of the storm had passed.

***

It was nearly an hour later when Renea could assuredly say that the worst of the storm was behind them. Slowly, she stepped out from the alcove where they had sheltered, putting her left foot out, then her right. Jac and Adher followed suit, their space shoes crunching on the well-rested Martian dust.

Gaining speed again, they began to head up towards the ledge Renea had seen on the map, following the tight ridge walkway. When they arrived, the ledge was wider than she had imagined, but this was perhaps because she had become used to such a thin and narrow walkway as the one, they had been walking on for hours.

As soon as she stepped out onto the ledge, Renea felt her body relax, crumpling beneath her body, and she sat swiftly, cross-legged on the spot. Soon, Jac joined her.

"I am exhausted." he stated, and Renea did not initially respond.

"I said I am exhausted." he repeated, folding to the floor.

"I heard you" Renea responded "We cannot stay here for long though"

Jac instantly moved to point a finger in Renea's shoulder "You are moving too fast, pushing us too hard. We need to slow down."

"We are moving as fast we need to Jac."

"Too fast."

"That isn't your call to make." Renea stated, and took a drink from her protein pack.

"Look at me! We are not superhuman, like you!" Jac stated

"I'm not…superhuman."

"Yes, you are."

Before Renea could respond, they were joined by Adher lumbering up onto the ledge behind them. Renea and Jac both turned to look at his companion, expecting to him to quickly rest as they did, but instead his vision was drawn elsewhere.

"The British are here" he stated. And in the unison, the other two turned to look where Adher was looking, and true enough, at the other side of the ledge stood the outlines of five men, some thirty metres away on the other side of the ledge.

"Good evening." said Tom Libretti.

***

Tom stepped forward, his tall and athletic build noticeable even under the pudgy orange British spacesuits.

"It is an odd coincidence to see you here, Renea." he stated, as the French woman started to sit up onto one knee and one foot from her cross-legged position.

"It's almost as if we're climbing the same mountain." she said in response. As Tom approached them, she stood up swiftly, and Jac did the same.

"You know, I'm glad you're here," Tom stated, "You make me feel as if this is all…meant to be."

"It is meant to be" Renea stated, trying her hardest to keep her composure "You are here to see me win, Tom"

"You know," Tom stated, as he continued to approach, now only about five metres away from the pair of them "I don't believe you."

"You cannot believe me if you want, that is up to you." she responded.

"You're a cheat," Tom growled, and they all felt the atmosphere suddenly switch "You let your friend die, Renea, and what's worst is that the damned IFSC let you keep climbing. But I know you, and how low you will stoop. When this climb is over, the whole world will see you for who you really are."

Renea moved towards him quickly, the two of them even in height, allowing them to easily look each other in the eyes.

"You should be very careful Tom," she stated, "If I'm as bad as you say, why antagonise me?"

"Hold on," Jac replied, and suddenly the short, lean Frenchman was between them, his hand on Renea's chest "Let's not be unprofessional here."

"No," Tom stated loudly "Listen to your lackey. You've only got to where you need to be, to where you are, because you've lied, or cheated, or murdered someone. I need you to know that. You'd be nothing, if you played fair."

Renea bristled at that, and tried to move towards Tom, but Jac kept him, holding her back. *Jac is small but strong.*

Tom turned away slightly, and smiled "You ought to rest soon. It is dark, and we both have half a mile of climb to the top of that cliff."

"You too." Renea responded, and Tom finished his turn, walking away. He rejoined his team as Jac and Renea watched, and then the five men the British team was comprised of disappeared around the corner, and out of sight.

"Dickheads." Renea growled, her body now vibrating with anger.

"Stop," Jac stated, moving his hand up to her shoulder "That was nothing. That was a pointless ruse. Tom Libretti is just insecure. He cannot admit we have a better team with stronger climbers. He is just saying words."

Jac was speaking sense, but Renea did not want to hear it.

"No," she responded, "he will use any opportunity in front of him to hurt us."

"Exactly," Jac stated "Benoit would not want you to listen to him".

"But I know Tom spoke the truth." Renea said.

"He did not." Jac stated.

"He was right about one thing," Adher cut in "It is time to rest. We have a big climb in the morning. We should rest here. It is large enough for tents."

Renea and Jac turned to each other, and then back to Adher.

"You're right," Renea stated firmly "We should rest. Keep pushing up the cliff in the morning, about half a mile before it flattens out and we start the trek. Tomorrow is a long day. We best be fresh for it." Slowly Jac pulled the bivvy bags they had brought with them out of Adher's backpack, and set them out.

Adher laid down on the ground, settling into his bivvy bag, and shutting his eyes, and drifting off to sleep. Renea and Jac entered their bivvy bags, turning to face one another. At first, Jac, laid out his hand in front of him. Renea took it in hers. They always did this on expeditions. Renea put her leg over his body, and in turn Jac placed his outside leg in between both of hers. They could not cuddle given the circumstances, but they did their best to press the glass sections of their helmets up against each other's. Eventually the two of them, almost half-asleep, let go of each other's hands, and held each other's shoulders in a hug. They held each other for some time, listening to the howling winds of the Mars mid-atmosphere, pushing and pulling bowls of red dust all around them. Renea was the first to fall asleep. Jac held on for a moment longer, taking in the irregularity of his situation, before he too fell asleep, exhausted from their climb.

Chapter Two

25th June 2085

The ropes were out. With the additional help of the ropes they were making good speed, the weaker Mars gravity allowing them to cover ground at a speed that they could only dream of on a large Earth cliff.

Adher moved to his left, to avoid a great big overhang. He followed the line set by the other two. The wind had died down at this point, although they were climbing in the dark once again, the days and nights being a little longer than on Earth. Above him, he could see the outlines of Jac and Renea, the rope running through his harness gently but suddenly angling in different directions above him. As he looked up, a small portion of rock came sailing past his face, and down towards the cliff bottom far below him.

"Sorry!" he heard Jac yell.

Slightly disgruntled, Adher continued to climb, resting when he found a suitable spot with good size hand holds. He took a moment to take in his surroundings; the great sandstorm from the previous evening had passed, and he could now begin to pick out pricks of light so many miles below, the dark night sky turning to a middle grey. The wind continued, but it was now gentle, giving a whistle past his helmet. He turned back to the great red slap in front of him, and continued to ascend, moving hand, then hand, then foot, then foot.

He looked up and above him; he could see Jac and Renea holding fast, Jac leading and Renea following suite not far behind.

Slowly Adher began to ascend again. He found that while he was not a natural climber, it was mostly a thinking game. He never felt the need to overthink anything, so he just 'did' climbing, and it seemed to work out well. After he moved his feet and his hands up, he came across one of the carabiners. As he passed above it, he pressed a button to side of it, releasing it from the rock face, and he tucked it into his pack. He began to brace himself for difficult climbing; above him he could see that the cliff face begin to overhang on itself.

Up above, Jac and Renea moved swiftly, Jac placing a carabiner in and then moving up past it like a spider, his movements very efficient, the Moroccan man barely showing any fatigue. He looked down at Renea, only a moment behind. Like a mimic, she followed his movements, raising right arm then left, pivoting on one foot, stepping and then standing up fully and continuing to move. He set another carabiner and moved past, and then suddenly, with no warning, it exploded out from the cliff face with a crack, slamming hard into the visor of Renea's spacesuit just as she was about to pass the device, and wrenching both of them from the cliff. The rope pivoted on the carabiner below the both of them, Jac falling further as he was higher. Renea stopped first, the force of the rope coming to a stop wrenching her body back and forth, and then the same for Jac, him dangling below her. Due to the shape of the overhang, they both dangled in mid-air, out from the cliff face.

Adher was pulled forward by the rope stressing from the sudden force, pressing up against the carabiner that was directly above him, two down from the one that had failed. He held out his hands, pressing them against the cliff face. This took some of the force of the fall, but not all. He slowly pushed himself away from the cliff face, and looked up to see the two climbers above him dangling in the open air.

Christ, he thought, *how are we going to get out of this?*

***

"I've got you!" Renea exclaimed. Jac dangled below her, swinging one way and then the other.

"Sacre Blue!" Jac exclaimed "Christ!". He was dangling some metres below her.

"Calm down!"

"Get me out of this!"

Adher began to press his weight away from the wall. As he limbered up, one of the drones flew past filming the event, and then flew away.

"Listen," Renea stated "If I can climb up along the rope, then I might just be able to connect up this carabiner with the one in my hand. Then Adher and I can both pull you up."

"Give it a go," Jac stated. Renea could understand his impatience. He was extremely exposed. The wind had died, but below them was an enormous drop straight down. *They could not see the bottom.* Slowly but surely, Renea moved one hand up over another, trying to pull both the weight of her and Jac hanging below her up the rope. Slowly she began to pull up, the rope now slack in her harness. Her hands felt the enormous pressure, the friction of the rope pulling on the inside of her hands. The tension of lifting both hers and Jacs' weight rippled through her body, and despite how muscular she was, she started to feel as if she was not capable of this.

She kept on crawling upwards when she felt a sudden click in her left hand, and she let go, both of them falling down the rope again. They swung for a moment, and then the weight of them slowed the momentum, and they returned to where they had started; both of them hanging from the rope in mid-air, below the overhang. They were both being held by one now straining carabiner, whilst Adher was stuck against the one below; and they only had the two carabiners in the wall.

She looked down towards Jac. Their eyes met for what felt like an eternity. *We have to get out of this. We are not going to die here.*

"This is familiar," Jac stated after a moment "This is exactly what happened to Benoit."

"This is different," Renea stated, "I'm going to get you out of this."

"This is how Benoit died" Jac replied grimly. He started to squirm in his suit, his limbs flailing haphazardly. The rope began to creak slowly, and pivot around in the carabiner above them, that was holding the full weight of both climbers.

"Stop!" Renea yelled. Luckily, Jac seemed to hear her, and slowly stopped moving around. He calmed, and lay backwards in his harness. When his eyes met Renea's again, there was a dead look within them.

"I suppose," he stated slowly, putting emphasis on every single syllable as they left his mouth "there is one way out of this."

"Go on," Renea said.

"Do you still have that knife on you?" he asked.

"Don't be silly," Renea said, "There'll be more ways than that out of this."

"It's the best way out of this, and to guarantee we can keep on climbing. You'll be able to haul your weight up the rope, and to safety."

"I can't let you do that, Jac. I can't climb this mountain without you."

"You can," Jac responded "You know you can. You are superhuman, I always said so. Every once in a generation, there comes along a sportsperson, Michael Phelps, Alex Honnold, Roger Bannister, who breaks all the records. Like they were designed to do that sport from the moment they were born. You are that person for this generation. I realised that a long time ago. I've followed you this far believing that, and you would be letting me down to turn it on me now. Now Let Me Go."

"I won't," she was taken aback by Jacs honest outburst, but tried not to show it. There was a moment which felt like an eternity where the two of them hung there, not looking away from one another.

"You can't carry my weight up that rope, and you know it." Jac stated eventually.

"Weight." Renea repeated quietly to herself. She looked around, all around at the situation. She looked at Jac, and then at Adher, and then up at the carabiner above her. She had an idea.

"Adher?" she asked, "Can you take the weight of another backpack?". Adher nodded from his uncomfortable position. "Brilliant" she stated, unclipping the backpack on her back "I'm going to throw mine to you. Should equal out the weight on either side of the carabiners." With that, she unclipped the buckles keeping her backpack attached to her, and with all her might, flung it at Adher on the cliff face. The bag hit his shoulder; he spun and caught it with his other hand. He felt the rope loosen slightly, pulling him down away from his uncomfortable position, and drag Jac and Renea up ever so slightly on the other side of the carabiner. Adher clipped the bag around his waist, below his own back.

"Right," Renea said "Now for the tough bit. Unclip that carabiner next to you."

"You are having a joke." Adher stated over the comms.

"I'm not," Renea stated "At the same time, push off from the wall with all you might."

"No."

"The velocity of the swing should be enough to catch us, and on the return swing we will be able to grab the wall." Renea explained.

"That will not work."

"It wouldn't work on Earth, we're on Mars. We're lighter here. It will work."

"That one quickdraw will be carrying all of our weight. They are not designed to do tha.t"

"We're lighter here. And it will only be for a moment."

"I do not like this idea."

"Just do it Adher," Jac cut. The Moroccan man looked between the pair of them, and then sighed, even visibly from their position.

"Sod it." came the response. He hit the button on the quickdraw next to him, disengaging it from the cliff face, and pushed off the wall with both knees as hard as he could, sending him flying across empty space below the overhang. He collided with Renea hard sending her flying away from the cliff face. Then they felt the movement of the swing run through the room, and grabbed the rope below them, both of them grabbing it at once. They used the power in their wrists to swing Jac out further, the three of them swinging below the pivot point of the one quickdraw remaining in the cliff face; the one above their heads.

On the return swing, Jac swung furthest, pivoting not only on the quickdraw but Adher and Renea's position too. He reached out with all he was worth, almost popping out from the harness, he reached, and he reached, and as they approached the cliff face, he held his hand out.

And he grabbed it. Then, fast as lightning, grabbed the cliff face with his other hand. Then he held on. Adher held onto Renea. Renea held onto her rope. Then, Adher let go of her, and Renea nodded. As if it had been rehearsed, she placed her boot on his thigh and pushed him away from the cliff face with as much force as he could muster, before he swung in past her on his own rope. He reached out and grabbed the cliff face, grabbing it with both hands, and pulling himself into a safe position. Renea, now taught to the cliff face, but a few metres away, leant over, as Adher leant out from his position – and their hands met. Using their joint arm strength, Adher hauled her in towards him, and she got one, no, both hands on the cliff, and in the same moment, the quickdraw above their heads gave way from all the stress. It fell away, leaving the three of them all holding the cliff, and nothing keeping them to it.

Jac instantly bolted himself to the cliff face with another quickdraw and Renea did the same. Adher took a moment to understand what he'd just achieved, before he did the same.

The atmosphere relaxed a little, as Jac began to climb up towards them. He came alongside Renea as Adher decided to move up ahead of them.

"Well done boss." he said. The two of them embraced in a hug as best as they could, given they were both lumbered in space suits, with huge backpacks attached.

"One request," Renea stated, as they started to come apart "Do not use Benoit's name like that again."

Ten months earlier

K2. The second highest mountain on Earth, on the border of China and Pakistan. They called it The Savage Mountain. That certainly seemed apt right now. The winds were howling around them, reaching forty, fifty miles an hour. Small dots of snow howled past,

Their team leader was Benoit Ravenel. He was the most accomplished climber in French history. He held the European speed record on Everest, Elbrus, Denali, Annapurna, and more. And here he was, right in front of them. He was a tall man, with broad shoulders, a thick moustache, and no hair elsewhere on his head; even his eyebrows were close to gone. Looking at his shape and his frame, you would have thought he was veteran Rugby player, but he moved with a lightness and nimbleness that was unbefitting of a man of his figure. In the right light, he did look like a fictional invention, an adventurer from an old Herge comic or a Jules Verne novel.

Renea Bessant knew that she would follow him wherever he led her.

That said, they had known each other for years. Every time she had found success; he had been there by her side. Her mentor, his apprentice.

This attempt at the speed record of K2 was the culmination of their career, one of the few records they felt they could beat.

When Renea first signed up to this challenge, she had been overwhelmed with enthusiasm. They had claimed the speed record on Everest only the year before, but now she felt a twisting nervousness in her gut. That time they had had a big team – but here on K2 they only had herself, Benoit and two sherpas. Not the biggest team even in ideal conditions.

And the conditions were definitely not ideal. Around them the wind howled, carrying large flakes of snow and sleet. Renea felt like the man from old Michelin adverts, unable to move for burden of clothing around her body. The climb had been long, and hard, and it felt increasingly as if they were not going to be able to make the speed record. The storm that they were on the edge of was not letting up, and moved in southwards from Kyrgyzstan in a way that they had not expected.

In some ways, Renea was relieved; they were near the top, but they were not there yet. Above them lay one of K2's most challenging features; The Bottleneck, a couloir of thick ice and snow build up which occasionally give way. And it had been gaining in size due to the storm.

"We need to move quick!" Benoit exclaimed "Keep heading up whilst the storm is only moderate! The big storm clouds are not due for another few hours! We could be up and back to Camp 4 in no time".

Renea admired his optimism, but she did not feel as if she shared it at this current time. She placed her ice axe into the ice wall as they moved along the narrow snow, path, and leant forward to far, slipping and falling on her face into a foot of snow. One of the two sherpas gave her a hand up.

"Ok," Benoit stated, turning to look at the three behind them "Place your quickdraws into the ice. They are on a specific setting to which they should burrow into the ice face." He demonstrated by clicking one into the cliff face, and then climbing up onto it, the rope leading through. For a moment, he was soloing, before clipping in a second quickdraw into the ice face, and continuing to ascend. Renea looked up, following her mentor's feet and hand movements, noticing the specific line he took as he climbed, something she always did, even after climbing with him for so many years.

Slowly, she put her gloved hands and booted feet onto the ice, and began to follow suite, as Benoit led the way up The Bottleneck. The wind and snow continued but it was certainly manageable. As

Benoit moved up the face, he continued to place in the quickdraws, pulling them from a rack on his belt. *That must be very heavy,* Renea thought, *but he moves as loose and as free as ever.*

Benoit placed another quickdraw in, and began to clamber up into an overhang position as Renea followed closely behind, one quickdraw back. Then, suddenly, the quickdraw between Renea and Benoit, started beeping, and without any further warning simply fell out. Then Benoit found himself dangling down below her, his arms and legs flailing, before he quickly calmed himself down. Renea herself was yanked from the wall too; both their weights now being held by the single quickdraw below Renea. Both the sherpas were pressed up against the same carabiner, trying to counter the weight of the two Frech climbers dangling above them.

"I'm sorry!" Renea exclaimed loudly "I thought I'd checked all the equipment."

"This isn't your fault!" Benoit shouted back.

"I can haul you up!" Renea exclaimed, and tried pulling the rope carrying Benoit's weight up towards her in a fireman's pull style. After a couple of pulls, she realised that was futile, and her arms gave way, the rope becoming tense again under the big man's weight.

Then Renea tried pulling hers and Benoit's weight up the rope, hand over hand. She very quickly gave up on that too, her arm joints and muscles now thronging from the exertion.

"Damn," she stated, looking around quickly and then down at Benoit "I'm sorry, I'm out of ideas."

"It's ok, Renea, just stay calm, I'll think of something." Benoit explained as he hung there in the open air "Mingma!" he exclaimed, getting the top Sherpa to turn to him "Can you take both of our weight?"

Mingma nodded, and he and the other Sherpa let go of the ice cliff by their hands and feet, allowing themselves to hang loose on the cliff face. They didn't budge anywhere.

"No, sorry!" Mingma exclaimed "You are heavier than us".

Benoit looked up from the position he was hanging in from Mingma to Renea. Renea met his eyes, and she could see a determination that she was familiar with.

"Renea," he stated, "You've been excellent." and from his backpack side pocket he pulled a small climbing knife.

"No!" Renea stated, and she started squirming in her hanging position "Stop! There has to be some other way!"

Benoit started cutting the rope above him, keeping him hanging below Renea.

"Well," he said "It was excellent. Not just to be a mountaineer, but to have the exact career I wanted to have."

"Stop! Please!"

"Goodbye Renea." Benoit stated, and cut the rope. He fell from his hanging position, plummeting fifty metres to the bottom of The Bottleneck, landing square on his back. There he lay, unmoving. For a moment, Renea gasped, hoping she'd awaken from this awful dream, at any moment, but unfortunately, she did not. She gasped again, her body feeling as if the

Benoit Ravenel lay contorted, unmoving and pale, a trail of blood coming from his head which stained the snow below him. Bessant was alone on K2, unsure of what to do next. Unsure of how the world would react when she got back to base, whether she made the summit or not. To her, her entire life was over.

Once she was back on the wall, she continued to climb, unsure whether that would have been what Benoit would have wanted her to do.

Present time

Renea continued to reach up, her hand following one after the other, when Adher, who was now in the lead of their party, held is hand up.

"Stop!" he exclaimed "We are at top!"

"What does that mean?" Jac asked over the coms.

"We are at the top of up" Adher stated.

"We" Renea struggled to say, as she continued to ascend the climb "We are at the top of the cliff. We must be." She looked up to see Adher now continue to ascend too, and then suddenly, disappear out of sight. Renea smiled inside her helmet at this realisation, and then she too began to see over the top of the cliff face – they were at the end of the climb. Adher was dancing like a mad man at this change.

Renea clambered up onto the top of the cliff, and stood up, their rope still running through their harness. After a few more seconds, Jac appeared behind her, and stood up fully. Her legs felt strange – they were on the ground once again, but she must remember that they were over eight kilometres above sea level. *They had just done a roped climb the same height as K2.* Without the three of them having to say anything, they began to unclip the rope that ran between them, and Renea moved over to stuff the rope into Adhers' backpack.

"Easy boss" he said as she continued to stuff the rope into his pack "Now all we need to do is walk".

"For twenty-four hours straight without stopping." Jac stated as he joined them.

"We will make a start," Renea said, "But I am certain we must now have a lead, to have come the way we have come."

"Unfortunately," Jac replied "We have no way of knowing that until we bump into them. Both those teams have competent navigators and strong climbers. Both those teams have more members than us. More heads to put together in difficult situations".

"Let's not focus on that," Renea nodded "Let's put one foot in front of another, and get to where we need to get to. I know about two miles forward from here, there is a rocky outcrop, which we ought to bear left around. At the start, there is a ridge of smaller rocks, maybe forty, fifty metres high each. We ought to spend the night there."

"Aye," Jac agreed "Let's get there."

***

Adher led the trek, he moved naturally, moved efficiently, calling out breaks, as well as any features that he could spot, telling them about how different features were made, as well as star patterns or anything else his eyes strayed upon. Around them, the day was disappearing, and whilst they were able to make out stars and the planets' twin moons, Phobos and Deimos.

"You sure do know a lot about this crap," Jac chimed in as Adher was continuing to regale them with the history of Deimos.

"It's my job," Adher responded "I was guide in Atlas Mountains. Taking rich Europeans trekking up Toubkal. They ask all kinds of student questions about sky. I find out the answers to be better at my job."

"I see," Jac responded, panting a little from the trekking "What was the most interesting thing you found out?"

"A planet in the nights sky is obvious because it is like one bright star that seems out of place. But it does not flicker, like a star."

"I never knew that."

"And Mars is even more obvious, because it is red."

"Oh wow."

"I see it many times from Morocco," Adher confirmed "But I never thought I would be on it, walking on its mountains."

"Neither did I friend, neither did I. Tell me Adher, do your mis- oh wow!" Jac's flow of thought was interrupted by the sight of the first of the 'teeth', huge, jagged rocks sticking out from the summit, running in a row to one huge rock behind them.

"This is it," Renea cut in "We ought to sleep here tonight."

"Ok boss." Adher responded, and slowly he came to a halt, before unclipping his bag and placing it down. He got onto his knees, and unzipped the bag, pulling out his sleeping bag. Jac and Renea did the same, as Adher started to take in some water and nutrients juice he went off to sleep. Despite how chipper he had been about starting the trek, he was soon off sleep, leaving Jac and Renea on their own. The two of them didn't fall asleep immediately, letting the dull drone of Adher's light snoring brush over their comms units. Instead, they sat up, their backs against small rocks that they found nearby. They were some thirty metres away from the sleeping Adher.

"Thank you, today." Jac said.

"What do you mean?" Renea responded.

"You saved my life." Jac told her.

"I did. But I was saving my own life."

"I gave you an opportunity to get out of the situation, and you ignored it. You didn't let me die, even though I asked you to cut me free."

"I couldn't do that to you; you're my best friend".

"You did that to Benoit."

"I…we didn't think we had another choice It was different." Renea bristled at that last comment. There was a brief silence. "You know, you said something quite interesting whilst we were out there."

"Yes?"

"About me being a superhuman?"

"Oh yes ha-ha!"

"What did you mean?"

"Well, within every generation there are a handful of athletes who are superb at what they do. Truly exceptional. They take everything that we thought we knew about a sport, and turn it on its head."

"And?"

"And you are one of those people. You need to be aware of yourself, Renea."

"I AM aware of myself. Can we talk about something else?"

"Of course,"

"Adher?"

"If we must."

"He thinks Mars has giant rats living under the surface of the planet, in caverns. He thinks they have created an intelligent society, away from the human race."

"Oh god."

"Mars Rats."

"Yes, I've heard the conspiracies elsewhere. I thought he was brighter than that."

The two of them smiled, and simultaneously burst out laughing.

***

As the laughter died down, Renea turned to Jac, and said "and what about you?"

"What about me?"

"What do you believe?"

"Well, to be honest with you, I think the galaxy, perhaps the whole universe, is bursting with life. We just need to go out there and…find it."

"Truly?"

"Truly. It has to be out there somewhere. I mean, think about it…eight planets in our solar system, one of them has the conditions to support complex life. Another one almost has the conditions to support life, and with a bit of scientific tampering, has after a time. Surely it can't be that challenging for it to occur naturally elsewhere."

"I mean, surely though, Mars supporting life is because of people playing God. Tampering with the known order of things. This planet isn't supposed to have a breathable atmosphere."

"It doesn't"

"It will within a hundred years. What I mean is that we are using a technology we do not fully understand."

"And yet…you're here?"

"I'm getting paid." They both laughed. Neither of them said anything for a little while.

"Thank you for saving me today" Jac eventually stated "Even if that idea was madness"

 "You were willing to let yourself die, Jac."

"I know, but it seemed like there was no way out of it. Like what happened with Benoit."

"Yes, a lot like what happened with Benoit."

There was silence again.

"Too much like what happened with Benoit" Renea then stated.

"You think that…"

"Maybe we happened to have two faulty AI quickdraws?"

"Honestly, what are the chances that on two of the most important climbs of your life that those things could go wrong twice in the same way? Those things never go wrong."

"Unless they're tampered with".

"Unless they're tampered with," Jac agreed "And both of these climbs, we've been up against the same rival team."

"We have" Renea nodded, and then swallowed and looked away. "This has been a very interesting conversation, Jac. Let's continue it in the morning, I need some rest." It was clear Jac wanted to continued talking, but Renea did not allow it. She moved away after the mentioning of a "goodnight." and went to settle to sleep on the far side of Adher.

Jac sat up for a further moment, until he decided to do the same, cuddling up with Renea in the same way that he had done the previous night.

Renea's thoughts lingered on Jac, and then on Tom Libretti, then on the Olympus Accord and the political pressure that lay on them. Then it turned on all the climbing behind them, then still ahead of them, until it lingered on nothing at all, and she fell asleep.

Chapter Three

26th June 2085

Renea had hoped that the trekking section of the ascent would be easier than the climb. Adher had begun to take the lead of the trek, occasionally looking back and checking that Renea and Jac were right behind him. As she had been back when she met Adher in the Atlas Mountains of Morocco, they always were. She had, in her head, been looking forward to the trek, but now, after what had happened with the other teams, and Jac's near death experience, she was mentally exhausted. She stopped for a moment to take on some water – her pack now felt noticeably lighter than before, and if honest, she was unsure if they had enough for the descent at the end. Perhaps she had misjudged it.

As they ascended, they had taken a left around the huge boulder that Adher had pointed out to them before they slept. From there, they had headed up the trek, facing bright sunlight paired with more wind, followed by a sudden chill as they passed behind the huge rock and into its shadow. As Adher moved up ahead of them, Jac caught up from the rear so that he was walking alongside Renea. They were both panting from the exhaustion.

"Renea" he stated, "Are we going to talk about our revelation last night?"

"Revelation?" she asked

"That someone tampered with the quickdraws. Twice."

"Someone?"

"Must I say it?" Jac asked.

"Yes."

"Tom Libretti."

"Why would he do that?"

"I don't know, Renea, because he's a professional looser? Because he's jealous? He was there on both incidents. He had every reason to sabotage you."

"He wouldn't stoop that low."

"You were willing to fight him two days ago."

"And I would have won."

"I'm really not sure you would have."

Renea turned to Jac and stopped him, placing her hand on his chest. Jac stiffened and there was a sudden palpable tension in the air between them.

"Jac" she stated, "If I move on this, and I'm wrong, then my career is over."

"Don't be so over-dramatic."

"I'm right, if I did choose to kill Benoit, then turning and blaming Tom, and being wrong, will see me out of this sport forever. No sponsor, no coach, to support team will want to touch me. It's bad enough as it is."

For once, Jac had nothing to say. He knew she was right.

"We keep quiet about this, Jac," she continued "And we just keep on moving. Thank the stars that we survived yesterday's incident, and put this period behind us."

"That does sound like a sensible idea." Jac nodded. Unfortunately, it was not to be.

Adher, who was still some way ahead of them, passed by the end of the huge boulder to their right, and suddenly a figure, no, several figures, stepped out from his blind spot. *It was Tom Libretti and his team.* The nearest one, a large man with dark skin and broad shoulders, grabbed Adher and threw him down.

"Adher!" Renea exclaimed, and, despite being over-encumbered by her chubby spacesuit, began running up the mountain side towards the commotion. The winds were coming in again, and the air was filled with red dust. *The drones were going to have a very hard time seeing them now.*

"Ah, calm down" Tom said "We're just having some fun."

Slowly, Adher began to sit back up from his position on the floor. Renea moved over to him, and helped him stand up. Tom stood and watched.

"All of this sabotage, this confrontation, is it worth? Are you that keen to protect your country's name?" Renea asked.

"The Olympus Accord?" Tom asked "I don't care at all. I don't care about my country, and I know you don't care about yours either. This is just a façade. We're using this opportunity for self-glory. Renea, this is about me, beating you."

"Are you surprised to see us?" Jac asked, as the pair of them stood up "I think you thought we'd be dead."

"Oh" he replied, "I figured you'd failed."

"That's not what I meant."

"Careful now, Jac." Renea cut in.

"I don't see the problem," Jac stated. *He was going to go for it,* Renea realised.

"This quickdraw," Jac continued, holding up the failed AI quickdraw in his hand "It's yours."

"I don't think so." Tom responded

"Well, it was ours. You tampered with it, somehow." Jac stated

"A likely story, spread a looser. Not even the chief looser, a supporting looser." Tom stated

"Well, each quickdraw with an AI input will have a log of who accessed it," Jac replied "So when we get down to ground level, we'll be able to see who inputted its instructions last."

"Oh, will you?" Tom asked

"Yes." Jac responded.

"And what if I was to prevent you from doing that?" Tom asked, and quick as lightning, pulled a red rock the size of an apple from the ground, and slammed it hard into Jac's helmet, cracking it. Jac fell back, dazed from the attack, and dropped the quickdraw. Renea rushed to her friends' side, and quickly clambered over him, putting one hand on his shoulder, before reaching into her backpack, and covering the gap with a paste which froze solid. Jac relaxed as he realised that the integrity of the spacesuit had not broken. Renea pulled him up, and turned to see Tom and his right-hand man, the one who had pushed Adher right behind them.

"Careful," Tom stated, "Be very careful now."

"Looks like you're going to have a fight on your hands" Jac said

"There's three of you," Tom replied "Six of us. Not too much of a fight, really."

"It won't be us you're fighting." Jac responded, nodding at the distance. Tom and several of his men turned at once to see a growing cloud behind them. *Another storm.*

***

"Damn!" Tom exclaimed, and turned to see that Renea and her team were already turning to start to make a move up the mountain, away from the incoming storm. The broken quickdraw was at Renea's feet. Renea and Tom simultaneously leapt for the device, but Tom was too far away. Renea reached out with her long arms, grabbed it, pulled it in and clasped it to her chest. She stood back up just as Tom came roaring at her - she lifted up the quickdraw, and swung it into the glass of his helmet as hard she could, the force knocking the quickdraw once again from her hand.

The helmet cracked, and Tom fell back, some of the glass going inwards into his face.

"Get me the sealant!" he screamed at the nearest man.

"I don't know which of us has it!" that man replied. Renea, panicking, with Adher and Jac now getting smaller and smaller as they ascended the mountain, turned to look for the quickdraw. But now that storm was upon them. Red sand was all around, and she could not see the quickdraw. The sand engulfed Tom and his team, the blond Brit still flailing around as he writhed from the bit of glass helmet now stuck in his face, the integrity of his suit compromised.

Renea turned away from him, and did the only thing she felt she could at this point; walk roughly in the direction of up. As she walked, she started to feel her thoughts overtake her, the wind and sand buffeting her spacesuit as she slowly put one foot in front of the other. Although the gravity of Mars was only a third of what it was on Earth, she was so tired, physically and emotionally, that she could no longer tell that. She found herself after so much adversity, alone on a huge mountain, millions of miles from her home. She could feel the tears start to roll down her face.

She stopped, looked up the mountain, or the thirty metres she could see, and wondered whether there was much point. Suddenly, there was a force behind her – it was an arm. Jac fell into one side of her, and then Adher the other.

"We've been looking for you everywhere," Jac stated "Time to get out of here and up to higher ground, get away from the storm to protect our suits." Renea slowly nodded, feeling unable to say anything, and slowly started to put one foot in front of the other again.

They kept on moving upwards, following the route that both Adher and Renea had memorised at this point. Every so often they stopped to take on extra water and protein, and then they turned and kept moving. The trek seemed to take hours, which was very much what they had expected, but none of them had truly been ready for the reality of walking in a straight-line up hill in an eighteen-hour stint. There was no peak on Earth that was quite like that. Eventually, after what felt like a millennia, the storm died down, and they were no longer being buffered by the wind and the snow. It was still daylight, although the clear Mars sky, home to zero light pollution, was greying now.

"Nearly there, boss." Adher stated, pointing up at a clearly definable mountain peak above them in the distance.

"That's so close." Renea stated.

"And the British team are behind us." Jac added

"Oh, for certain."

"No word on the Nepalese team?" Renea asked, turning to Adher.

"No word." Adher responded.

"They could be anywhere," Jac said "They came up from a totally different starting base."

"Then let's not worry about them," Renea said, "it's us against the mountain."

"That's what I like to hear," Jac said "Adher, lead on."

Adher smiled, nodded, and began to walk up towards the summit, his steps now larger, with a spring to them that they did not carry in the storm. Renea hung back, and turned to Jac.

"I'm sorry," she admitted "I left the quickdraw."

"It doesn't matter," Jac replied "I saw you break Tom's helmet just before that storm hit. He's done for."

"I don't know about that, he's a very wily guy" Renea said

"Oh, I don't think we'll be seeing him again," Jac responded "Something in my gut tells me so."

"I wish I had your certainty." Renea mumbled.

"Do not give him thought. He was a monster." Jac added.

"He was. But one I'd known for a long time" she responded.

"How did you even meet him?" Jac said

"Well," and Renea took a deep breath, thinking slowly back to a very different period of her life "We were friends once".

***

Ten years earlier

Tom Libretti was lean with blond hair, and an arm span as long as his height head to toe, he was almost the perfect build to be an exceptional climber. As his dad drove him down the long, winding road from Edinburgh out to their destination, he felt a knot build up in his stomach. This was most unusual knot of unease, something he would have not normally felt. It had not begun here, it had started back in York where they had set off from, and only increased on the drive up to Edinburgh. As they approached the European International Climbing Arena, where the trials were to take place, it only got stronger.

Scanning in and getting settled into the competition area was easy enough. Tom said very little, as his dad got them sorted with timings and a competitor sheet. A man who worked at the climbing arena led them down to the main room, which had a few very serious looking judges to one side, as well as athletic-looking teenagers of all sizes filled the room, some with parents to accompany them, and some without. Tom's dad settled him on a bench, and they took in the sights around them; huge orange, blue and white walls covered in plastic climbing holds of all shapes and sizes. The trials had already begun, and whilst the judges were watching like hawks, most of the competitors talked amongst themselves.

"Nervous?" Tom's dad asked.

"Yes, a little." Tom responded

"That's not like you." Tom's dad stated

"I know," Tom replied, "I just…I've never been in a competition like this."

"Just do your best, Tom, that's all I ever ask of you," Tom's dad stated, smiling warmly "Oh and make sure you bring home at least a Bronze medal." They both laughed lightly at that comment. "I suppose it doesn't help that you're on second-to-last." Tom's dad said.

At that, the ears of a nearby girl pricked up. She was a teenager, like Tom, but clearly a little older, and even taller than he was.

"Hello." she said in a light French accent

"Hi," Tom said. He took in this competitor - she was tall, brunette, physical fit and confident but with awkward facial features; her eyes were small and her chin and nose both seemed too large for the rest of her face. All of it together was striking in its own way though. "I'm Tom" he stated, standing up to shake her hand.

"Renea" the girl responded.

"This is…this my dad, he drove me up from York, where we live"

"Ah" Renea responded "I flew on my own. I am from Dijon in France. I am French"

"I guessed that part" Tom responded. The joke cut out any tension and they both laughed.

"I heard you say you are second to last?" she asked.

"Yes, that's right" Tom said.

"Well, that's good, I am last" Renea stated "We best get comfortable"

The competition whiled away as the two of them set together, observing all the climbing that they could see in front of them. The pair were equally fascinated by all that they saw, taking in risky moves on the bouldering competition, and who was most entertaining on the speed climb. Tom's dad had long since found an old crime novel in the arena's book donation pile which he was pouring through, now on at least chapter four.

All of that was cut to a stop when Tom's name was called, and he walked up to the bouldering competition. His job now was to traverse across a set of large plastic holds in a set time. Before he knew it, the nervousness was cut out from underneath him and he was on the wall, pivoting and moving. Now he was actually there, doing what he had set out to do, all anxiety was gone. He was in his element. As he moved across the traverse, he could hear whooping and cheering from behind him, loudest of all, his father, and his new friend Renea. *Glad that people were actually watching him.*

He had finished it in almost the same time it had taken for him to walk across the arena floor to get there, or at least that's how he felt. Then he had to do the speed ascent; get up a roped wall as quickly as possible. Finding himself at the bottom of the wall, he heard the bell go and it was almost muscle memory to him, as he moved up the wall, hand over foot, and occasionally foot over hand. Before long he found himself descending down again, and back on the ground. He headed over to his dad, unclipping from the wall as he walked.

Then, as he walked, he heard a huge cheer, and turned. Renea has already finished the bouldering traverse course. In seconds. Then he stood, dumfounded by what he was seeing, as she practically flew up the speed climbing route, at a speed that would probably make a chimpanzee blush.

The noise from the onlooking crowd was enormous; twice what it had been when Tom had made his attempt.

As Renea came back down from the wall, she was beaming from ear to ear, and walked straight up to Tom, giving him a hug. Despite his inner disappointment, he did embrace her in the hug, and then slowly to effortlessly followed her over to the medal podium next to the judges.

"So," Tom's dad said in the car on the way back "Second place. Not too bad. That's a silver medal, they don't hand those out for nothing, you know."

Tom said nothing.

"She was fast, that French girl." his dad continued

Tom said nothing.

"What was her name, Renie?"

Tom said nothing.

"No, it was nicer than that. Oh, it was Renea, wasn't it?"

Tom said nothing.

"A pretty French girl. I can't wait to tell your mum you met a French girl at the climbing competition. She seemed to really like you, too."

Tom said nothing.

"We'll have to get over to Fontainebleau at do some climbs over there. Maybe we could meet up with her. I'll take the van; we'll make a proper trip of it."

Tom said nothing. At last, his dad noticed.

"Oh Tom. You're having a sulk, aren't you? Because you didn't win". Tom did nod at this, at least. "Well, I must say, it's ok. This is normal. As you get better at something Tom, whatever it is, you must realise that you'll come up against better and better opponents, and some that are so good that they'll beat you."

Tom said nothing.

"You need to look on the bright side. You climbed well; you deserved that silver. And you made a new friend. Now let's get home, and your Mum and I will take you out to celebrate."

Tom still said nothing. All his thoughts, positive and negative, lay with Renea Bessant.

***

Present time

They were closing in on the summit.

Renea could feel it.

It was within their grasps, and the last few hours of the trek had been in their favour; the sun was up above, dimly lighting the sky, but it had begun to fall, darkening the atmosphere around.

Still, they continued to put one foot in front of another, and keep trudging forward. Renea could sense the protein powder and water tanks in her backpack getting lighter and lighter as they continued up the mountain. Jac's slick pacing had become more of a drawl, and even Adher's relentless workhorse style and slowed slightly. Renea was tired. Not just of the walk, but of the near-death experience, and the run-ins with Tom Libretti. She graciously welcomed the end of this peak.

As if sensing her internal negativity, Jac fell in by her side as she continued up Olympus Mons.

"So," he said smiling "We are maybe…half a mile from the summit?"

"Must be getting close that, yes," Renea replied, "It does steepen a little at the very end."

"So, what are you going to do when you get to home?" Jac asked

"Ooo" Renea pondered this question comically as they walked along "I think I'm going to call my Mum from the base, and then head back to the debriefing camp for a big glass of wine?"

"I was thinking I'd have the big glass of wine back at the space port waiting to go back to Earth." Jac said

"I'm not sure I'm able to wait that long," and they both laughed at that "I'm not superhuman."

"Yes, you are," Jac stated, and the tone of the conversation changed "I said that."

"But you're wrong," Renea replied, "You put me up on the pedestal that I don't deserve."

"I don't understand." Jac said simply

"I'm just lucky." Renea explained "And I work hard. So do you. So does Adher."

"I mean," Jac responded "I see where you're coming from."

"I just think…I'm not who you think I am Jac."

"No, no I know. You made that clear."

"I'd like you to know that you could be the person you think I am."

"Hahaha, I suppose."

"No, it's true. You work hard, you understand routes, techniques, you know how to motivate people. You could be leading your own elite teams."

"I learnt all that from you."

"No, you didn't. You worked out a lot of that from yourself."

"I see what you mean."

"I'm not a superhuman. I'm nobody special. I just work hard, do what people expect of me, and home for the best." Renea reaffirmed.

"I get you" Jac replied, before pondering. "Adher" he said, "What are you going to do when you get home?"

"Me," the Moroccan responded from up ahead "I am going to bed."

They both laughed.

***

They had been right – as they approached the summit, it began to steepen. They found themselves clambering up towards the top of the mountain on hands and knees once again. The wind had picked up yet again, but this time it was nowhere near as aggressive as the two storms that they had experienced. As they began to scramble up the sheer red rock face, small parts of it began to break off. Now they were on four limbs once again, Renea took the lead over Adher, and Jac took up the rear. She moved hand over foot, and then foot over hand. She felt as if each movement took all the energy she had left.

"We're two hundred metres from the summit." she stated over the comms.

"That's less than an hour."

"I'm tired." Adher chipped in.

"We're not stopping now." Renea stated firmly. She continued to lead the way, the three of them moving slowly yet still slickly up the mountain face. They said nothing else for several minutes. In between the motions of grabbing a hand hold, moving up her feet, pivoting, transitioning from foot to foot, Renea's mind began to wander. She thought back to the start of this trek, the climb with which it began, to their near-death experience towards the top of the cliff, to the run ins with Tom Libretti, to now. In the most bizarre way, it seemed to have tied together so many of the significant points in her climbing career. *Whether she would have chosen for it to do so or not.*

Within the next movement, she found the ground becoming shallower once again. She was able to stand back up, and walk. The cliff curved around her feet – the summit was in front of them. As she walked upwards, the top of the cliff became apparent. There was a large sideway rock lodged in the ground, about the same size as a small lorry. A natural summit stone, how wonderful.

Renea smiled and rushed forward, breaking into a run, as she closed the forty, no thirty, no twenty metres to reach it.

Then, suddenly David Sherpa from the Nepalese team stepped out from behind it, followed by the other members of that team. Renea stopped in her tracks so quickly that given the weak Martian gravity she nearly fell on her face from the momentum her body carried.

"Oh." was all she could manage, as she stood up and took in the sight in front of her.

"Hello sister." David Sherpa stated firmly but warmly.

"How…how long have you been here?"

"Just over five minutes, sorry." He seemed genuinely apologetic. Renea couldn't find anything else to say. She sunk to her knees, and remained there until Jac joined her and helped her up. Adher was shaking hands with the men in David's team.

"You did your best," Jac reminded her "Don't despair that we didn't come first. Rejoice that we got here."

"I…. suppose." Renea replied, and then slowly she began to relax

"We're on the summit of the tallest mountain in the solar system," Jac reminded her with a nudge "Not many people get to say that. And think about how many young climbers will be inspired to follow in your wake and achieve something this amazing"

"I suppose you are right." Renea replied, and then she turned and took in the view; the night sky was filled with stars, the sun now resembling a simple dim light not much brighter than the other stars in sky near the edge as it prepared to disappear for the next twelve hours. In the sky not far from the sun there was a bright, unwavering light. *Home*, Renea realised. *Earth.*

Renea walked forward, placed her hand on the lorry-sized stone in the ground, and Jac followed suit. David Sherpa approached the pair of them without caution or ego.

"So," he said, "What are you two going to do next?"

"Well," Renea replied, looking at Jac and then back at the sherpa "I think we're going to retire from this. Find a new avenue."

"Any ideas sister?" David asked

"Well, maybe coaching." Renea responded on the spot.

"That would be a shame sister," David stated, still joyous of tone "I always look forward to seeing what you two do."

Renea was taken back by the positivity shown by a rival climber.

"Well…thank you," she responded, "And what about you?"

"I suppose I'll look for something to do back on Earth. The seven summits record, perhaps."

"Sounds interesting," Renea replied, "We might make a move for the base now."

"Very well sister," David stated "Oh, before you go, I passed the British team this morning. On their way down."

"Oh." Renea replied.

"Well done for dealing with Tom Libretti and avenging your mentor." David stated firmly.

"I…I…I don't understand what you mean." Renea tried her best to sound surprised.

"I think you do." David stated.

"We have no evidence though." Jac chipped in. David stood there, smiled, and then quickly hopped his backpack off his pack and placed it on the ground in front of them. He opened the backpack, and lifted an object out of it. *The tampered AI quickdraw.*

"Oh lordy," Renea stated, astonished "this was our quickdraw Tom tampered with."

"Benoit Ravenel was a good man. I'd always suspected the story involved foul play sister. I hope this will help make things right."

Renea took the quickdraw from David and stuffed into her own backpack.

"Thank you so much." Jac stated, shaking David's hand. Renea paused for a moment, before embracing the short lean Nepalese man in a hug.

"Thank you," she said "and you should be so happy for yourself, what you have achieved for your country."

"Thank you," David responded, grinning "this is a victory not just for me, but for all of Nepal."

She turned, Jac followed, and then Adher took up the rear.

***

They clambered down the trek once again, the mountain now seemingly falling away in front of them. There remained a tension in the air, the three of them not speaking much.

"What's on your mind?" Jac asked Renea eventually.

"This quickdraw," she replied "It's not enough to prove what happened to Benoit."

"I see."

"David didn't mention whether Tom was amongst the British team as they passed each other."

"I get you."

"And so, I'm worried that we won't get anywhere by fighting for Benoit's name. And mine. And if Tom is dead, then I actually AM a murderer."

"We will just need to get back to base and face the music, either way, Renea. We know the truth now; we did not before."

"Oh Jac, you are too good to me. I don't deserve a friend like you."

"Well, it helps that I really fancy you."

Renea laughed out loud, and so did Jac. They continued walking as this conversation went.

After a little while, they died down "Are you sure you want to leave this?" Jac asked.

"I do," Renea said "the last year has been so much. I've had to deal with so much negativity on so many fronts. This climb has only amplified that. I need to stop, and find something else. For my mental health. There's no point being this 'superwoman' climber if I can't face getting out of bed in the morning."

"That's a very good point." Jac replied

"I'll find something though. I might get a job coaching, or something. Get fresh talent into the sport. Teach them how to be good climbers. And good people."

"If that's truly what you want to do, Renea, then I will do the same."

"Thank you, ever so." Renea responded, smiling.

"And just think of the work you'll get, being a legendary Olympus Mons record holder." Jac said

"But Jac, I didn't get to the top first."

"No, you didn't," he replied "But you did get the first female ascent. And we hold the speed record. No one's ever going to take that from you."

"Sacre blue, Jac, will you ever stop being amazing?"

"I'll try not to." Jac responded.

As they moved further and further from the mountain's summit, their minds began to wander.

"What does this mean for the future?" Renea asked

"I guess this means Nepal has political control of Mars now." Jaq responded.

"Well, that won't feel weird at all." Renea responded, and they both started laughing.

They turned forward and continued to walk down Olympus Mons, back to its base.

THE END

The Man in the Mountain

By Alex O'Neill

(Based on an original idea by George O'Neill)

Date: 2450

Location: New Aberdeen (Earth)

Chapter One

5th October

It was a cold autumn morning. Quantum physicist Maria Smith walked into the High Court of Justiciary in Edinburgh, Scotland, on maybe one hour's sleep. Grey bags sat under her eyes, and she clutched a lukewarm Americano coffee close to her chest. She'd donned her one formal suit-dress that vaguely fit her (she was not a person for formal attire) and no amount of cold shower and caffeine this morning would make her feel ready for the day ahead. This is not exactly where she saw herself as when she had moved to the UK four years prior. As she entered the room, she followed behind her ex-employer, Dr. Jodie Connors, who was the primary defendant of the case. Dr. Connors exchanged a brief glance at Maria, and then her lawyer, a broad-shouldered man with almost no hair but an air of being 'far better than Dr. Connors deserved,' sat down in between them.

Maria chose not to look their way again, despite them being in this together, technically.

Across the hearing sat several people, most notably the Vice-Chancellor and Pro-Vice Chancellor of New Aberdeen University, and more worryingly, several members of the government. Maria managed to recognize the Home Secretary as well as the Defence Secretary, people responsible for governing major parts of the country. The Lord Justice General of the Court peered down her hooked nose and halfmoon glasses at Dr. Connors.

"So," she stated, "Court is now in session." There was a long pause, which for Maria seemed to go on forever. The Lord Justice General then continued "For the sakes of the jury, we are gathered here due to a national-level inquiry into the unlawful activities of the New Aberdeen University Quantum Physics research department, between the dates of 2nd and 9th July.

That was August 2450 on their timeline project, more commonly known in the Newspapers as 'The Michael Project.'

A couple of titters went up amongst the courtroom. Maria shifted uneasily in her chair. The Pro-Vice-Chancellor had she—yes, just her—locked in a death stare. Why her?

Maria looked away, trying to focus on anyone else in front of her to break the tension, but it was no use. Eventually, as the court reading continued, she locked her eyes back with the Pro-Vice-Chancellor and decided to put up with it.

"We must first examine the intent of the activities conducted by Dr. Jodie Connors and her team. The experiments that took place during that time were, if the prosecution is to be believed, intentionally kept as secret from the University's senior management. Now, is it correct that the nature of the experiment would be required to be cleared by said management in order to be granted approval?" The Lord Justice asked.

"Correct." The Vice-Chancellor responded, "Which it was not."

"Thank you, Vice-Chancellor." The Lord Justice responded, "Do you wish to respond on this matter?"

"I do." Dr. Connors' lawyer stated, and he stood up. "It is my client's understanding that the university management had approved any research into teleportation technology until such time as The New Cold War was ongoing."

"That is correct, Mr. Green" The Lord Justice responded.

"And on 18th December 2449, my client made a request for funding to run testing on a teleportation device with heightened capabilities—a request which was then approved by the university senior leadership unanimously."

"The team for Prosecution can now respond on this matter" the Lord Justice stated. Maria looked to her right. Past Mr. Green and Dr. Connors sat a very serious-looking military man, a General, perhaps, or Lieutenant-General of some kind, and a well-dressed female lawyer.

The lawyer stood up.

"My client states that the term 'heightened abilities' does not accurately describe the altercations made to the teleportation device used for 'The Michael Project,'" she stated crisply. "We'd argue that this machine's primary purpose was not even teleportation, and it is not accurate to describe it as such."

"Understood," the Lord Justice responded. "It is understood by the panel that the experiments conducted by the department were not just unlawful, but also, in the prosecution's report, reckless and lethal."

"Permission to respond," Mr. Green said. "My client does not agree with the use of that second word and would like you to justify its use."

"Very well," the Lord Justice responded. "Is it not true that the deputy Lead of the project tragically lost his life during the experiments?"

"Adam Rehange's death was not a result of anyone's misconduct but his own," Dr. Connors interrupted, and the court began to stir. Maria felt uneasy at the use of Adam's name in any context. She saw the jury begin to turn and look at each other. She saw the Pro-Vice Chancellor move and whisper something into the Vice-Chancellor's ear.

"Dr. Connors, I must warn you not to speak out of turn again," the Lord Justice said, "which would allow us to move onto the principal claim made against you; the charge of second-degree murder in the 'Michael Project,' of Dr. Adam Rehange."

The court fell silent.

How has it come to this? Maria thought.

***

Three months earlier. 3rd July 2350

It was a bright but cool mid-week morning, and a strong sun penetrated the huge, double-glazed windows found across the University of New Aberdeen, creeping out from behind a mass of white and grey clouds. So much for a sunny July.

New Aberdeen was a quickly developing city built on the southern border of the Cairngorms National Park, intentionally built to be an economic hub north of Glasgow and Edinburgh.

The university sat right in the middle of the city and boasted a huge dome based on St. Paul's Cathedral from London. The main building was painted a bright white, rather than a drab grey like the Cathedral. Behind the main building lay a maze of science laboratories and cafes. The whole place looked so clean one could eat their dinner off it.

Dr. Adam Rehange sat alone in the University cafeteria, working a marble between his fingers. He was a well-muscled, tall, blond man, now in his late twenties; but gave off a healthy glow that often allowed him to pass as a Master's or bachelor's student. He wore a baggy green hoodie and grey jogging bottoms, and large black rim glasses. Over this informal dress he wore a gleaming white lab coat, which he easily filled out with his broad frame. Between taking sips of his morning smoothie, he placed the small marble under his thumb. As he pressed down, the marble went spinning out from under his thumb and across the table, and then onto the floor.

It moved almost faster than Adam's eyes could follow it, but as soon as it hit the floor, he leaned over and scooped it up. His eyes darted around to see if anyone had spotted him; the cafeteria janitor—a squat middle-aged lady with curly hair—frowned at him, shook her head, and carried on cleaning.

"Hello, Blondie" came a loud voice. Adam knew instantly who it belonged to. Maria Smith, his lab assistant, on the work he was doing with Dr. Jodie Connors. Maria was a chubby woman, perhaps a couple of years older than himself, with thick brown hair, big eyes, and an even bigger voice. She sat down opposite Adam, her arms spreading to more than half the small table.

"Are you drinking puke?" she asked, looking at the smoothie in his hand. Adam smiled and looked down at the Kale and Spinach-based concoction. "It's a health smoothie," he responded.

"You're trying too hard," she stated. "It doesn't hurt to get a Burger King from time to time."

Adam smiled. He was usually a very serious person, but he knew that with a select few people, he could drop his guard. Maria was one of them.

"Doing anything interesting this coming weekend?" Maria asked.

"Not particularly," Adam responded. "Going for a hike. Need to do my weekly shop. Big run on Sunday."

"You know, you could always relax." Maria asked.

"I don't do relaxing. It stresses me out, not doing anything."

"My mum would love you."

"I'm sure she would, if I one day got to know her."

"You'd have to get to know me first."

"I do know you."

"Not in that way"

There was then a moment where neither of them spoke, and then Maria looked up at Adam, catching his eye.

"To work," she stated, turned on her heel, and walked away. Adam sat in his seat for a moment, smiled as he looked back down at the table, and pushed the remains of the smoothie around in his glass. He breathed in through his nose, and then stood up to follow her, quickly jogging to catch up as she reached the other side of the dining hall. Maria pushed open the door for them, stepping out into the early morning sun, both wincing a little. Adam soaked in the sights of the university; a spectacular building, and while he liked to pretend that you got used to it—that's what he told his students— he knew that you never truly did.

***

Adam and Maria clocked in for the morning. Roger, the gentleman who operated security, buzzed him in, and handed him a locker key. Adam had always thought Roger looked like the human version of a pug: small, with thin brown hair and large, dark eyes. Maria followed quickly after, smiling and winking at Roger, who smiled back and handed her a key, too, as he buzzed her in.

Maria followed Adam into the elevator, and as they descended, she smiled at him. Adam looked ahead, and then caught her eyes, then looked away again.

"Do you ever think about the fact that no one has a clue what we do here?" Maria asked.

"I think it's best that way. Not many high and mighty academics would like to know we're what we're building down here."

Adam thought slowly about the situation. The experiment had been self-funded by the head of their project, Dr. Connors, who had handpicked Maria and Adam from PhD programs she taught on. Adam was brought on to support the research, and Maria as a practical lab technician. Their world, overnight, had changed. That said, Adam had never looked back, never questioned why Connors chose him. He had known—he had always known—that he was going to do something special with his life.

The elevator finally reached its destination, and Maria and Adam stepped out.

Adam smiled, nodded at Maria, and headed into the changing rooms. He put his bag away, removed his jewellery, and replaced his thin reading glasses with prescription safety goggles.

Dr. Connors met him as he entered the lab. She was a tall, thin woman with small, brown eyes and wiry brown hair. She looked like everyone's marmite, firm-but-fair schoolteacher. Adam had found her very affable and well-humoured, as far as genius scientists went. He had read all her books and had picked New Aberdeen (amongst other reasons) because he knew she worked there.

"Big day," she said with a smile. "Our first living subject."

"You got it?" Adam asked, glad to see his mentor so upbeat.

"I had to sneak it out of the environment study building last night," Dr. Connors stated, "But if anyone had challenged me, I would probably just ask if they knew who I am."

Adam laughed. Dr. Connors was not a complete egomaniac, but she certainly knew she was famous and would not be afraid to flaunt her fame if it helped. Adam believed, passionately, that she wanted to make the world a better place, and therefore he didn't mind.

***

They approached the machine together, and Maria moved around, placing reflectors in position. They had found that using the machine created an enormous amount of excess energy, some of which converted into light that they had to reflect away from themselves to prevent blindness. This was something Dr. they would have to iron out before running a demonstration for the entire faculty.

Maria joined Dr. Connors and Adam, giving a quick thumb-up. She passed a big cardboard box to Dr. Connors, who pulled out a large black rat.

"Right," she said, smiling. "We shall call you…Rattus?"

"I think it looks like an Adam," Maria stated.

Adam shook his head, looking at Dr. Connors.

"You know," Adam stated. "I'm happy to try it. I really don't see why the animals get to go first."

"Too much paperwork," Dr. Connors said firmly, a twinkle remaining in her eye.

"The first living creature to travel in time is a stinking rat. It won't sound particularly good when I tell this to my grandchildren," Adam said, looking at Dr. Connors, who then turned away to look at the rat, giving it a gentle stroke.

"I think I'll name him Michael, after my ex-husband," she said, and Adam had to smile.

"Ok. So, Maria, get ready." Dr. Connors waved her right hand. Maria rushed to power up the machine.

"Adam, get the video recorders ready." Due to the light, they wouldn't be able to record much, but they needed everything they could get, should there be testing issues, some teething problems with the machine, for example.

Adam set up four video cameras facing into the machine, and then, using a sliding ladder, switched on a fifth camera that looked directly down. Dr. Connors placed Michael into an open box, and then inside the time machine.

The three of them stepped inside a control room, as the time machine powered up.

"Godspeed, Michael-the-rat," Maria said, her accent barely separating the words.

Dr. Connors leaned forward and sorted out the settings. "Ok, let's start small, with one centi-second. It won't mean much to us, but we can use the cameras to observe any change. We don't want to put Michael through more than we need to in case the experience is painful."

"Are you sure you want to go with a jump that can't be observed by the naked eye?" Maria asked.

"I do." Dr. Connors nodded. "Let's not run before we can crawl." With that, she pulled the switch, initiating what they had coined "the jump."

There was a huge flash of light, which was successfully reflected by the mirrors. Almost as soon as it had started, it was over. The time machine powered down, a deep hum resonating through the entire spacious laboratory. It wasn't to worry; they had the finest soundproofing that Dr. Connors's considerable wallet could supply.

Adam smiled when he saw all the cameras and mirrors remained unharmed.

Dr. Connors was the first to step out. She moved quickly toward the box, almost at a trot. Adam was close behind her, while Maria hung back. Dr. Connors and Adam peered into the box.

Michael was missing.

"What?" Dr. Connors asked no one in particular. "Was he vaporized?"

"Vaporized?" Adam was confused.

"Get the video footage now!" Dr. Connors's voice suddenly rose.

Adam scrambled to the top of the sliding ladder, unplugging the camera before coming back down. He turned to Dr. Connors, about to speak, when she nodded behind him.

"I see him!"

Adam turned to see Michael pressed up against the inside of the machine, well outside his box, uncomfortable but alive. Dr. Connors picked up Michael once again, stroking him to calm him.

"He's very startled," she stated. "But I don't think this caused him any physical harm. Mental, maybe, but he's not exhibiting any unnatural behaviours."

"Do you think he actually travelled?" Adam asked.

"I don't know, but he couldn't have climbed out of his box. It's far too large."

"Then maybe…maybe the machine affected his mass?"

"It's not impossible, but this is conjecture. We don't know, not yet." Dr. Connors stated. "You know what I'm about to say. Play the footage, Adam."

A few moments later, Michael had been placed safely within the control room, and Maria was left to attend the lab. Adam and Dr. Connors headed into her research office down the hall.

Adam connected the chip from the video recorder to the computer, while Dr. Connors set about making them both a coffee.

As Dr. Connors came round, she allowed Adam to sit in her swivel chair to operate her computer and stood behind him, looking over his shoulder.

"Ok, this is at a fiftieth of normal speed," Adam said as he hit play. The footage played slowly, the light present to a degree, though dimmed using Adam's editing skills. Michael-the-rat sat nonchalantly in the box, positioned in the middle of the screen. Suddenly, as the video played frame by frame, Michael vanished.

"Stop the recording!" Dr. Connors exclaimed. "Where did he go?"

"I don't know."

"Play the next frame," Dr. Connors ordered, and Adam hit play again. As soon as Michael disappeared, he reappeared in the corner of the camera, pressed up against the inside of the time machine, right where they'd found him.

"Damn," Adam swallowed. "He didn't climb out of the box."

"No, Adam," Dr. Connors shook her head. "It would appear that he teleported."

"Did we—did we just invent the teleport?" Adam asked.

"No," Dr. Connors stated firmly. Her usually approachable demeanour dropped, and she became instantly sterner. "But we might need to look at the drawing board again."

Adam and Dr. Connors headed out of the office. For the next few hours, Dr. Connors returned to her laboratory and poured over the recording, noting, slowing the footage down again and again. Adam was sent away to the library to do some reading, and then the pair of them attended a meeting with Dean Booth, where Dr. Connors continued with the lie that their work involved testing power cells for Edens. She sent Adam away to update their costing sheets to help cover the lie; everything they did had to help cover the lie, down to making the laboratory look like it was made to test power cells.

Adam headed downstairs, back into Dr. Connors's office, and began filling in sheets and sheets on his laptop, the bags under his eyes increasing.

"Adam," came a loud voice, and he looked up to see the curvy outline of Maria filling the doorway, her lab coat removed, just wearing a-white shirt and grey suit trousers. "Are you ok, pal?" she asked.

"I feel like a failure… Dr. Connors picked me for this project, and I can't even get it right. I can't even figure out why it's not working."

"You're being hard on yourself," Maria stated. "Too hard on yourself. For god's sake, Adam, Dr. Connors can't figure out why it's not working either, and she's like the Einstein of our times."

"I suppose," Adam responded, smiling slowly.

"You look tired," Maria said.

"I am tired."

"Go home. Get an early night. I'll finish this off."

"Yes, ma'am," Adam said, standing up and smiling to himself. *Maybe there was something to Maria*, he thought, *she was certainly a good person.*

"I know you like being told what to do. Otherwise, you wouldn't have put up with Dr. Connors for so long," Maria stated, and then blushed ever so slightly. "You know, maybe tomorrow night, you could spend some time with me?"

"You wish," Adam smiled, and stopped as he passed Maria. The two exchanged a brief hug, which was warm and momentarily fulfilling, then Adam cleared his throat and headed out of the door. He stopped in the doorway. Maria watched him for a moment.

"Actually… maybe we could watch a film tomorrow night?"

"I would like that" she responded with a smile.

"How about I meet you at the New Aberdeen south Holo-theatre at 8 p.m. tomorrow?"

Adam headed out the door, up to the changing rooms, and picked up his stuff, placing his jewellery back on. Then, before going out of the building, he quickly opened the lab door and saw Michael-the-rat in his box, squeaking away. Adam nodded at Michael, quickly looked around the lab to make sure that none of his stuff was left inside, closed the lab door, and went out of the building, back to his home.

***

The following morning, Neil Booth, Dean Booth of their college, an overweight and flustered looking man who somewhat resembled Winston Churchill, sat down with Dr. Connors and Adam.

Adam wasn't listening; he was looking out of the window.

As he tuned back into the conversation, he heard Dean Booth mention a reduction in the annual budget to acceleration particle machine funding.

"And of course this would mean a further reduction to the Eden expansion research in D wing, too" he continued. This didn't mean much to Adam, but Dr. Connors face reddened slightly at this.

"But that's my project, I backed it, and funded it, with my own money," Dr. Connors stated.

"Money that you've borrowed from us over the years," Dean Booth responded.

"I have," Dr. Connors replied. "But have I not given you results? Have I not put this university on the map?"

"You have… but in the last few months we've barely seen you; there have been conferences and boards where we've needed you. You've either been on the press tour of your latest book, or been uncontactable, away doing research on this teleport project" Dean Booth explained. As the older man mentioned the word 'teleport,' Adam's eyes shifted over towards Dr. Connors, who caught his eyes and then looked away.

"We will, of course, be conducting a full review of your progress very soon," Dean Booth stated. "Most likely before the end of the next working week"

"We… we need more warning than that," Dr. Connors responded.

"I'm afraid I can't hold off the rising tide any further. The amount of funding we are allowing for such a secret experiment without any visible results can only go on for so long" Dean Booth stated "The Vice Chancellor wants to be involved, and I can only put him off for so long. So, it's either me, or him."

"We should discuss this again on Monday, perhaps," Dr. Connors stated.

"Hmmm," Dean Booth said, and then sat back into his chair, and Adam could see the man was relaxing somewhat. "Yes, we can do that."

Then Dean Booth stood and showed them both the door, which Adam and Dr. Connors promptly used to leave.

Once they were in the corridor, Adam and Dr. Connors exchanged looks. Neither of them said a word, but they fully understood each other.

"I need to meet someone," Dr. Connors finally said, "What are you doing for the rest of the day?"

"Lectures, for the most part. I hold some office hours for my first-year students between three and five, though they never use it—I could meet you after that?" Adam asked.

"Sounds good," Dr. Connors responded. "I'll see you this afternoon."

***

Tired faces filled the lecture hall. End of the week, very nearly the end of term. A chubby-faced young man with square glasses sat right at the front, propping his face up with his hands. A couple of young women toward the back, both in makeup and with blond hair, were having a conversation on their own.

Nevertheless, when lecturing, Adam came alive. One of his few true escapes. Sadly, this lecture, week nine of ten in 'Introduction to Scientific Ethics,' seemed to be grabbing nobody apart from one or two of his nineteen-year-old students. There were a couple of the girls on the front row, one with loud fuzzy hair, and the other with sleek ginger hair, who seemed to be paying strict attention to Adam, just not to what he was saying.

"Of course, we've established that harm is unethical," Adam continued, "so I ask you to consider this question: should we avoid any studies that may potentially harm people? What if there is no way of testing the success of technological advancement without the potential harm of animals, or even people? Should we pursue it?"

He left the question open to the entire room. It all went quiet. A couple of people glanced at their watches. It was 3 p.m., time to wrap up.

Adam held the room longer than he was usually allowed, whenever he could. Out of the corner of his left eye, he saw Maria enter the room and swiftly take a seat.

"Yes," replied a small, skinny student with scruffy blond hair. There was a murmur around the lecture hall, and one scoff of "of course he'd say that."

"Why?" Adam asked, one eyebrow raised. "What kind of technological advancement could possibly justify the decision to hurt someone, erm, Jason?"

"Well," Jason responded. "That person could use themselves in the experiment or maybe find someone who is willing to be harmed."

"That's very true. I supposed we need to account for that recklessness in human nature. But a human life is worth a lot."

"I agree," somebody else added, and Jason shook his head.

As Adam scanned the room, he saw a tall girl with wavey brown hair put her hand up. Adam pointed at her and said, "Emma, go ahead."

"I just don't think we should have that power, you know, as people," she said.

"Can you expand what you mean?" Adam asked.

"We're all sat here, in this university hall, discussing whether we should use up lives to make scientific advancements…are our lives not good enough now? Is humanity not the most prosperous it's ever been?"

Adam moved to respond, but instead it was Justin who countered her first.

"So, should we just stop?" he asked.

An interesting debate, this, Adam thought, *at least there are a couple of brains in this place.*

"We have so many scientific advancements that we're on the cusp on, or almost on the cusp on. Ways of improving our FTL drives, our terraforming, mass-cloning, teleportation, maybe even time travel," Justin stated.

"I hate to interrupt, Justin, as this is fascinating, but there is no evidence that time travel can be achieved. The height of Chinese scientific research poured all their resources into it in the 2290s and achieved…nothing. Let's debate science, not myths, here. Anyway, let's continue this next week. Remember, I want the submission of your module essay by the *start* of that lecture, and I will return it marked by the fifteenth of August. I'm sure you all just need to make the finishing touches anyway."

As the lecture hall packed away, Maria swiftly hopped up onto stage to meet Adam.

"Ooo, Adam" she said, "You are a bit of a dark horse, aren't you?"

"What do you mean?" he asked, as he started to pack away his notes into his leather satchel. "Let's debate science, not, myths, here" she stated, trying her best to imitate Adam's clipped English accent.

"Well, that's right" Adam responded.

"If any of these kids knew what you were doing, they'd worship you" Maria said. Adam placed his hand on his lip, aware there we still a number of students passing by them to leave the hall.

"Then maybe it's best they don't" Adam stated.

"Are you excited for tonight?" Maria asked.

"I am" Adam said, "But I can't finish early today, I need to meet Dr. Connors."

"I'll come with you" Maria added.

"Sure, come with me."

The two of them turned to leave the room, filtering behind the students making their way out. Maria followed Adam down the corridor, all the way through the university campus to Dr. Connors' office. Adam knocked and then opened the door. Dr. Connors stood there, behind her desk, on one side of the room, and on the other stood a man he did not know. The man, arrayed in an all-black military uniform that Adam couldn't identify, looked like a gentleman spy who had escaped straight from a 1900s spy film: handsome, greying, with a warm smile and thick moustache.

"Ah…Adam…and Maria" Dr. Connors "You're early."

"I decided not to hold my office hours this week" he responded.

"Well, it's high time you two met anyway" she said.

"This is Captain Andrew Rosewell" she said "He's the man who's made all this possible. He's with military intelligence, and he's helping fund the experiment. His division were the first people to approach me with the idea."

"Adam Rehange, I assume? And Maria Smith?" Captain Rosewell said, swiftly turning on his foot and heel to firmly shake Adam's hand. He then turned and did the same to Maria.

"You started this?" Adam asked.

"Yes" Captain Rosewell stated "My unit have great interest in the progress of your little operation. There's a great many things Victoria II's splendid military could do with a time machine. Anyway, as Jodie said, this has been an unexpected pleasure, but I really must be getting back to command."

And, as quickly as they'd been introduced, Captain Rosewell nodded, turned to the door, and marched away. Adam was the first to speak once he was out of earshot. "So" Adam said, "This is who we're really working for, it would appear?"

"Well," Dr. Connors responded, "there was never any need for you to know."

"What about trust? Respect? I lecture in scientific ethics, for god's sake! Do you think it would have been useful for Maria and me to know this was secretly a military operation?"

"Some of the greatest scientific discoveries have been made in the name of war. All the work on the Manhattan Project and the work of Robert Oppenheimer was supported by the military. They used science to change the world, Adam, and we can, too" Dr. Connors explained.

"We're not at war anymore!" Adam exclaimed.

"There's always a war brewing, Adam, you know that. And the country that invents the time machine, and holds those time machines, will be untouchable—which country do you think would be most likely to use it well?" Dr. Connors explained.

"I need space…to think."

"Take the weekend, both of you" Dr. Connors stated "Adam, I'm sure you'll understand, in time—" but he had already gone, and Maria with him. Dr. Connors stood alone in the room, staring down the empty corridor, watching her two colleagues disappear out of sight.

Chapter Two

6th October

The trial continued, and as more and more people in a position of influence came to testify, Maria could see the jury turn to one another and begin slowly discussing the situation. She tried to read their lips, to see what was being said, but there were too many conversations, and it was all too hard to follow.

Dr. Jodie Connors sat stone-faced, and Adam, sitting next to her, was not much brighter. Maria looked between the two of them, nodded, and then turned back to the Lord High justice, and then— wait! Adam! For a moment, he had been sat there, sour faced with the rest of them. And then Maria blinked, and he was gone.

Dr. Connors saw that Maria was staring past her and then turned to see the empty space Maria had been looking at.

"What?" she asked, eyebrow raised. Maria paused for a moment, looked down at the ground, and then quietly stated "Nothing."

The Lord Justice stood up and began to speak again, so their attention snapped back to him.

"We would now like to address the statement made by Dr. Connors and Miss Smith in their defence. Dr. Connors, you stated that you were... coerced by another entity, one describing themselves as a member of the British Secret Services?"

Dr. Connors turned to look at Mr. Green, who spoke on her behalf.

"My client states that she was funded and approached by a member of military intelligence who asked her to complete this task. He visited throughout the process of the creation of the time machine and held multiple private meetings with her."

"Was anyone else present at these meetings?" the Lord Justice asked.

"No."

"Where these meetings recorded in anyway?"

"No."

"Were there ever any other members of 'military intelligence' present?"

"No."

The final 'No' hung for a moment over the room, and then the jury frantically began discussing. Dr. Connors caught the eye of the

Vice Chancellor and then looked down. Then slowly, she looked at Maria, their eyes meeting, before she looked away again.

She had messed up, Maria knew.

July 2350

That evening, Adam and Maria met at the Holo-theatre in New Aberdeen. The cloudy sunshine of the morning had long since disappeared, replaced by an urgent wind. Adam didn't mind too much; he'd donned a thick down jacket and met Maria downtown. When she met him, she was holding chips in a cone, one of the many small over-priced takeaways in this area of the city. The film was long, an American summer blockbuster called 'Attack of the Immortal Space Pirates 7,' and it filled the Holo-theatre with explosions, monsters, and all manner of flying sailing ships.

As they walked out, Maria was smiling, whilst Adam remained slightly more straight-faced. They began to walk down away from the Holo-theatre towards a nearby park, but it was getting late.

"Wasn't that great?" Maria asked "I mean, what a cliffhanger! The next one won't be until 2354, sadly, but I can wait."

"Not the sort of thing I usually watch; I'm more of a documentary man."

"I suppose they can seem a little infantile, but you're supposed to watch them ironically, like, laugh at them as they go along."

"Really? I didn't get that vibe at all."

"Well, that's because you watch documentaries. Anyway, you're a university lecturer; isn't watching endless documentaries too like work?

"I watch more than just documentaries on theoretical physics—that would be daft" Adam admitted.

"What do you watch?" she asked.

"Historical, geographical, some on literature, some on sport, well, quite a lot on sport…"

"Sport?" she asked.

"My second love," he stated.

"After?" she asked.

"After physics, obviously!" he smiled.

As they talked, the two of them headed into the park, and Adam stopped walking, taking a moment to turn and look at Maria.

"Today had me thinking" he said slowly, sounding out each word, one at time, "whether this is really what I want."

"What do you mean?" Maria asked, smiling slightly "Adam, this isn't even a date."

"No, I like this." Adam said "I mean what we're doing with Dr. Connors. I'd always had my doubts, but still, deep down, I knew that a time machine would advance our society. It could be used to write so many wrongs."

"We could be famous," Maria added.

"We would; there would be no doubt," Adam said.

"It would have to go public, eventually," Maria added, as they stood in the corner of the well-lit city park.

"Unless… this Captain Rosewell… no, it's unimaginable," Adam pondered and began to look away.

"What? What are you thinking?" Maria asked.

"I'm thinking…that they might keep it a secret, even once it's made. Why bother the rest of the world with a time machine? Why share that power?"

"Yeah…" Maria said, her voice hushed now. "A working time machine, in the hands of one country's government, off the record, unknown to everyone else, could—could do anything."

"It's too dangerous," Adam said. "Let's speak to Dr. Connors on Monday."

"We need to make it public ourselves. Dr. Connors isn't going to just get us to leave."

"This is all speculation," Adam responded. "And it's not working…yet."

"We are this close!" Maria stated, holding her thumb and index finger slightly apart, "Michael-the-rat, he moved. We did *something* yesterday."

"Maybe we need to give Dr. Connors a chance," Adam stated. "Our hands are still the safest. We speak to her on Monday, and then we give her Monday."

"Adam, I don't trust her anymore," Maria said. "We need to do more than that."

"What do you suggest?" Adam asked.

"This weekend," Maria responded. "I'm going to find out what I can about this Captain Rosewell and who he represents."

"That's not a bad idea, and—oh, hello" Adam said, looking past Maria with alarm.

Slowly, a figure appeared from the shadows of the park. It was a big man, hunched, but without the hunch, the man would be as tall as Adam. He grinned, and smiled slowly at Maria, but then grabbed her with one hand, and thrust her up against the wall with the other. He pulled out a dagger, but Adam thumped the man as hard as he could across the forehead. The man fell back and staggered, before slowly standing up and attempting to take a swing at Adam, who swiftly moved out of the way, and then grabbed the assailant and threw him to the ground.

The man, who had greying hair and a chapped lip, took a deep breath in, and, taking a last look at Adam and Maria, stood up, turned, and scampered off into the night. Maria turned back to Adam and hugged him tightly. Adam just stood there motionless.

"Jesus," she stated, and slowly let go of Adam, who continued to just stand there.

"Everything ok?" she asked.

"All good," Adam responded. "Just…nothing. I suppose he didn't see both of us when he approached."

"Probably not," Maria agreed "Can you…walk me home?"

"I can," Adam stated, and the two of them hooked arms, Maria leading the way into the dark streets of New Aberdeen.

***

On Monday, Maria, and Adam both settled into their coats, their walk into the office more sombre, neither one of them wanting to really discuss what happened on Friday night.

"We run another test. Now."

Adam and Dr. Connors headed out of the office.

"Maria," Dr. Connors said as they re-entered the lab, "we're running another test. Is Michael ready?" Adam noted a nervousness in Dr. Connors' voice that had not been there before.

"He is." Once again, Maria moved forward with the box containing Michael and placed it in the centre of the time machine. Adam switched the cameras back on.

Dr. Connors moved swiftly into the control room, followed by Adam and Maria.

Dr. Connors' hands hovered above the control board. "We need to put Michael's destination in to match his current location."

"In terms of longitude and latitude?" Adam asked.

"No, er... no, that doesn't matter. The landing destination needs to read 'same as starting position.' See, look—we didn't put anything last time. That must be where we went wrong…"

"You think?"

"Yes," Dr. Connors replied, "and the small jump in time was mirrored with a small jump in space. We've got to manually take out the jump in space. You know, ask the machine not to do it."

"And if you're wrong?" Adam raised an eyebrow. "That's a theory. We've got no evidence to support it."

"Then we've invented a teleport device, not a time machine."

"Michael disappeared. For a frame of that recording, he was gone; no puff, no bang, just gone," Adam said nervously. "He no longer existed."

"That might be the effect of a teleport. The atoms that formed Michael temporarily disappeared and then reappeared elsewhere."

"Maybe. But we ought to increase the time jump to be certain."

Dr. Connors nodded. "Good idea. Maria, increase the jump time to a second."

"Putting it up to a second, Dr. Connors."

"God, I hope you're right, Adam. I want you to be right."

"Me too, boss."

"Hit it, Maria," Dr. Connors ordered, and Maria flipped the start switch.

The time machine flickered into life once again, roaring, and ready to go. There was the same flash of light, shining only for a moment, then flickering away.

When it was completely gone, Michael had disappeared. He did not reappear.

Adam and Dr. Connors ran into the lab as Maria scrambled to power everything down. Adam looked round the inside of the time machine, while Dr. Connors looked under every box, and into every nook and cranny within the entire lab. Maria soon joined her.

"He's not here," Dr. Connors said after a couple of minutes.

"Damn." Adam groaned and sat down on the inside of the time machine, just next to the box.

***

A few moments later, Adam and Dr. Connors were back in her office, with a recording of the most-recent test. Adam hit play. Just like last time, Michael disappeared. But then, even playing at a reduced speed, he did not reappear. He was just… gone.

"Adam, what on Earth? Tell me you're seeing this, too."

"We teleported him."

"We did not teleport him! That machine is not set up to be a teleport. It sends objects to one of two places; the same destination as it set off from, or nowhere, in which case the machine reverts to sending to where the object set off from. Either way, it seems to want to teleport the object somewhere else."

"Then maybe… maybe we should specifically put in coordinates. Longitude and latitude, like Maria suggested."

"We could put in the longitude and latitude of right here, but to put in the coordinates of anywhere else on the globe, to jump the object in space and time simultaneously, would require a redesign and a rebuild of the existing machine. We don't have time for that, and I don't have the patience." Dr. Connors was firm. "I have spent too much time on the exact details of the post-build theory to be looking at a physical rebuild."

"But we are already jumping objects in time and space," Adam stated. "Somehow."

"What do you mean?"

"That first jump, with Michael, he moved in time and in space. It was minuscule, but it was still a jump in both dimensions," Adam explained.

"Go on."

"And perhaps the second jump was too big. The machine couldn't handle it. Vaporized the rat," Adam explained.

Dr. Connors' eyes widened. "And maybe the two don't exist without one another. Maybe we can't jump things through time, without also jumping them through space. And because we didn't set the location, it tried to jump it through space while getting it as near as possible to the original destination. Second time round, when we asked it to stay in the same place intentionally, the machine vaporized the rat."

"It's possible." Adam nodded. "All we need to do is improve the machine, and theoretically, we could do bigger jumps…"

"Exactly," Dr. Connors smiled. "But this is all a lot to think about. I need to go over the math's again. Look at the footage—from every angle. We'll call it a day for physical testing, but I need you to get this written up, beat by beat, into some form of report."

"I can do that," Adam nodded before turning from the office, and then turning back. "You know, this is a lot."

It was several hours later, and Adam sat in the university cafeteria, eating some cheap chili con carne served on a plastic plate. All that money and the catering was awful.

Out of the huge glass pane windows that surrounded the cafeteria, the sun was sinking just below the horizon. A few kitchen staff moved about behind the serving, clearing away the cooking trays and vats.

A plump young janitor moved between the tables with a mop and bucket. A couple of undergrad students sat far away from him—a couple ogling each other while they pushed their chili meals around on their plates, letting them run cold.

Adam recognized them; they were physics students who had been in a module he'd lectured on earlier in his PhD. He was unsure whether to make eye contact.

One of them, the lad, smiled and waved. The girl followed suit.

Adam smiled, nodded, and looked back down at the unappetizing food. It was getting late. There was a moderately comfortable bed waiting for him at home.

As the young couple left, the janitor went over to clear the mess that remained on their table. Adam was in the middle of the cafeteria, completely alone.

Suddenly he heard a scream, and his head snapped towards the kitchen. One of the staff dropped a pot of boiling water, and in the confusion, a black rat with no tail ran out from underneath the serving stations.

"Pass me that pot," Adam exclaimed, and the kitchen worker threw the small pot to him. Adam caught it and chased the rat between the tables.

Michael—Adam was sure it was Michael—dodged and dived, but the janitor turned to face him, which caused the rat to double back on himself, right into Adam's path. Adam slammed the cooking pot on top of the rodent, trapping him inside.

"Got you," Adam grunted. "Slippery bastard."

"Keep an eye on the rat," Adam ordered the janitor and headed into the kitchen. A couple of the staff were still shaken. Adam turned to them and nodded at a big man, the sous-chef.

"Where did it come from?" Adam asked.

"He popped out from that ventilation shaft." The man pointed at the bottom of the wall where a small ventilation shaft had been popped off its hinges. Adam crouched down and inspected it. The inside of the ventilation shaft had claw marks on it, as if Michael had struggled. Really struggled. And trapped within the ventilation shaft entrance itself was Michael's tail. It lay there, lifeless.

"Anything?" The sous-chef asked. Adam pulled Michael's tail from ventilation grate and stuffed it into his breast pocket.

"Nothing. Poor thing had got caught and had to ram its way through; tail came off in the process."

"Is that normal?" the sous-chef asked.

"I'm no biologist, but I believe so," Adam hedged. "It's probably just a stray, nothing to worry about, no lawsuits, I'd say.

I'll take the thing to the lab and destroy it humanely." With that, he walked away.

Just as Adam left the kitchen, he walked out into the dining room and caught sight of Dean Booth passing beyond the end of the room, walking down a corridor. Dean Booth looked briefly into the dining hall as he passed and caught sight of Adam. Both men stopped. Dean Booth walked into the room.

"Everything ok, Mr. Rehange?" he asked, as he got close enough for the other man to hear him. It took Adam a moment to respond, his hand clenched tight over Michael-the-rat, eventually responding "Yes, of course, why would things not be ok?"

"Because you look nervous, and I can see the sweat on your forehead." Dean Booth stated.

"I've just been at the gym after work; you know me," Adam replied.

"Also, you're holding a giant black rat in the university cafeteria," Dean Booth added "It appears to have no tail."

Bollocks, Adam thought.

"I was wondering if you had some kind of reasonable explanation for that?" Dean Booth asked.

"I erm…" Adam stuttered, before coming back to his senses "It's a…we're using it in an experiment."

"I see" Dean Booth stated, now moving closer to Adam so that he could talk more quietly "I must admit, Adam, that this experiment of yours is starting to use up my patience with yourself and Jodie."

"Sorry," Adam blurted, not sure what else to say.

"I would quite like to see this teleport device that you've been working on, which takes up so much time and money and yet delivers so few results."

"I'm afraid that will not be possible" Adam said.

"Why not?" Dean Booth asked.

"It's not… complete."

"I know that," Dean Booth said. "I'd like to see it anyway."

"I, you know, really shouldn't. Dr. Connors wouldn't be happy if I showed you it without her present."

"Well," Dean Booth stated, slowly smiling "Don't tell her."

I'm not going to be able to get out of this, am I? Adam thought. Slowly, he moved one converse-covered foot behind the other, and shifted his weight, trying his hardest to think of an excuse out of this situation. Nothing came to him.

"You're starting to seem a little too resistant to this, Adam," Dean Booth stated.

The threatening tone of the last sentence snapped Adam back into it.

"Oh, well, then, let's head down and have a look."

A few moments later, and Dean Booth followed Adam hurriedly down the steps from the upper floor of the particle physics labs. Adam held Michael-the-rat, now tailless but with his wound bandaged, opening each door with just one arm.

"You know, I'm sorry to have put you all the way down here, working on this teleport," Dean Booth stated "But needs must. Even our allies can't know we have these."

"So, you've said before," Adam responded.

"You've had an interesting history, I suppose, haven't you, Adam?" Dean Booth asked, "To come into academia having been an almost famous… triathlete?"

"Pentathlete," Adam corrected him.

"Haha, I bet your parents are proud of you."

"I don't really speak to my parents much anymore," Adam responded. He didn't like making small talk with someone he didn't necessarily like. Dean Booth, for example, was prone to switching from calculating stares and intimidation to jovial small talk in a moment.

"That is a shame, Adam," Dean Booth continued, as they arrived at the right door, and Adam scanned his card into the door next to it, allowing them both into the lab. As they entered, Dean Booth took in sight of the laboratory, its central dome with glass casing in the centre of the room, and the large control room tucked away to one side.

"Blimey," Dean Booth stated, before turning to look at the other man "This looks like no teleport template I've ever seen."

"Just take a look," Adam said, handing Dean Booth Michael the rat, who looked at Adam as if he'd just handed the other man excrement. "Take a look. I'm sure you'll find it's all in working order, and that we're on time for delivering the project."

Dean Booth headed over to the centre of the room carrying Michael, and Adam darted into the control room. Dean Booth walked over to the glass cabinet and set down Michael, who scurried away out of sight.

"Well," Dean Booth stated, touching the glass door and then inspecting the door release mechanism. "I'd need to see all the full specs, but this looks like a complete machine. I assume you were testing it on the rat and didn't want me to know ahead of time of announcement?"

Oh, thank God, Adam thought, *we might be ok here*.

"Yes, that's right," he responded. Then Dean Booth popped the glass door to the machine open and stepped inside. He smiled, and nodded, taking the contraption in. Then he stopped and his face fell.

"This panel" he stated, "It has a destination."

"Yes, that's right," Adam responded quickly "Where we send the subject."

"But it has a time, not a place!" Dean Booth stated, and turned to stare Adam directly in the eyes. "This is a time machine."

Before Dean Booth could even do anything, Adam hit the huge green button on the control panel, and the glass doors closed around Dean Booth.

"You're a liar, Adam Rehange! You know damn well the repercussions of this! Let me out now," Dean Booth stated, "You will let me out, and you will let me out now!"

"I can't do that," Adam said to himself, too quietly for Dean Booth to here.

"When the world finds out about this, this whole university is screwed!" Dean Booth exclaimed. Tears started to appear in Adam's eyes, as he became aware of what he now had to do. He turned, slammed the destination scale up, 100 years into the future, and pressed launch. The machine began to count down, and Adam groaned. Dean Booth was battering on the walls of the machine for Adam to let him out, but there was no choice now. He had simply seen far too much. The light in the room increased, and increased, and Dean Booth began to scream, not in pain, but simply overwhelmed by fear of what was going to happen to him, and Adam turned away, unable to look at what was going to happen, and began to crouch down on the floor, facing away.

Then, in a moment, the light was gone, and Adam stood back up, his hands shaking, his face teary, and looked at the empty room in front of him, Dean Booth now catapulted a hundred years into the future.

What had he done?

Chapter Three

7th October

The trial continued, with various members of the university board and senior management appearing to protest their innocence against the claims made about wrongdoing made by the university. As the day progressed, Dr. Connors sunk further and further into her chair.

"It must be addressed," The Lord Justice stated, sitting forward, "that the accused, in their personal statement, claimed that the actions of Mr. Adam Rehange were in some way understandable and justified."

Dr. "We would like to state that the individual in question was under stress due to the situation he was placed in," the lawyer answered.

"A situation that he had willingly put himself, from what we understand," the Lord Justice explained "And the fact that he also most likely took the life of Neil Booth, Dean of the college of theoretical physics at the University."

Maria shifted in her seat awkwardly. *The focus of this court should not be on Adam,* she thought. *It should be on Dr. Connors if it was on anyone.*

As the scene droned on, Maria found herself staring out of the window, not taking on the grey noise of the trial anymore. She thought of Adam Rehange, his passion, his kindness towards her on so many occasions.

She zoned back in when Dr. Connors stood.

The Lord Justice stated, "that we now prepare to hear the statement of defence." Maria realized Dr. Connors was going to give her own statement.

"I wanted to plead my case with the court," she said clearly. "That while there has been significant damage as the outcome of this experiment, we *need* this technology. We need it to help us to overcome our problems and move forward. Can the British government not see the potential that this has machine has? It would change the globe; it would make the United Kingdom a world superpower once more—it would put us back on the map! The Russians, the Chinese, the Americans, the UN, the ISA would all want what we have at our fingertips!"

There was a lot of murmuring from everyone in the court—this was not what they'd been expecting.

"I beg you to consider a fully funded, public, time-machine program," Dr. Connors stated.

"We were so close… we got it working, even! It just needs fine-tuning."

"This trial is not a sales pitch," the Lord Justice stated. "You understood the implications of this experiment when you began."

Dr. Connors took a deep breath and sat back down. She turned and looked at Maria for the first time during the day. Maria just stared back and shook her head.

****

Maria had been sleeping when Adam came to her apartment, eyes wide and sweat on his usually composed face. He had clearly been crying a lot.

"Adam!" she said.

"I need to—I need to talk to you," he said, and pushed his way past her into her apartment.

"Woah—what is it?" Maria asked, turning and grabbing him by the wrist, so that he couldn't ascend her stairs. He shook her hand off, being stronger than her, but this angered her.

"Adam, stop, you're being weird!" she exclaimed.

"I've, I've done something" Adam said, his usually steely composure completely gone, as he was unable to look Maria in the eyes. She grabbed his hand, and this time she held onto it.

Adam stared at her and didn't say a word.

"Just calm down, Adam," Maria then said, unsure of what could have rattled Adam so much "Let's go upstairs… I'll make you a cup of tea or something."

Adam said nothing in response. Slowly, he allowed her to lead him up the stairs, and into the small living room of her flat. He took a seat on her two-person sofa, and she moved over to her Kitchenette to switch the kettle on. He continued to avoid eye contact. His right knee shot up and down, tapping his heel on the hard wood floor with anxious energy.

Slowly, the kettle boiled, and Adam continued to say nothing.

"If something has happened," Maria began "I can help."

"I…I can't begin to explain," Adam stated.

"Whatever it is, Adam, I *can* help. Is it the machine? This job?"

"I suppose," Adam responded.

"Then tomorrow, we leave… you and I let this machine go. We hand in our notices and Dr. Connors can find someone else."

"That's a nice idea," Adam responded softly. "But now I don't think I can leave this project that easily."

"Well," Maria said, her eyes widening as she stepped away from the boiling kettle. "Whatever Dr. Connors has on you, whatever bargaining chips she has over you, we can just reveal everything, the machine, the lies, Captain Rosewell, all of it."

"She doesn't have anything on me," Adam stated and turned to look her in the eyes for the first time. Maria froze where she stood. The kettle went off behind her. "I need this project to be a success. I *need* the time machine to work" he stated grimly.

"Adam, what do you mean?" Maria asked.

"I was so close to famous," Adam stated, "to being the next big British sport star. Pentathlon. I'm surprised that more people don't know me, sometimes, but then history very rarely remembers the losers.

"You're not a lose."

"And I let it take up my whole life, every moment from when I woke up to the moment I went to bed. Training, coaching, and promoting my brand. I was never there for my own friends and my own family. And there was one time, the summer of 2326, one month before the Olympics, when I'd gone to the cinema with my sister in Glasgow. She'd been scared to walk home alone, and I told her, I insisted, that it'd be ok. That it'd be alright. One rainy

Wednesday night in May, in Glasgow city centre. I had training early the next day, and of course, I couldn't miss it. So, I ducked off straight after the film, barely even said goodbye."

"Whatever happened" Maria interrupted "wasn't your fault."

"She died," Adam stated. "Because I wasn't there. She was attacked and she fought back. I don't think the guy meant to kill her, but she was a fighter. A knife came out, and it was all over as quickly as it started. She died, for the contents of her purse."

"And you want to go back and change it?" Maria asked, "We don't even know if that could work." By this time, the kettle had finished boiling and had completely settled again.

"Then we can make it work. You don't understand the mess I'm in, Maria, you really don't." Adam stated "I went to that Olympics and sat on the reserves bench for the summer, and then in October, I injured my knee training, and that was it, I was out. I looked for something else. Something else to throw my obsession into, and after sports, it had always been physics. I applied to university and worked my way up, first class student from undergraduate all the way up to the PhD, where I got the attention of, of course, Dr. Jodie Connors."

"She headhunted you," Maria stated.

"And you," Adam responded. "I don't think she's ever been very coy about it. She's a world-famous scientist, she knows she can use people. And I appealed to her because she somehow knew my background."

"And she put two and one together?" Maria asked.

"She knew I'd stop at nothing to make her project work, no matter how illegal it was," Adam stated gravely.

"Then leave," Maria said again. "Just run away, with me. She can't complete that project without us."

"It's too late," Adam responded, turning away from her to look at the window.

Maria turned away and headed back over to the kitchenette. Slowly, she began to pour herself and Adam two teas.

There was quiet for a few moments, and then suddenly Adam stood up, stating, "I have to go. This was a bad idea."

Maria moved in front of him, holding the cup of tea up in front of her so he couldn't just push her out of the way.

"Just stop here and calm yourself down, Adam," Maria stated "I can understand why you're upset, but you're a good man. In that park, you saved me. You shouldn't hurt yourself over mistakes you made years ago now."

"And what about mistakes that I've made just now?" Adam stated angrily.

"What do you mean?" Maria asked.

Adam paused, and then more calmly stated "I've made mistakes right now."

"That doesn't matter."

"I did something I shouldn't have done."

"That doesn't matter."

"I killed Dean Booth." Adam stated.

Maria dropped the cup of tea on the floor. The enamel mug smashed across the floor, flicking the tea everywhere.

"I... you... Adam... what?" Maria stuttered.

"He found out about the time machine," Adam said "He found out, through me, so I tricked him. I lured him into it, Maria.

"Where is he now?" Maria asked.

"God knows," Adam responded, pushing past Maria and almost knocking her off her feet. He was now between her and the door. For a moment, Maria panicked. Then, Adam placed his hand on the door handle and pressed it down.

"I hoped coming here would make me feel better, but if anything, it's made me feel worse," he stated, opening the door and turning to look back at Maria one last time. "Be seeing you," he said, stepping back out into the rainy night.

As soon as Maria had digested what had just happened, she followed Adam down the stairs, and she caught sight of him, a now-hooded figure in the dark and the rain, visible under the dim streetlights, getting smaller and smaller in the distance.

"Adam!" she screamed "Adam! Come back! Don't be an idiot!" The figure that was Adam did not respond, but only got smaller, and smaller, until he disappeared into the night.

***

Adam stepped into the control room, turning the machine on for the second time that evening.

Adam took a swig from an old whiskey bottle he had kept in his locker, set up the controls for a ten-minute jump into the future, removing longitude and latitude and landing back in the same spot. He didn't need the rat.

Adam adjusted the cameras, stepped back into the control room, and set the machine in motion. Then he hopped out again with enthusiasm and stepped into the time machine. The machine began to whir into life and hummed with noise. Slowly but surely, light surrounded him. Michael-the-rat squealed from his box, panicked and unable to understand what was going on.

Adam looked up, embracing the light. A feeling of energy enveloped him, like a solid coating. It tingled every skin particle, like nothing Adam had ever experienced.

Adam felt it burning up, the heat increasing. What seemed like a moment in the control room was an eternity inside the machine.

Adam closed his eyes and smiled. His feet began to lift off the ground; his heels, and then his palms; he felt entirely weightless. He felt the energy, the sound, the temperature increasing all around him, and he embraced it. The burning brilliance increased and increased, with what must have taken a second from outside, the machine seeming to take an eternity from within it. Just when it became too much for him to bear, he heard a jagged ripping, and everything went black. He was no longer inside the University of New Aberdeen. He had gone somewhere else entirely.

***

The following morning, Dr. Connors and Maria entered the lab, almost simultaneously, to find the cameras set up and still running.

Dr. Connors searched the control room and found a terrified, tailless Michael running in circles inside his box. The control panel reading showed a planned ten-minute jump with no change to the location.

"What the hell? What happened here? Where is Adam?" Dr. Connors asked.

"There's footage," Maria shouted. "It's still recording—almost thirteen hours of it." "Switch it off," Dr. Connors ordered. "Load it up on my computer now."

"It won't be fast," Maria said.

"I know. Just get it done. Was this Adam?"

"Either that, or we had an intruder."

"No, there's no sign of a forced entry. And apart from us, Adam was the only one with the code to the doors. We left together yesterday, so unless you snuck back in, this was him."

"This was him, then," Maria headed out to upload the file to Dr. Connors's computer.

"Please tell me he didn't get in that thing without supervision," Dr. Connors whispered.

Dr. Connors searched the control room and spotted a piece of paper with Adam's scrawled handwriting: "Michael travels 1 centi-second—jump across the machine. Michael travels 1 second—

jumps into the green cafeteria." Dr. Connors read it and then read it again.

"Ah, damn," she whispered to herself and began to panic. Adam must have come across Michael after she'd left. The machine had jumped the rat in space; if Michael had landed in the green cafeteria, he'd jumped almost three hundred meters.

Dr. Connors frowned and headed out of the lab. She swung into her office, where Maria sat at her desk, uploading the video file.

"Which way is the green cafeteria from here?"

"West," Maria said.

"On the first jump, Michael was pressed up against the machine on our left, from the control room, which is…westerly?"

"That's right," Maria confirmed. Dr. Connors handed her Adam's note.

"Oh my god. What does this mean?"

Suddenly there was ding, and Maria checked the computer. "The video... It's ready to watch."

Dr. Connors and Maria sat side by side, watching the video screen intently, unsure of what was about to happen. They watched as Adam stepped inside the time machine. Everything seemed normal. The time machine flicked into life, then Adam was surrounded by light and disappeared. Gone.

They fast-forwarded ten minutes, but he was still nowhere to be seen. They waited another minute. Dr. Connors hit the fast-forward, and they sped through the recording at about fifty times the regular speed. After another few minutes, there was still nothing.

Dr. Connors and Maria slowly turned to look at each other and then go back to the screen. Dr. Connors cut to the end of the recording, where the lab looked exactly the same.

They sat in their seats, not saying anything, for quite some time.

After a while, Dr. Connors spoke. "I have had an idea, but the ramifications are not pleasant. We programmed the machine to ignore latitude and longitude, to avoid confusing it. Even to the same measure, the subject could end up in a slightly different spot. You follow?"

"Yes," Maria replied.

"So, to avoid that, we wanted the subject to end up in exactly the same spot in space, yes? The issue is the Earth is always moving. It's always spinning on its axis and it's always rotating around the sun. The machine calculates not to throw objects into space due to the Earth's orbit; it might fail to factor in the Earth rotating on its axis. That means whatever's west of us is coming toward us at an incredible speed."

"Ok...."

"About two hundred eighty meters per second, if my memory serves me correctly," Dr. Connors said. "So, when we jumped Michael across the time machine floor, he landed in the same place he set off. But everything else on Earth had moved two-point-eight meters due to the rotation."

Maria nodded.

"And then when we jumped Michael for a full second, he might have been gone for that second, but he landed in the green cafeteria, which is two hundred eighty meters west of the lab. So, when Adam jumped ten minutes, it would have landed him—"

"Landed him west of here," Maria finished. "But wait, you're saying he's ok? That the time machine definitely works?"

"It works," Dr. Connors smiled.

"Then…where's Adam?" Maria asked.

"He'll be wherever's one hundred seventy kilometres west of here." Dr. Connors searched on her laptop to work out exactly where that was. But when she saw where, her face dropped.

"Where is he?" Maria asked in a whisper.

***

Ben Nevis is the tallest mountain in the United Kingdom, located in the county of Inverness-shire in Scotland. This natural beauty, composed of thousands of tons of metamorphic and igneous rock, sits at the very edge of Loch Linnhe and near the town of Fort William. It stands a fine 1,345 meters above sea level and is what remains of a Devonian volcano. One of its sides, Glen Nevis, is the steepest slope in Britain. Thousands of tourists visit it every year, which prompted the opening of a pub at the mountain's summit in 2039.

In English, its name is Venomous Mountain.

Underneath all that rock, all that wildlife, all those people, in the base of Ben Nevis, a man appeared.

The man appeared from nowhere and all he could see was blackness. The weight of the mountain pressed upon him, the stone running through his legs, where two objects were attempting to fill the exact same space. He was bleeding out, running out of oxygen, deep in the base of Ben Nevis.

He tried to reach down to his pocket for his phone, but he could not move.

He tried to work out where he was, but with the lack of oxygen, his head began to pound. He had been in a lab… somewhere… somewhere that must have been far away. But now he no longer knew where he was.

He gritted his teeth, and tried to remain calm, thinking about his friends, his mum, his dad, his sister. Trying to fight through the pain, he focused on his happiest moments. He would not go calmly into the darkness. Recent memories rose up, and he clung to them. A machine, a machine that had puzzled him beyond belief, that he had spent his academic life working towards, from school through to doctorate.

That was it, a time machine. Memories started to come back to him. He wanted to invent time travel; and he had done so. He'd certainly go down in the history books, that much he knew. He could just see himself, standing on a plinth, holding a Nobel Prize in Physics, where he would join his childhood heroes—scientists like Curie and Newton, Einstein, and Hawking—on the next generation of physicists' bedroom walls.

The man smiled. He had made it.

Then the man in the mountain, whose name was Adam Rehange, closed his eyes, rested his head on a stone, and smiled no more.

Epilogue

Dr. Connors was led away from the High Court, closely followed by Maria Smith, both in handcuffs. A line of policemen kept the press, the protestors, and the anti-protestors at bay. Dr. Connors raised her hands so that the press could not get a clear photograph, but Maria did not do the same. A grey-haired policewoman with narrow eyes held Dr. Connors by the shoulder, leading her down to the car. The policewoman bundled Dr. Connors into the front of the car, before her colleague, a larger man with no hair, bundled Maria into the seat next to her, and the two police officers got into the front of the car.

Slowly, but surely, the car began to make its way through the crowd surrounding the High Court, with police officers in riot gear slowly moving the protestors back. Dr. Connors turned and looked at Maria up and down, and then looked away, out of the window.

There was a pause, a beat, a moment, where Maria almost expected tears, and maybe even an apology.

But when Dr. Connors turned back to Maria, her resolve was steely, with no sign of emotion.

"Do you ever wonder who he was?" Dr. Connors asked,

"Adam?" Maria asked, eyebrow raised. What was she on about?

"No, Rosewell!" Dr. Connors exclaimed; the car was beginning to pick up speed as it left the High Court behind.

"He was some man," Maria stated, "And he ruined our lives."

"He must have… belonged to a foreign spy circuit. He knew of Adam's past, my past, he knew the inner details of the University's most secure areas," Dr. Connors explained as the car drove on.

"He was very good at his job. He knew you were a new-age Nationalist, and he pulled on those strings," Maria stated bitterly.

"He could have been Russian perhaps, or French. The Germans have been jealous of our new age of scientific endeavours for decades now. Although it wouldn't surprise me if he was Japan's man, either. I wouldn't put it past the Indians to try something—"

"I don't think it matters," Maria interrupted, with a sharpness that took Dr. Connors aback. "He won. This incident will dethrone the UK as the leader in temporal physics, and its allies. That is what he wanted, and it's what he got."

"Oh, come on, do you really think that's the case?" Dr. Connors asked.

"I'm sure of it," Maria stated and turned to look out the window. On the pavement next to them, a calmer crowd had gathered to watch the procession of police cars taking them through the streets of Edinburgh. Maria watched the faces of the people stood on the pavement, some frowning, some angry, some sad, a few young men pointing and laughing.

In amongst these faces, for a moment, Maria saw Adam Rehange, his face completely neutral. Slowly, as Maria's eyes followed Adam's, he smiled. Then she blinked, and he was gone.

"Yes," Dr. Connors stated, and Maria zoned back into where they were, the police car, in the middle of Edinburgh. "We've opened Pandora's box, you see, we've opened the lid on time travel. It'll be hard for the British government, or any for that matter, to put a lid back on that."

Maria turned to look Dr. Connors in the eyes and saw that the older woman was almost smiling, despite being in the back of a police car. It seemed almost like she expected Maria to return that smile. Instead, Maria lunged and swung her handcuffed hands as one, hitting Dr. Connors hard in the face, and there was a sudden crack—she had broken Dr. Connors nose. The smaller woman made no attempt to try anything back, and just sat, clutching her nose.

"How do you live with yourself?" Maria asked. Dr. Connors didn't respond, and the police car drove on in silence.

THE END

Omniscience

By Alex O'Neill
(Based on an original idea Ted Marois)

Date: 2949

Location: Meridian Station Designation EON-1

Chapter One

Tara tightened her hands at the end of the arms on her allocated seat. She felt constrained by the huge seat belt coming over both of her shoulders and clipping into a strap just over her crotch. The lift shuttle was full of people, but Tara stared at the roof, not wanting to make eye contact with any of them. She held the arms of her chair tighter as the shuttle began to pick up speed.

"Care for some sweets?" came a sudden, warm voice.

She looked to the man seated to her left, his warm smile out of place against the crisp white EON Corporation uniform. He was a middle-aged Asian man with dark, piercing green eyes, a round, youthful face with a warm smile. He had a slight belly, but carried himself well, clearly a tall man when stood.

"I'm sorry?" she asked.

"Sweets?" the man held out a bag of Jelly Babies. "I find they ease the stomach during the climb up the gravity well. They help with the transition."

There was a heartbeat of hesitation before she reached into the bag and took a candy, putting it into her mouth.

"Thank you," she said.

"Better?" the man asked when she started sucking on it. The taste was sweet and satisfied her whole tongue, and she did feel a little more relaxed. To her surprise, it was helping her feel better. "I'm Gabriel Sen, Medical Officer on the trip."

"Tara Dean, Engineer," she said.

"What is the mission, anyway? The boys upstairs didn't tell me much when they reassigned me onto it. Just said they needed a medical officer assigned as soon as possible. All they said was 'experimental and dangerous.'"

The ship tumbled beneath them as they at last broke free of the atmosphere. "It's an FTL engine test, a prototype of the new Mark 4 engines," Tara said, the Jelly Baby dissolving away in her mouth.

"Ah," Gabriel nodded. "Those projects. Travelling to other galaxies... and here I thought our own galaxy was big enough," he chortled. Then he looked at her curiously, "So how does it work?"

With an eager laugh, Tara almost forgot her dread of space. "How much time do you have?"

"Approaching EON-1 docking facility," announced the ship's AI. "Estimated time of arrival, ten minutes."

Gabriel smiled. "I guess that's your answer."

"When a conventional FTL ship travels faster-than-light, it bends space time around it, creating a bubble that lets it bypass the speed of light." Gabriel seemed like a smart man, but she tried to avoid any deeply technical terms as it wasn't the field. "The Mark 4 engine is a step in a different direction; by stimulating exotic matter at the right time, you can open a hole in the fabric of our universe, and move the object in question, in this case The Infinitum, across dimensions in the form of pure atoms, which..."

"Allows for nearly instantaneous travel between one point and another anywhere in the universe," Gabriel nodded, surprising Tara. He smiled placatingly. "I minored in relativistic physics. Oh, and I've seen films, I guess. It's a fascinating theory, but it would mean a large number of our accepted physics models would have to be wrong in order for it to work."

"Believe me, it works," Tara narrowed her eyes. "We tested this and tested this. Now all we need to do is a field test. EON has decided to use the Mark 4 on a regular deep space mission to prove its applicability to the company's processes."

"A lot riding on this for you, then?"

"Well, yes, but I'm only an FTL engine specialist engineer," Tara responded, "The representative from the Mark 4 development team is Dr. Asif Calabash; he's the Science Officer with us on this specific trip, and he's the one whose livelihood truly rides on it." She had worked closely on the FTL project, alongside several other great minds, to understand the effects on a transport ship such as theirs.

"PREPARE FOR LANDING," the AI pilot announced, the ship shuddering as thrusters maneuvered into the EON-1 docking facility. The space station acted as the corporate headquarters for the Meridian Corporation, allowing them to oversee every aspect of their operations with keen eyes.

The shuttle settled onto the hangar floor. As the rear ramp opened with a hiss, Tara instinctively held her breath in case they accidentally vented into space.

"Another sweet?" Gabriel offered. She took one gladly.

"Tara!" someone cried, and Tara was barely out of her seat when someone pounded up the ramp and practically tackled her. There was a woman on top of her, a woman she knew well.

"Ela," Tara grunted, struggling to stay on her feet. "Too tight; you're going to kill me."

"Oh, don't be so serious," Ela laughed, loosening a little but still holding onto Tara. "It's been years since I've seen you; I think I've earned the right to be excited." She glanced at Gabriel and gave Tara a not-so subtle nudge. "Look at you, getting back into the dating game. Who's the handsome older man?"

Gabriel cleared his throat, "Gabriel Sen, medical officer assigned to Mission 104. I'm assuming you're Ela Treen?"

The small woman nodded and let go of Tara, much to the engineer's relief. "That's right. I'm a co-pilot and navigation officer of The Infinitum."

"Nice to meet you," Gabriel said, smiling.

"Nice to meet you, too," Ela responded, shaking his hand. "This way, you two. Captain is just finishing pre-flight."

They followed Ela across the hangar deck and over towards The Infinitum. Tara turned her head and took in the sights and smells of the place, knowing it might be the last time she would be anywhere resembling normality for some time.

The Infinitum stood alone across the hangar from the other ships: large, brown, and streamlined, with small cockpit windows at the front and large rocket exhausts at the rear. The main deck sat at the front in an almost spherical shape, and with small windows at the top where the living quarters were located. It looked important when first glancing at it, but lost interest soon after, so that no one else in the hanger paid it the blindest bit of attention. Few people knew what it was, to be fair.

As the three of them approached the ship, Captain Clare Peters stepped down off its gangway to greet them. She wore a faded maroon jumper over her captains' uniform that brought out the paleness of her skin and her observant dark eyes.

"I don't believe we've formally met," she said, her eyes falling on Gabriel, who walked at the front. "You must be the new medical officer."

"That's correct, Gabriel Sen," Gabriel said, his large face sporting a broad smile, and stepped forward and shook his new commanding officer's hand.

Peters turned to Ela. "Show Officer Sen to his quarters, please."

Ela followed Gabriel up the gangway and up into The Infinitum, leaving Tara alone with Captain Peters, though she didn't quite know what to say. Captain Peters doesn't seem like someone you can easily make small talk with.

"Tara, engineer," she stuck an awkward hand out and shared a short, firm handshake. "I worked on the first FTL prototypes myself."

"I started in engineering," Captain Peters nodded with approval, "It's good work. Welcome aboard, Tara."

***

After Tara had been led into the ship, she took a turn to the left and headed down into the dormitories area. As she paused for a moment, she closed her eyes and tried to imagine the ship taking off, not still, like it was currently. Then, slowly, she heard a voice creeping into her head.

It didn't register as words to begin with, as the voice sounded so unlike anything she knew as a voice, it was deep, raspy, like that of a monster from a horror film, but real, true, come to life in her head.

"Tara" it said, slowly and alluringly "I need you."

The voice seemed to be creeping up louder and louder, as if it had been at the end of the corridor, but now its owner was stood right behind her. The hair on the back of her arm began to stand on end, and her knees locked, her legs now stiff in a way that would not move.

"Come and find me," the voice said, almost impossibly loudly, and Tara made herself turn, opening her eyes to find… an empty corridor. She dropped her bag, and the metal clip on the outside of it clanged loudly on the ship's metal floor. Gabriel popped his head out of the dorm he had chosen, some twenty meters away and looked her up and down.

"Are you ok?" he asked.

"I… I'm fine," she responded. "Just nervous."

"Well, if you need a check over, please just say," Gabriel responded.

"It's just… anxiety" she lied.

"Ok," Gabriel nodded. "I still need to read personal medical logs. I can make that my next job!" He smiled and disappeared back into his own room.

Tara crouched, grabbed her bag, and carried it into the dorm she had chosen. Slowly, the tremors in her hands now calming, she placed her bag down on the bed and started to empty out her clothes. As she set out her effects on the bedside table, a commotion outside of the ship caught her attention. A couple of station workers, two men in grey overalls, were uncoupling one of the fuelling roads was wired up to The Infinitum.

As the nearer, smaller one started to activate the winch to reel the rod in, the larger man moved over the edge of The Infinitum and began to uncouple the road from the outside of the ship. As he did so, and the metal clip lifted away from the hull, Tara heard the other man yell "No! It's not switched off yet!" and fuel blasted out, sending him flying backwards, across the immediate area of the hangar into the other man. The two men then fell onto the control switch, inadvertently switching the fuel line off, and the ends of the jet stream of the fuel pissed out of the end before it flopped to the floor.

Swiftly, Gabriel ran out from the entry ramp to The Infinitum and tended to the two men, whilst more people in boiler suits ran out and started to clean down the spillage. Everyone looked frantic. Tara turned away from the window and looked down at her own stuff laid out on the table.

She held out her hands. They were shaking.

This trip is cursed, she thought.

***

Tara had met the rest of the crew after unpacking: first, Ela had led her down to the main deck, where she was greeted by a fresh-faced young man, who quickly rose up from his chair and placed his hand in hers.

He stated, "Troy Marven." Troy had deep blue eyes, and a chiselled jaw line, looking like an archetypal handsome fighter pilot

"Pilot. You must be Ela's ex. I can see why she kept you quiet," he added.

"Tara," Tara responded. "Engineer."

Troy moved away, and Tara turned, bemused, to Ela.

"Yep," her friend stated, "He has that effect on everyone."

Tara stepped forward and took in the view: the main deck was a huge, open area, with blinking white lights. A large spire ran through the middle of the deck, and down onto the engine deck below: the Mark 4 FTL engine. It was built through the rest of the ship.

Around the engine, two men scurried about, one short, one tall. The tall man was the first to notice them. He came over towards Tara and shook her hand firmly. He was bearded and broad-shouldered, with kind eyes and comically small glasses that perched on the end of his long nose.

"Simon Holme," he beamed. "First Officer and support for Dr. Calabash… you must be Tara Dean?"

"That's correct."

"That's Dr. Calabash," Simon gestured to the man still standing at the machine. "He tends to keep to himself for the most—"

"Only when there are strangers," Dr. Calabash interrupted. "This isn't a stranger; it's the engineer: Tara."

"He's a little bit eccentric," Simon winced, "but he's the best in his field."

"I can hear you!" Dr. Calabash exclaimed.

"That's a good sign," Simon chuckled. "He doesn't even respond to people he doesn't like."

"I see," Tara nodded, and took a step back. She stumbled into a body behind her and quickly turned to find a tall, strong-looking woman with thick brown hair and very pale skin towering there. The woman blinked and slowly smiled.

"Tara," she held her hand out to the woman nervously.

"Nicola Trench," stated the brunette, shaking her hand. "Security Officer."

"Don't scare our engineer, please," Captain Peters said, walking onto the deck without really looking at anyone. "She'll think we're all mad onboard this ship."

"We are, aren't we?" Ela asked playfully.

"Not always—Ela, you have duties, don't you? Tara, get some rest and have something to eat. Be prepared for launch in the morning."

***

During dinner, Tara sat alone, taking in the sites out of the starboard window. From the small dining area, littered with basic metal and plastic furniture, like a prison, she could see men and women rushing around in boiler suits, pilot's clothes, the occasional military uniform, and the odd business suit. One man in an ugly neon green outfit wrestled with a large clamp, struggling to pull it out from a ship which was readying to depart. A man and woman ran over to join him and together they pulled the clamp out. The two then turned and gave the man a scolding for attempting to do it on his own.

Across the bay, a skinny black man in a business suit talked hurriedly to a large woman in a military uniform. The man waved his arm vaguely in the direction of the ship that was taking off.

"Quiet in here," came a voice, and Tara looked up to see Simon sitting down at the table opposite her.

"Sir," Tara stated, sitting up straight, to which Simon waved his hand.

"Not in here," he replied firmly. "How are you finding it so far?"

"We haven't started…" Tara responded, "But I don't enjoy flying or space particularly."

"Some people might say you're in the wrong line of work," Simon stated, half-smiling.

"I like being an engineer. I like fixing things. And working with Meridian Corps allows you staff benefits that other engineering jobs simply can't give you," Tara explained.

"Yes, but about eighty percent of the engineering work with Meridian is on long-distance space voyages, like this one. Are you able to put up with that?" Simon asked, one eyebrow raised. Maybe she had been a bit too open with a superior officer.

"I can deal with it, particularly when there's a good crew," Tara said, not quite meeting Simon's eyes. "But… it does intimidate me, having history riding on our backs."

"To a degree," Simon replied. "FTL engines have existed for some time now. This is just a new type."

"But, sir, doesn't that scare you?" Tara asked.

"It could do," Simon replied. "But Dr. Calabash is the best at what he does. He might not be the chattiest man onboard, but he is a safe pair of hands. We went through initial training together…obviously we studied different courses, but I've known him for a long time. Once I heard he was attached to this project, I request transfer."

"Are you talking about me?" Dr. Calabash asked, joining them at the table.

"Always," Simon stated firmly, smiling.

"It's rude to talk about people when they're not present," Dr. Calabash stared blankly. "My mum would always say so."

"True," Simon replied, "But if we all followed that advice, how would anything ever get done?"

Tara smiled at this. Fair point.

"Tell me, Tara Dean," Dr. Calabash said. "How well do you understand the principles of the Mark 4 FTL Engine? You see, there have been sceptics towards this project, hence why the Meridian Corporation have decided to test this one under relatively low-key conditions. The research consistently proves that their scepticism is misplaced, however, as—"

Simon waved his hand to get Dr. Calabash to stop.

"There's a time and a place, dude," he stated. "Let the poor woman eat her dinner."

"How is Ela doing?" Tara asked

"She's doing well," Simon replied, eating up the last of his dinner. "When we're not in movement, though, she takes her fair share of the cleaning and cooking. There is a rota of sorts, but she likes taking on more than her fair share. Unlike some" He raised an eyebrow at Dr. Calabash with this final comment.

"She likes to be busy. She always did," Tara responded.

"I do," Ela stated, appearing in the kitchen doorway. "Have you three finished eating?"

"Yes," Simon stated, standing back up and brushing himself down. Dr. Calabash quickly followed suit, copying Simon's movements almost to the letter. Tara smiled at Ela, who smiled back.

"Let's go chill out," Tara said. "You've done enough today."

Tara and Ela went up to the mess room, where Troy and Gabriel were sitting together, drinking, and playing some convoluted card game called 'Space Pilot's Gamble.' Both men turned and smiled at the them when they walked in, which reassured Tara; for a moment, the atmosphere had seemed thick. There had been public scepticism about this new FTL method. Both men were dressed in t-shirts and casual trousers, and music was playing. Gabriel pulled a bottle from his coat and passed it to Tara, who took it in both hands.

"Careful," Gabriel warned, "Sip it first. Then you'll get used to it, trust me."

Tara took a sip and tried to let the liquid lie on her tongue. It was spicier than any curry she'd ever eaten. She spat it out into her sleeve almost instantly.

"Hell," she muttered, and the others started laughing.

Gabriel smiled, took the bottle back and passed it across to Ela.

"So," Ela said, taking a swig, "What do you think of the rest of the crew?" She was noticeably more accustomed to Gabriel's spicy brew.

"Damn..." Tara replied. "No small talk at all, then? Straight to it..."

"You know me too well for that," Ela responded.

"Well... Captain Peters seems like she knows what she's about. I understand why she's been put in charge of this mission," Tara began.

"True," Ela nodded.

"Simon and Dr. Calabash, I haven't really got to know yet...they seem to go off by themselves quite a lot? Are they... ?"

"No" Troy responded quickly, "They just don't have any other friends," and gave a quick and awkward guffaw.

Ela shook her head.

"No," she agreed. "They're just old friends, like me and you. Meridian needs people who can trust each other on this mission."

"Very selective, I guess," Troy stated. "I suppose they'd have to be for a mission like this."

"What about you?" Tara asked, turning quickly towards Troy, and Ela gave a gentle smile, out of the pilot's line of sight. "How did you manage to get yourself here?"

"Well…" Troy hummed thoughtfully. "Where to start… I, well my parents, sent me to the best piloting school in this quarter of the galaxy. But I don't like space, I don't like science… damn, I don't even like piloting all that much. I just want my name in the history books."

"Your fifteen minutes of fame," Gabriel said, smiling, and handed the younger man the spiced drink.

"Exactly," Troy nodded, and took a quick swig. His face convulsed for a moment, and then he spat the drink out all over his lap and wiped his mouth with his spare sleeve.

"Just disgusting," he stated, and they all started laughing. The game continued late into the evening.

***

Not long after Tara had awoken from her second sleep, Captain Peters called all of them onto the main deck, where she stood in the middle of the room. Simon stood near the machine, perusing it over the end of his tiny glasses, while Dr. Calabash moved around it quickly, brandishing a clipboard. Nicola stood silently at one side of the room, just off Captain Peters' left shoulder. Ela and Troy remained facing away, looking out into the vastness, keeping the ship moving. Both of them seemed completely engaged, clearly loving their job.

"We are preparing to make the jump in ten minutes—I would suggest you all take a seat," Captain Peters commanded. "Dr. Calabash will fire up the FTL engine and then we will be ready to make the jump immediately.

Tara moved over to a seat as the ship began to increase in speed, and just across from her was the ever-amiable Gabriel, who smiled and nodded.

"Exciting, huh?" he asked absently, more to himself than to her.

Dr. Calabash and Simon disappeared below the command deck via a set of stairs to program the hyperspeed engine. Nicola took a seat next to Captain Peters in Simon's chair. The two very serious women exchanged a quick glance and began to plug themselves in to their seats and then Gabriel, Tara and the two pilots quickly followed suit. The ship continued to pick up speed, and soon Calabash and Simon returned from below deck and slipped into seats behind Tara and Gabriel.

"Deep-space guidance systems... online. Radio communications systems... online," Troy read out. "Defence weaponry systems... online. Sonar and radar short-range communication systems... online. All rear-facing thrusters... online. Ship's computer and backup computer... online. Life support systems... online. Self-destruct systems... online. Internal heating systems... online. All systems checked, Captain."

"And launch," Captain Peters stated. "In... three... two...."

"We're starting our acceleration process, Captain," Troy said, turning to look at his superior officer. "We're going to need to reach three times the speed of sound in order to make the engines hot enough to launch."

"Understood,"

"We're approaching the speed of sound," Troy smiled.

Tara started to feel goosebumps on her skin, and the g-force pressed up against her face as if she were in a fighter plane.

"Understood."

"We're approaching twice the speed of sound."

"Understood."

"We're approaching three times the speed of sound."

"Initialize the hyperspeed engine," Dr. Calabash stated.

The whirring hum began quietly, then got louder and louder, until Tara felt the noise inside her head. The ship began to shake, and the room began to stretch, pulling one way and another. Tara's hand clamped down onto the seat she was sitting on, feeling her breakfast rising up in her stomach, pressing against her oesophagus.

Tara's head moved all around the room, unable to focus on anything. Then her eyes met Gabriel's.

"Now you see why I drink the spicy brew," she heard him say, but his mouth did not seem to move. Tara could barely keep conscious, and then they hit hyperspeed. The following moment lasted forever and there was no time at all. Tara felt nothing, no g-force, no feeling of sickness. No light, no dark, no cold, no heat, no happiness, no sadness. Nothing.

The ship pulled out of hyperspeed, and light filled Tara's eyes once again. Everyone still sat where they had been sitting and where they took off and looked exactly how they had appeared before the engine started.

"Is that it?" Troy asked.

"So it would seem," Captain Peters snapped. She unclipped her seatbelt and moved over to stand by the control panel.

Outside of the ship's front window they could see a solar system, but not one they recognised. Below them, but not very far below, as a medium-sized rocky planned, a similar size to Earth perhaps, but rocky, brown and barren. In the distance there was a star, but only just. It was a darkened, tiny prick of light in the distance.

"Ela, where are we?" Simon followed after the captain. "We're not at our original destination point. Where are we? What planet is that? And that sun out there is dying – it's a brown dwarf"

"It's not. There's no brown dwarf star within the entire sector," Ela responded, quickly unclipping her belt and scrambling over the monitor in front of her. She brought up a map. "This a unique system… there isn't one that matches it on our records."

"Broaden that to the ISA's wider records," Captain Peters ordered.

"Still nothing, Captain."

"I suggest we open comms," Simon said, and Troy bolted out of his seat, moving over to the main control panel in front of the hyperspeed engine.

"Any line?" Captain Peters asked, tension laced in her voice.

Troy moved over and held down a large button, which gathered no reaction.

"No initial response," he said looking between Simon and Captain Peters.

Tara looked askance at Gabriel, who returned that same look to her.

"No response," Troy stated again. "But if we—"

The young pilot stumbled as the entire ship shook, then was thrust off his feet and slammed down onto the ground as loose elements rattled and echoed throughout the control room.

"What was that?" Simon demanded, scrambling towards his chair.

"Possibly turbulence," Captain Peters moved over towards the main control panel to pick the young pilot up off the floor. As the two were partway up, another smash shook the ship, and they both went over. Tara gripped the arms of her chair and grimaced.

That was no turbulence.

"I know what that was," Tara admitted, as Nicola picked up both Captain Peters and Troy, one on each arm.

Captain Peters and Simon turned to look at her in unison.

"It's an asteroid impact. I've experienced it before."

"Tara's right," Ela confirmed, "I'm picking up multiple small unidentified objects moving around on the scanner."

Captain Peters nodded and looked around the control room.

"Ok. Everyone back to their seats."

The crew complied and just as Captain Peters closed her seatbelt, the ship shook again, setting off a loud alarm.

"WARNING! CRITICAL DAMAGE!" cried the ship's computer.

"I think we ought to land," Simon cried.

"I don't think we'll get much choice," said Dr. Calabash, "That hit took out our left thruster. I can't imagine we'll be able to get back to jump speed without it!"

"Then we're in agreement," Captain Peters commanded, "Head down to the planet, quickly and steadily."

Troy nodded and chartered a course. The ship creaked and teetered as it began to change angle, moving down towards what appeared to be a barren, fiery planet.

"Looks lovely," Gabriel muttered to Tara as he buckled himself down. "I might take the wife her for our anniversary."

Tara said nothing, still gripping the arms of her chair for dear life.

"We're clear of the asteroid belt now!" Ela exclaimed as they began to approach the planet.

"Good," replied Captain Peters. "Now, bring us in slowly."

"I'm trying my best," Troy responded. "With that thruster gone, the other two thrusters are burning through their fuel at a dangerously fast rate."

"That's fine, we'll siphon it through when we land," said Captain Peters.

"Slow it down now!" Simon ordered. "We're coming in too fast!"

"That might be easier said than done!" Troy shouted back.

"Ok, deploy brake wings," Captain Peters ordered, and Troy hit a large blue button. As the ship drew closer to the planet, the wings on the side pivoted, increasing their surface area to slow their descent.

"Brake wings deployed. Killing speed," Troy hit a button cutting the ship's two remaining thrusters. "Speed is at approximately three hundred miles per hour and declining. Ten miles until impact with planet."

"It's still too fast!" Captain Peters cried. "Deploy parachute."

"Deploying parachute," Troy hit another large button, this one pink, which fired a large EON-branded parachute out of the back of the ship, just above the central thruster.

"Nine miles," Simon announced, "We're still going too fast!"

"Employ emergency brake thrusters," Captain Peters shouted. "Get that speed down!"

Troy swivelled in his chair and hit a large yellow button…which proceeded to do nothing.

"No response, Captain, First Officer," his voice shook.

The ship continued to plummet through the atmosphere. Tara swivelled in her chair to look down at her own monitor screen, and she saw it.

"They're, erm, the brake thrusters are down," she stated nervously, turning back to the rest of the room to address the others. "That asteroid must have hit them, too."

"Ok," Captain Peters responded, "then we're going to have an entertaining landing. Troy, I'm going to need you to skim it."

Troy looked at Captain Peters, then over at Simon, exchanging nods with both. He pulled on the ship's steering to flatten their descent as much as he could. The ship was now almost parallel with the planet's surface. Slowly, he pressed down on the steering as the ship began to slow ever so slightly. He pressed a little more, gripping tightly to the steering stick. The bottom of the ship slid against the planet's surface, rocks and stones banging and clanging beneath them.

"Gently," Simon told Troy, "Nicely done."

Troy sweated as he waggled the steering stick, pulling the fast-moving ship between towers of stone that littered the planet's surface. The ship hit a boulder and twisted within its trajectory, but kept moving further down towards the surface, riding along the top of the gravel. Then it happened: the parachute caught on one of the stone towers, pulling the whole ship to pivot to the left, before the strings snapped and the ship was flung hard into the base of another stone tower. It flopped to the ground and then it was still. They had landed.

Chapter Two

Initially, it was darkness. In her sleepiness, Tara once again began to hear a voice that she didn't fully recognize. Even though she thought she was asleep, the voice seemed to penetrate her ears, her mind, an unstoppable force.

"Tara."

What do you want? She thought, speaking back to the voice.

"You're here," it said.

Tara woke up in a shot. Her eyes looked all around, and she breathed out hard. It was so cold. The shock and horror of the descent had left Tara bewildered, but she wanted to know where they were. As soon as she moved, the lights switched on the main deck, and Gabriel blinked awake next to her.

Slowly, the others began to rouse and unclipped their seatbelts. Nicola walked over to Gabriel and Tara as they brushed themselves off.

"Any serious damage?" she put a hand on Tara's shoulder.

"Couple of bruises," Gabriel smiled in thanks.

"Walk it off," Nicola nodded, before she went to check on Captain Peters.

Simon walked over to the pair of them, nursing a wound on his balding head. He nodded at them. "It's not too bad."

"It looks bad," Gabriel disagreed, raising an eyebrow.

"It could be bad," Simon admitted hesitantly. "Maybe. I'm not a doctor."

"I am," Gabriel reminded him, "I'd put it under an icepack and keep from any strenuous activities. Get yourself in the Medi-bay once the ship is up and running, but right now we might need you."

"Guys!" Ela cried from across the room. "It's Troy… I think he might be dead. He's not breathing!"

Troy lay on the floor with his body curled up into a ball. Captain Peters and Gabriel ran over to join Ela by his side, and Gabriel quickly checked for a pulse, then shook his head.

They unfurled Troy's body and found a huge bruise on his forehead and bleeding coming from the top of his head.

"Severe blunt-force trauma to the head," Gabriel stated. "His seatbelt must have been faulty. Damn."

Ela looked over at Tara and shook her head as a tear slipped down her cheek. He was gone, nothing they could do. Ela walked away from the commotion around Troy's body and towards Tara. The two women embraced in a hug, slowly and tightly putting their arms around each other. Tara held that hug for a while, longer than she had expected.

Tara had never experienced a crew member's death before; it was rare, even in deep space travel.

"I don't think we'll be laughing about this one when we get out of it," Ela said in her ear.

Tara didn't respond, merely blinked tears from her eyes. In her field of vision was Dr. Calabash, who unlike the others was tinkering with the hyperspeed engine which ran through the centre of the control room. After a moment's tinkering, he stepped away, and the lights of the room came on at once.

'SHIP'S COMPUTER ONLINE. LOCATION: UNKNOWN PLANET. BREATHABLE ATMOSPHERE. PLANETARY EVOLVED LIFE SIGNATURES: ONE' blared the ship's computer.

Tara and Ela broke apart from their hug and Simon moved over to stand next to Dr. Calabash, whipping across the main deck in a second.

"Damn," Simon whispered, peering over the console. "A breathable atmosphere. That can't be right. What are the chances?

"What are the chances?" Dr. Calabash shook his head. "I don't really know. Mathematically, very unlikely."

"Computer," said Simon, "What is the make-up of this planet's atmosphere?"

"PLANETARY ATMOSPHERE IS 78% NITROGEN, 21% OXYGEN, 1% ARGON AND LESS THAN 1% CARBON DIOXIDE AND OTHER GASES."

"That's like Earth. A lot like Earth," Simon announced.

"That's *exactly* like Earth," Tara stated as she walked over the engine to join them. Maybe it was the shock of Troy's death. Perhaps they were all imagining this.

"Then we might have found Earth's twin?" Calabash asked.

"It didn't look like Earth from the window," Ela joined them.

"One life form..." Simon wondered, looking between them. "One. On the whole planet."

"We need to find it," Tara said. "We need help."

Captain Peters stepped between her and Ela. Nicola and Gabriel joined them on the opposite side of the hyperspeed engine.

"That computer will only count sentient life on its scan, which means it's a person, of sorts," Captain Peters said. "That person could represent a threat, even to the seven of us."

"Seven?" Tara asked.

"Troy's gone," Peters snapped. "And since we have no idea how long we're going to be here, I suggest that we give him a proper burial, here, on this planet. I won't lie to you—this is a bad situation. But we didn't get this far as people to give up in the face of despair. We are officers of Meridian Corps, and we are better than that. Tara's right, we need to find this life form, as soon as possible, and see what they know—even force them to help us if we really must. We also need to make repairs to this ship, using whatever parts we can. There are the materials to fix the damaged thruster in the mechanic's bay… and a spade to dig a grave for Officer Marven. Let's hope this life form, this person, could lead us to fuel and we could bring that back to the ship. I think we could get back off planet with a repaired thruster, but not enough fuel to get to hyperspeed. Of course, even resolving that, we, and the ship's computer, have no idea where we are."

"Could we not send a signal out for help?" Ela asked.

"Yes, we could," Captain Peters responded, and she turned towards Simon. "First Officer, will you do the honours?"

Simon leant forward and pressed a couple of buttons in a precise arrangement on the hyperspeed engine.

"Opening comms now," he added quietly.

"COMMS OPEN" the ship's computer reported.

"Hello," Simon stated. "This is First Officer Simon Holme of The Infinitum, a deep-space exploration and transportation ship commissioned by the Meridian Corps. We have crashed on an unidentified planet with a breathable atmosphere. Please send help. We have seven crewmembers remaining, with one casualty upon landing. Over and out."

***

They headed outside the spaceship, and Gabriel, Nicola and Simon began digging a grave, turning up dirt with a set of spades from the ship. Tara stood behind the others, watching this slow process. Slowly and carefully, the three diggers lowered Troy's body into the hole, then stepped away. For a moment, the seven of them stood around the body, saying nothing.

"Flight Officer Troy Marven," Captain Peters began. "Troy was a young man, taken before his time, through no fault of his own. He was a sound man, a brave man, who stepped up to the mark when his superior officers needed him."

"Here, here," Simon added.

"He will be remembered fondly by his last crew, who now wish Troy a gentle ride into whatever life there is after this," Captain Peters finished.

"To Troy," Gabriel stated, and the rest of the crew repeated him. Gabriel then filled a shovel with dirt and threw it onto Troy's body. Nicola and Simon quickly followed suit.

The others went back inside, but Tara remained. She took in the planet: breathable air and soft, crumbly soil, but grey, rather than brown. The sky was bright and barren, with no clouds as far as the horizon. That could mean there were no, or very few, water sources. The air was still, with no wind to tell of or even discernible weather of any kind. The air was warm, a little warmer than earth, and there were no birds, no insects. It all felt remarkably calm and still. Not how you might imagine a wild unexplored planet. This was clearly not a terraformed planet, and had no obvious human visitations here, and yet, there was a person here, somewhere. Tara headed back inside when suddenly Ela grabbed her jumper.

"Tara!" she exclaimed. "We've got a message from the lifeform!"

Tara moved over to join the others, who stood around a console that Simon had managed to lower.

"Hello. I have received your message. Welcome. I will be found at the source of this signal," it read.

"Damn," Captain Peters gasped. "Computer, can you trace this signal?"

"SIGNAL IS BEING EMITTED TWELVE MILES FROM OUR CURRENT LOCATION," the computer informed them. "SENDING LOCATION TO YOUR HANDHELD DEVICES NOW.'

"This is excellent," Captain Peters smiled from ear to ear. She turned to look at the rest of the crew. "We need to track down this individual—this could take a day—and make sure they lead us to fuel. And we need to fix the ship. I suggest that we split into two teams, an A team of myself, Security Officer Trench, Medical Officer Sen, Navigation Officer Treen and Engineering Officer Bainbridge will accompany me across this planet's surface. Science Officer Calabash and First Officer Holme will remain here to fix this ship to the best of their ability."

"Shouldn't I remain here?" Tara asked. "Broken thrusters primarily fall within my job description. First Officer Peters is stronger than I am and the most experienced in field expeditions."

"True," Captain Peters replied, "but if we obtain fuel, I need as many fit and able people with me as possible. First Officer Holme has received a head injury, and it would do him best to stay here."

Simon grimaced slightly, clearly keen to join them on the adventure, but then nodded at Peters.

"Ok," Tara responded, "let's do this, then."

***

Their journey was long but not exhausting. The planet was warm enough that soon they had all removed jumpers and coats. The air of this planet felt safe, almost nice. Like Earth's atmosphere, but without the clogging of Methane, Carbon Dioxide, and what Tara's dad had liked to call 'human stink.' While the planet was not home to humans, it certainly could accommodate them with the right terraforming equipment. Perhaps she would tell them all about it when they got home. Or perhaps she would keep quiet and hope the human race left this planet well alone. God knows what they would do to this place.

It was several hours later when Tara noticed Captain Peters and Nicola walking up in front, out of the earshot of everyone else. Tara walked up between Ela and Gabriel, who were engaged in a conversation about echolocation devices.

"How's it going?" Ela asked. "You've been at the back for a little while."

"It's going fine," Tara responded. "I'm just taking in the planet. Isn't it fascinating?"

"It's ok," Gabriel responded. "I've seen better. I grew up on Proxima Centauri C."

"The Super-Earth?" Tara asked.

"That's the one," Gabriel replied. "An amazing place to live."

"I prefer Earth myself," Ela responded.

"You're a home child?" Gabriel raised an eyebrow.

"No, Mars. But I never liked Mars; there was never anything there for me."

"I must admit, I don't meet many Martians who like Mars," Gabriel said. "You should ask my wife about Martians after a couple of drinks, and she's off, let me tell you."

"You'll find we're the same as anyone else, really," Ela said. The three of them continued to talk as they walked across the surface of the barren planet.

***

As they walked along, Tara dropped behind, walking a significant distance behind Ela and Gabriel. She felt as if something were creeping along behind her, but she couldn't see or hear anything. It was like the empty frame of a person was walking up behind her. She felt suddenly more aware of everything as this entity seemed to get closer to her; the crisp crunch of her boots on the planet's surface, the wind whistling past her ears.

"Tara," came the from earlier voice, from nowhere in particular.

"Who—" she asked, "Who's there?"

"Such a lost little girl," the voice stated. "Not even knowing who she is."

"You don't scare me," Tara replied, her voice trembling.

"Of course I do," the voice replied. "Why would I not?" The voice increased in volume, until the moment when Tara could almost pinpoint its location, and then it was gone.

Slowly, Tara turned and began to walk forward towards Ela and Gabriel, but then she felt the pricks of five fingers touching the back of her neck. When she turned, there was no one there. And yet the fingers pressed down further, and further, until they felt like they were inside of her.

She felt the back of her neck and nothing there. Tara screamed, and Ela and Gabriel came running. The hand inside her held her up, her feet lifting from the ground. As Ela and Gabriel reached her, the hand simultaneously disappeared, and Tara fell to the ground.

Ela sat her up swiftly and brushed the hair from her face. "Tara!" she exclaimed. "What was that?"

"Rapid heart rate, but her vitals are all normal," Gabriel chimed in, looking in both of her eyes with a small flashlight.

"I don't know," Tara stated, wide-eyed and struggling for each breath. "I just don't know."

***

Back onboard The Infinitum, Dr. Calabash and Simon were both rotating around the damaged FTL engine. Dr. Calabash leaned up to the control panel and then hit a button.

"Ok, Simon, get out of there," and like a bolt, Simon slid out from underneath the FTL engine's control. The two men were now stood on the outside of it, and then slowly the machine flickered into life.

"Ok," Simon responded, a smile beginning to creep onto his face. "We've got it!"

"I think that means we can get home," Dr. Calabash stated. As Simon headed over the control panel, he heard a *bing* noise from the computer at the back of the deck.

"Go and see what that was, please," he told Dr. Calabash, as he sat down and began to plug the comms in to speak to Captain Peters.

"First Officer Holme to Captain Peters," he stated. "Please come in. This is an important message. We have managed to get the FTL engine back online, over."

"Holme," came the fuzzy reply, "that's good news. We are nearing the—we are nearing the life form now, over."

"Good luck with first encounter, over." Simon stated.

"We are losing our battery power," Captain Peters replied. "We must-we must reserve radio contact for absolute emergencies from here on, over."

"Understood, over" Simon replied. When he turned around, Dr. Calabash stood completely motionless.

"Simon," he said, "I left this monitor to run a long-term scan on the dirt we gathered from the planet. It should be able to tell us whether we are on a planet it recognizes, and what planet it is closest to, should it not?"

"And?" Simon asked, one eyebrow raised.

"It's a one hundred percent match with planet Earth" Dr. Calabash stated.

"But… that's not possible," Simon argued, motioning to the bleak landscape outside the ship windows. Then Simon composed himself. "It's not possible, is it? Tell me this can't be Earth—I mean, I was there two weeks ago, it didn't look like this. There's nothing, nothing that could have done this to Earth."

Dr. Calabash took a deep breath in through his nose, and out again, before he spoke.

"I have one theory," he said. "You're not going to like it."

***

It was another few hours later when Captain Peters stopped them all, and huddled the five of them together, just before a large dune. "According to the readings on this chart, the life form that sent that message should be just over the crest," she stated.

"Got it," Tara nodded.

"Nicola and I have pistols in our packs. That should help with the… persuasion. But let's hope this individual is cooperative and can help us."

"Understood," Ela responded, and she exchanged a worried look with Tara.

Tara tried to swallow down her nervousness.

"Now, listen," Captain Peters stated, the tone of her voice becoming blunter. "We don't know who this individual is, their background, how they came to be on this planet alone, or how much they can help up. We don't even know if they'll be able to understand us. So, we need to treat them with extreme caution. They might not have seen another person for quite some time. Let's show them we can be trusted. Follow me." And with that, Peters stepped up onto the dune and started up, followed by Nicola, then Gabriel, then Ela, and finally Tara.

One by one, step by step, they moved towards the brow of the dune. What they saw when they reached the top stopped them dead in their tracks.

It was an old, ruined cathedral, smoke billowing from every door and every window, yet they could not see any fire in the ruins. The smoke trailed off and disappeared into the empty sky, as if it were not natural. As if it were not meant to be. The building itself was ancient and enormous, greater than any church Tara had seen in her life. And yet it looked old, as if it had sat abandoned on this planet for hundreds of years.

Gabriel sidled up between Tara and Captain Peters and frowned, taking in the sight that lay before them.

"I guess you're going to give me bad news," he said, his voice quivering.

"We're going in, Gabriel," Captain Peters responded.

As they approached the Cathedral, the air began to get colder, as if they had stepped inside a fridge, and before long, a freezer. The smoke around them began to billow and move, and it appeared to Tara as if it was forming arms. Tara stopped, aghast, but when she looked again, they were gone. She turned to Ela and saw in her eyes the same fear and confusion, and then recognition of what they were seeing. The two of them nodded and then carried on forward.

They had entered what was left of the cathedral's main doorway when Captain Peters announced, "We're right on top of the signal." She did not turn around.

As they stood in the main chapel of the cathedral, the smoke around them started to funnel between them: their arms, their legs, even through their hair. It was almost as if it were driven by wind. But there was no wind. Slowly the smoke moved out from amongst them, and started to encircle the five of them, moving faster and faster, acting like a hurricane, but, again, no wind.

The smoke began to come together, filling into a large pillar of dark mist, coalescing into a solid shape that eventually became a figure. The billowing and moving of the smoke stopped, and in front of them stood a slim, faceless figure neither male nor female; tall, but no taller than the tallest of them, Nicola.

"So," it said with the same voice Tara had heard in her head earlier. "I believe you've been looking for me."

Chapter Three

No one moved or said anything, for what felt like an eternity to Tara. This figure, whatever it was, must have been the human race's first-ever recorded extraterrestrial life. The first non-human sentient life in the known universe. And it was terrifying.

Captain Peters stepped forward slowly, moving towards the figure. "My name is Captain Clare Peters of The Infinitum. I come from the moon Titan, in the Primary Sol system, a moon of Sol 6, Saturn. My crew and I have crash-landed here, and we need help. We don't have the necessary fuel required to leave this planet and get home. We were wondering if you would be able to help us find the necessary materials to leave your planet in peace?"

The figure said nothing for quite some time. It did not look specifically at Captain Peters, nor at any of them in particular. Instead, it continued to stare straight ahead, to the back of the main chapel.

Eventually it spoke. "What material do you require?"

"Ah um…" Captain Peters began, "Some kind of liquid hydrogen? Is there anything like that on this planet? Kerosene, maybe?"

The figure was quiet again.

"There is plentiful Kerosene on this planet," it stated.

"Fantastic," Captain Peters responded, clearly nervous. "If you could just tell us where it is, and then we could be on our way."

"You do not need to find it. I already have it. I anticipated your arrival here from the moment you crashed," it stated.

"Well… that's excellent—are you willing to give us the Kerosene we need?"

"Of course," the figure replied, "but it will cost you."

"We don't have money" Captain Peters replied sternly.

"No," stated the figure, before pausing. "It will cost you two lives."

"What? What do you mean?"

The figure didn't move, but it began to laugh. The unearthly cackle echoed through the Cathedral, shaking right through Tara, and she felt herself moving towards the back of the group, wanting very much to be at home.

"We are Officers of the Meridian Corps!" Nicola exclaimed, "You will not threaten us in this way!" She drew her pistol from her bag, holding it to the figure's head. The figure's head moved for the very first time, turning to lock eyes with Nicola. Suddenly, faster than anyone could react—faster than anyone could blink—a stream of smoke shot out from the figure and grabbed the arm that held the pistol. Nicola screamed and fell back onto the ground in front of them.

When she sat up, she looked down at her left arm in astonishment. Her hand was gone. The end of her wrist was now just a stump, with no marks at all, as if it always had been.

"How—" she exclaimed, "how is that possible?"

"As you can see," the figure stated, "my power is far beyond yours. I need to live to sustain myself. You can either give two of you willingly… or I'll kill all five of you."

"You!" Ela exclaimed, charging forward, moving to punch the smoky figure, when Captain Peters placed a firm hand on the younger woman's chest, and pushed her back gently.

"Stop, Ela," Captain Peters stated. "I'll do it, if someone must."

"But Captain," Gabriel began, "we need you!"

"No, you don't," Captain Peters responded. "I joined Meridian twenty-four years ago to better myself. To make something of myself. I would say, and I'd hope you agree, that I've done that."

"Your leader shows great courage," The figure stated, "I respect that."

"Just get this nonsense over with," Captain Peters stated, dropping her pistol to the ground next to her.

"I need two," The figure replied.

Captain Peters grimaced, when suddenly she found Nicola standing at her side.

"Nic," Captain Peters said, her eyes locked on Nicola's. "I'm gla—" the figure snapped his fingers, and both women dropped to the floor dead, their necks broken.

***

The other three stared down at the two dead bodies, failing to comprehend what was really happening.

The figure said nothing, but just snapped its fingers again, and the remaining crew felt their bags fill with weight.

"The jugs in your bags," it said, "are now filled with the fuel that you require."

Gabriel stared down at the dead bodies of Nicola and Captain Peters. His eyes were teary, and his body was tense. "You!" He looked up at the figure. "You didn't need to do that! They were good people!"

"I did," the figure stated, motionless. "I need lives, or I will eventually die. While I understand your plight, you must understand that I must place my own needs over anyone else. Would you not do the same?"

"I would let myself die rather than remain as whatever you are!" Gabriel exclaimed. His foot was extremely close to Peters' pistol, Tara noticed. She quickly stepped in front of Gabriel, putting herself between the figure and the older man. She turned and nodded at Ela.

"Come on, Gabriel," Ela said. "Let's go now. Don't aggravate it any further."

"Can I ask a question?" Tara asked.

"Yes," the figure replied. "It won't cost any extra lives. Your colleagues are more than enough to sustain me for now."

"Who are you?" Tara asked.

The figure went quiet again, almost as if it didn't quite know the answer to the question Tara had just asked.

"My name," It said eventually, "is the Omniscience."

"The Omniscience?" Tara asked. "As in you are omniscient. All-seeing, and all-knowing?"

"That's right" it replied.

"Then that's why you knew we crashed. You knew why we were coming to you," Tara realized.

"That's right again," it said. "I can see everything on this planet. And everything in the wider universe in which it exists."

"So, you know where we're from?"

"No," it said "And that's why I find you so intriguing. I do not know where you are from before you came to this planet. I thought I'd consumed all the humans. In fact, I know I had."

"What… do you… mean?" Tara asked, her brain thinking fast but her mouth moving slowly.

"Come on, Tara, let's just go" Ela said. Tara ignored her.

"As in humans are extinct. Right across the universe," it stated.

"You know?"

"I assured it. I consumed their lives," the Omniscience replied.

"That can't be," Tara responded, moving towards the figure. "We've all come from a world teeming with humans; we'd know if there were none. According to the ship's readings, it's still the year 2949."

"That's the current year on this world, too" the Omniscience stated.

"But that's not possible," Tara argued, "since we just saw people a few weeks ago. It's simply not possible."

"Tara," Gabriel said, putting his hand on her shoulder, and confused, she turned to look at him, looking at his deep brown eyes, and his kindly, reassuring face. "I've feared the worst since I first saw this planet. Tara and the Omniscience have confirmed my theory. We jumped much further than just across space on our test run, Tara. That's why the ship's computer doesn't know where we are in the universe, yet this planet is so familiar. There's a reason why this planet's atmosphere is perfectly breathable. There's a reason why the Omniscience knows we're human but doesn't know why we're here, on this planet."

"Say it," Tara growled.

"This is Earth," Gabriel said. "This planet is Earth."

Damn, Tara thought. *We're in a different universe.*

"There's another universe?" the Omniscience asked.

"You read my thoughts?" Tara asked.

"This universe you come from?" the Omniscience asked. "Does it have life? Does it have sentient life?"

"It's teeming with both," Tara replied, moving away from the Omniscience.

"Then I would very much like to visit it," The Omniscience responded, and began laughing again. "After I consumed all the life in this universe, I hauled up here, on Earth, where humanity began, living off the energy from all those lives that I had consumed. And, oh, I had not seen a human in ever such a long time. You have no idea how happy I was to see you when you landed. I would like to visit your universe ever so much."

"I cannot allow that," Tara responded. "I must protect my universe."

"Tara Dean," the Omniscience said. "I must admit, I quite admire you. I thought that the moment I felt you on this planet. You showed… promise. The potential to be more."

"That was you… in my head… on the way here?" Tara asked.

"It was, indeed," The Omniscience replied, "Timid little girl, at heart"

"Get out of my head, arsehole," Tara growled.

Ela was the first to move in the commotion that happened next. She dived for the pistol on the floor, and picked it up, rolling up into a crouching position, firing rapidly into the Omniscience. The bullets had no effect, firing off into the figure before ricocheting back, one cutting straight through Ela's throat.

Tara jumped and caught Ela as she fell to the ground.

"Come on," Tara said. "Stay with me!"

But Ela was already dead. Tara began to shake, her friend dead in her arms, and slowly placed the other woman's body onto the ground. Ela, her oldest friend, once her lover within Meridian, and the main reason she had ever agreed to this mission, was gone.

Slowly, Tara stood, and then locked eyes with Gabriel, who stood across from her. "We cannot allow this creature to leave its universe," Tara stated. "Our ship must be destroyed."

Gabriel quickly grabbed his radio from his pack, but The Omniscience grabbed him with smoke tendrils, holding him aloft, some twelve feet above the ground. "I need that ship to fly, dear humans."

Smoke began to fill Gabriel's skull, and his face reddened and reddened, until his skull blew into a thousand pieces, and his body fell limply to floor. Tara looked down at what was left of her new friend, Gabriel Sen.

The Omniscience turned and looked at Tara, who looked back at him.

"You need me," she realized. "You turn up at The Infinitum without any of us, Holme and Calabash are going to self-destruct that ship, keeping you here!"

"You're absolutely right," The Omniscience responded. "Maybe you are cleverer than you look, Tara"

Time slowed as she ran and jumped for the pistol that lay on the ground. The Omniscience made no move, but grimaced as she grabbed the gun and began to raise it towards her head.

An eternity passed before the muzzle touched the bottom of her chin—she pulled the trigger; the *click* indicated her success… and the gun was gone. It dissolved into small black atoms in her hand, as if it had never existed.

Tara gaped in shock, unsure what to do next, and the figure of The Omniscience dissolved into smoke. It rushed towards her as she stood transfixed and poured down her throat. In a last-ditch attempt to fight off The Omniscience taking over, she did the only thing she felt she could; she held her breath. An incredible heat rose up inside of her, followed by intense cold. She thought of her friends and crewmates who had given their lives for this mission: Troy, Ela, Gabriel, Nicola, and Captain Peters. She used their bravery and strength to hold in the burning now spreading across the inside of her body. Then she felt that heat rise up towards her head—

—And then she felt nothing at all.

***

Some hours later, Dr. Calabash responded to a knock on The Infinitum's door. It was Tara; battered, bruised, and alone. Her eyes were sunken with dark bags under them, and her skin was pale.

"Hello," Dr. Calabash said hesitantly. "We've managed to make temporary fixes to the ship's damages. Are you… are you alone?"

"It was the lifeform," Tara said. "He laid a trap. The others, they, the others… they all died. Their bodies… there's nothing we could recover—I only just managed to get away myself. But I… I got the fuel."

Simon suddenly joined Calabash at the door. "Christ, Tara, you look a right state. Get yourself down. Robert, get the young lady something from the kitchen." He took Tara's backpack off her and the three of them headed inside, the door to The Infinitum closing behind them.

Tara slumped in her seat in the control room, as Simon headed down to the engine room to refill the thrusters with the Kerosene. Calabash returned with a hot drink in a large mug which read 'Galaxy's No. 1 Pilot.' Tara smiled. That had been Troy's.

Simon quickly returned from the engine room and sat down opposite Tara. Hesitantly, he took her hand and held it for some time.

"It's ok, Tara," he stated. "It is over, and we are going to get home. Our friends haven't died in vain."

The three of them sat there, quiet for a moment, soaking in the loss of their fellow crew members. Then Simon, a few tears in his eyes, nodded at Tara and Dr. Calabash.

"I suppose I'm acting captain now," he stated. "Let's get off this godforsaken planet and leave the mess behind us."

He stood up and walked over to the pilot's seat, and the ship fired into life. Tara buckled in, and Dr. Calabash joined them, buckling into his usual seat.

"Computer," Simon stated. "Take us back to hyperspeed as soon as we're out of orbit."

"PLOTTING COURSE. SPECIFIC DESTINATION REQUIRED," the ship's computer stated.

"EON-1," Simon responded. "Let's get this baby home and fixed up."

Tara felt the ship beneath her quiver and strain as it began to take off, and then the jet engines kicked in. The ship sped up and launched into the atmosphere, and then into space.

Tara felt her arms naturally assume their position of being clamped onto the arms of her chair.

"LEAVING PLANETARY ORBIT."

"Ok, taking her up to lightspeed," Simon stated.

Tara felt her body go all weird once again, taking in the effects of a hyperspeed jump.

"9," blared the computer's countdown.

"8... 7... 6... 5... 4... 3... 2... "

Black smoke began to creep discreetly from Tara's ear, and she smiled. *A new universe,* she thought, *how lovely. So many humans. So little time.*

"I can't wait to fly," she whispered.

"1"

"LAUNCH CANCELLED."

Tara looked over towards the control deck. Both Simon and Dr. Calabash were staring at her.

"You," Simon stated, "You said you hate flying."

"I did," Tara responded, struggling for words. "But... I've changed."

"But what I'd really like to know," Simon followed up as he stared across at the ship's control panel. "Is why you currently register as two lifeforms on the scanner."

Everything that happened next took forever and also happened in the blink of an eye. The Omniscience poured out of Tara's body, which fell limp on the seat. Dr. Calabash leapt up out of his seat and grabbed a laser gun which had been kept under one of the control desks. He wheeled on the Omniscience, but it had entered him. The smoke funnelled into his ear until it had entirely disappeared, and Dr. Calabash stood there, no longer himself.

He grinned and turned.

Simon stood with his hand hovering above a large red button on the main control deck. In his other hand, he had placed a key into a nearby switch, which was labelled 'detonation.' The Omniscience's smile disappeared.

"Would you really do it?" It asked through Dr. Calabash's mouth and began to smile again. Simon's eye quivered, his hand shaking.

"Kill yourself and your friend to stop me? A heroic sacrifice to save humanity is not uncommon, I saw it happen countless times in this universe too, but could you really do it? To never see your wife, your children again? For no one to ever know what happened here? To never see the sun ri—"

"Enough!"

Simon slammed his hand down onto the red button, setting off a series of triggers across the ship. The Omniscience's smile disappeared, and Simon gained one in its place. And then they were both engulfed in flames. The control room, the mess room, the bedrooms were all covered in fire, as the ship was thrust apart in every direction. Simon held eyes with The Omniscience for as long as possible, as The Infinitum blasted into a thousand different pieces. Then slowly, they smiled together. And then neither man was anymore.

By the time it was done, only pieces of metal and bits of body lay strewn across the planet's barren ground.

THE END

Nomads of the Light

By Alex O'Neill and M. M. Dixon

Date: 3259

Location: Ark Designation DS7089

Prologue

{REDACTED EMAIL FROM THE DEPUTY HEAD OF STAFF AT ISA TERRAFORMATION PROJECTS, BEN TOLLEN, TO PROJECT LEADER PAUL MARTIN ON ARK DESIGNATION DS7089}

Dear Paul,

I hope you are happy with my suggestions regarding the Ark Designation DS7089 staffing, that of Karl Trystan to be the Operations Overseer on the trip. I believe he would be a suitable fit for the role.

Regards,
Ben

Dear Ben,

I do have some issues with Karl's appointment as I have looked through his digital record and it would seem to me that there has been some nepotism at play; he is the nephew of your immediate boss, is that correct?

I worry that, given his murky track record and some of the training records, he may not be up to the task of leadership on this job. Would it not be practical to put a more experienced supervisor in place for this, to match some of our more experienced technical team leaders that are on this voyage?

Thanks,
Paul

Dear Ben,

Thank you for your email and I appreciate your concerns regarding Karl Trystan. I believe that despite his murky training record, that Karl has the potential to be an excellent recolonization project manager and just requires an easy supervising role to begin with. The Ark mission DS7089 only must travel in what is effectively a straight line, from ISA Space station #12 to Orlan 3, past very few other planets. All the crew need to do, if they don't do anything they shouldn't do, is not fall out.

I hope that puts your mind at rest.

Thanks,
Paul.

The Story

Maintenance Log Entry/MDL32591105.1427.3/Krylov.Yavelda

The ark, DS7089, is set to land on Orlan 3 two weeks from now. As scheduled, the computer woke my crew and the pre-arrival supervisors so we can start prepping the ship. Most of the staff is still in prot-sleep but one maintenance crew member (Elliot T. Groka) died; standard ejection. Other maintenance crew members were fine with a little caffeine and food. I sent two to the med bay, but they're expected back to work after one more sleep cycle.

We looked over trucks 1-5 today. Minor problems with ragged hoses in truck 2 and major problems with the electrical systems in truck 3; the others tested normally. We'll split off a team of five tomorrow to repair the noted issues while everyone else checks over trucks 6-10.

The Goliaths' systems seem fine, but a full manual maintenance check is scheduled two cycles from now.

The Eden's system diagnostics also sprung no tickets. A full manual maintenance check is scheduled four cycles from now.

The ark's internal maintenance diagnostics showed several minor issues. We opened tickets for 17 hose replacements, three touchpad sensor replacements, and one set of door wiring. Fuel systems popped a non-specific error which I'll look into tomorrow.

External ark maintenance diagnostics showed clear; however, crew will walk the exterior for visual assessment two cycles from now as well.

Operations Supervisor Trystan's personal log, entry 354

We grow closer to Orlan 3 every day. I personally can't wait. This team of engineers—engineers, more like bison in boiler suits—seem to be able to do a lot, but one thing that they can't do is make this ship go any faster than a snail's pace. Yet another day where I have nothing to reflect on, nothing to really engage me—I truly pulled the short straw with this one. I heard that the transport ship to Epsilon 6 has multi-room saunas and swimming pools onboard! Swimming pools! Just my luck that the ISA chose Orlan 3 for me. They've piled it on me by waking me up early—are any other administrators on this voyage up yet? Of course not! Just me and Overseer Smyth, anyway.

Anyway, I digress. This day was, like I've alluded to, much the same as any other, except I'm no longer enjoying a rest. Oh, yes, we lost a crew member in prot-sleep. That was unfortunate, I'll admit. The side effects of prot-sleep seem to be continuing with almost all our staff, with two of the engineers even taking the afternoon off. I took this time to talk to our Operations Overseer, Marcus Smyth, who confidently told me that everything was still very much going to plan. I updated him with the progress as best I could (I don't like to maintain long conversations with the head engineer, so I get what I need from her and go). I long for a little bit more excitement with this job... of any kind, really. At least Smyth promised some reward at the end of this.

That's all I've got to report today if I'm honest. It might be different tomorrow, but I can't imagine it will be.

Maintenance Log Entry/MDL32591107.1440.1/Krylov.Yavelda

All maintenance crew members are back on standard cycles.

All critical primary system diagnostics and routine maintenance checks are complete. Two new tickets have been opened for the crew quarters: one is to repair the showers on level 2, which is a low priority since only maintenance and operations supervisors are currently awake and they can use the showers on level 3, which are working; the second is to fix the electrical connections in the level 2 break rooms; this issue is likely linked to the other ticket and has the same low priority.

Internal maintenance tickets on the trucks, Edens, Goliaths, and the Ark itself are all closed without incident, except for the fuel system hiccup previously noted. I checked that at 0800 yesterday and found a significant weakening in six joints. I rerouted one section and disassembled the joint to find that it was completely missing one of the pressure seals.

This could be an installation error… if so, I'll probably find the same error in the other five weakened seals. But I can't understand how these seals could be installed without such a critical piece as a pressure seal. Maybe the part was not included, but the installers went ahead anyway, thinking it non-critical, but those seals sell pretty well on the black market, so maybe they thought other things.

Regardless, we're now dangerously close to not having the fuel we need for the final manoeuvres.

I notified the Operations Supervisor, Karl Trystan, of all I had found and told him the best fix was to apply patches to absorb and further seal the faulty joints, per regs. There would be a small delay for other maintenance requests as the team accomplished this. However, he kept insisting on entirely draining and rerouting the fuel from this system to the backup system. I showed him the reg and told him how his plan might mean losing more fuel since we would have to access valves outside the ark. Plus, the backup systems have not had any diagnostics performed yet.

He seemed to understand and agree, but when I came back in the next cycle, he had had other engineers re-route anyway, without any notice or even any filed record.

I checked the backup system immediately and discovered the same issue as we had in the main system with seven of these seals. I patched everything, but we continue to lose small amounts of fuel. It would not be anything to worry about if we hadn't re-routed to the backup system, but now we can't afford any loss. We need to replace these seals to keep what fuel we have, which we can't do in flight. I could replace most of the joints in the primary fuel storage as we go and then re-route the fuel back, but with only 5 complete spares (the others lack the same seal), one joint would still be a problem in that system. I would pull one seal from the backup system then and locally reroute as I did the first time I was checking into this issue, but we would lose even more fuel with the system change. So, we have either a continuous slow leak in the backup or another larger loss as we route back to the main system and repair the final seal.

We'd already lost approximately 75% of our +10% reserves from the leak when it was discovered. Now the remaining reserves are gone, plus 2% of the fuel necessary to change course and route us to Orlan 3. I filed a report with the ops team, suggesting we land on a small planet along our route to repair the system and recover however much fuel we can, plus generate biofuel from our planting supplies, which won't be as clean but should work to get us to the settlement site. It's their call, but I can't see any other way.

Operations Supervisor Trystan's personal log, entry 356

Today we had a faulty fuel line in the centre right section of the hull which led to some leakage. Obviously, I suggested that we siphon the fuel and reroute it round, but the end result of this was Yavelda Krylov doing whatever she wanted, so I had to step in. I overruled her, but then due to unexpected fuel movements, we now have to land on a closer planet. Yavelda then tried her own solution, a series of absorbing fuel patches along the line, which to her credit, seem to have stopped that leaking, but she told me it was too late now.

The gall of this woman! To tell me what to do on my own shift! I wouldn't be surprised if she's also the one putting coffee grounds in the metal recycling deposit. Her Neanderthalic demeanour would certainly suggest so. I guess the best way to handle this is to relay it to the rest of the team and let them figure out what to do about her—I hardly believe that the operations team going to Epsilon 6 would have to put up with this. Wait until I tell the Association. A detour that we could expect to take up to maybe a week, and I know it'll be me who's got to stand up and explain this to our crewmates and then make the call to Marcus Smyth about it. I guess, sometimes, when you're in a leadership position, these are the things you've got to do.

I had a look earlier, and the nearest planet, the one we are set to land on, is logged in the ISA systems as 'Knittel 16' and has been designated un-occupiable. The stats make it comparable to Mercury, back in the Earth system, slightly cooler and slightly larger, but other than that, it's that planet's twin. What are we supposed to do there? Hopefully, the issues with the fuel line are a simple fix once we land, and then we can get back up on our way. People will hear about this, though, from outside, and the humiliation will be enormous when I get back to Alpha Centauri C.

We might have to stay on Knittel 16 for up to a week–and with limited fuel, we can only hope to sustain our position there for a very short amount of time, as it will maintain something the engineers call 'a cold bubble'. If something goes wrong further with the fuel-line fix, then the ship won't be able to maintain to the cold bubble, but I highly doubt that will happen. Tomorrow, I plan to reroute the back-up fuel into the left hull section, and we can only hope that the extra burst is enough to get us further on, and we won't need to land on from Knittel 16. Tomorrow morning, the first job for me and Yavelda (she won't be getting out of it), is to wake the rest of the passengers and crew to alert them to the situation. I won't be looking forward to it, but I can't imagine she will, either.

Maintenance Log Entry/MDL32591109.1413.1/Krylov.Yavelda

Supervisor Trystan has once again ignored everything I told him and ordered maintenance personnel to re-route what little fuel we had left. His reasons are impossible to understand, but the result is an additional 1-2% loss of fuel and further maintenance needs when we land.

I don't know how to make him stop forcing through decisions when he doesn't understand anything I've told him. I contacted his supervisor, Smyth, to file a formal complaint. Smyth, however, seems to believe that Trystan was acting within his rights and that the "unfortunate events" are because of "miscommunications" on my part. When I asked him outright to review Trystan's decisions, he brushed me off.

We have enough fuel to land on Knittel 16, which they approved. It is not a friendly planet, but, assuming no further supervisory meddling, we should be able to keep a force field, complete maintenance within a few cycles, and generate a little fuel from our food supplies. Now that we've lost even more, I don't know whether we can make enough, but we have to try, or we'll never get to the settlement planet. Crew members can remain in the ship and lead relatively normal lives while the fuel effort is completed, though it would have been ideal to keep non-critical personnel in prot-sleep, because now we all have to stretch our hours to address minor tickets—such as showers—that could otherwise have waited. I have a good crew, thankfully, and they're all willing to do more than they should be asked to, so we'll get through this.

Operations Supervisor Trystan's operations log, entry 358

We've been crashed on Knittel 16 for two days. Panic is in the air, although things have settled a little since yesterday. This planet is incredibly hot—not even terraforming material. It's become pretty clear that it's not going to be hospitable, even for the short amount of time that it would take for a rescue crew to arrive. I've managed to salvage the majority of my personal belongings within the hold of the main ship—many others foolishly threw theirs out on entry in order to lighten the load. The ship seems to be unrepairable; however, a group of the scientists, the boffins, have come up with a method to hoist the ship up above the transport trucks which were meant for construction once we arrived on Epsilon 6. We have managed to keep our transmat hatch system intact, which allows me to enter the ship and retain this log, but it seems to be one of only a few of the non-essential systems still functioning. We lost Operations Supervisors William White and Catherine Goode in their stasis pods in the crash, which leaves me in charge until rescue arrives.

However, the head scientist, Dr. Ella Goldberg, and the head labourer, Chris Sabah, have been enormous thorns in my side since we landed—insisting that I should have awoken the other Operations Supervisors when we detected the slightest threat to our journey. I reminded them that this would be against the ISA's over-management policy. It's clear to me that some people on this journey, even so-called 'department leaders,' have very questionable judgment. At least that oaf, Yavelda, is keeping quiet. I've had my suspicions of her commitment to the journey from its beginning, but at least she seems to have her head screwed on when in a difficult situation. She does like to glare at me from time to time, though.

With a rescue signal sent before we (crash) landed, we should only hope that rescue will be with us within the next week. We have forty surviving colonists plus me, six scientists, three engineers and nine labourers. That's less than a quarter of who we set off with, but if all goes well from here, it's still enough to make initial colonization, and we can call it a successful mission. There has been talk amongst the department leaders about a plan to move the ship, with the surface of this planet being too hot for us to stay even within the shade and staying on the dark side of the planet. But this is a debate that will have to wait until morning, as I am far too tired to oversee any decision of that kind right now.

MDL32591120.1405.2/Yavelda's 3rd log

As I look back over recent events, I can't help but wonder what I could've done, in this life or even in the last, to be cursed with so much bad luck, especially in the form of one Supervisor Trystan. True, he probably didn't cause the initial problems with the seals—

I don't think he's bright enough to work the black market without being caught—but he has compounded the problem so many times at this point, I have to wonder if he's deliberately sabotaging the settlement mission.

We are on Knittel 16, at least, and so we have a fighting chance to survive—well, those few of us who made it here do—until a rescue ship can arrive. And survival is all we can hope for on this bleak rock.

The landing did not go well. I haven't had time to look deeply into what happened mechanically because our efforts have all had to be focused on shelter and salvaging what resources we can. We crashed in the daylight area, with the ship flipped upside down, and I believe we only survived the day because of the additional heat shielding on the ship's bottom. However, the ship heated up enough (causing us to lose a few more settlers) that it became obvious we could not survive a week this way. We used the dusk to haul out what machinery we could salvage and the night to hoist the ship up onto the mining trucks with the two cranes we were able to salvage. We lost two of the maintenance crew to these efforts—one when a crane failed and one when a suit failed. My remaining crew is beyond exhausted, but we are sleeping only in very short cycles until we get as much survival equipment as operable and sustainable as we can. There are too many maintenance tickets to list here, but food and medical needs are the highest priorities after getting the trucks going so we can try to stay in dusk and avoid both the intense heat and cold—not that dusk is much better, but it is survivable in the ship or for moderate time periods in the suits.

Operations Supervisor Trystan's operations log, entry 369

Last week, we began our circumnavigation on the planet, following the rise and fall of the sun around the surface of Knittel 16. I thought we ought to stay in one singular location, but Sabah and Goldberg both argued against it and took a vote (a waste of time) amongst everyone, with the decision being to leave the area. Goldberg has assumed some kind of authority over the group, despite myself actually being the highest-ranking officer, which is not something I can really allow to slide—I have made the decision today to have to let her go from the ISA's employment once we arrive at our true destination, Orlan 3.

I must say, I am impressed by the ingenuity that it has taken regarding the circumnavigation system. The main ship is hoisted up by four transport trucks, with most of the essential life support systems stripped, and carried by the transmat underneath the ship, in the shade, while we all mostly work and live underneath. From there, we follow the rise and fall of the sun, as this planet is survivable so long as we stay at twilight, just as the sun sets. The ship keeps some power with solar panels that Yavelda Krylov had labourers drill to the roof of the ship. Yavelda has also approached me and Dr. Goldberg about leaving a series of communication antennas behind so deep-space scans might pick up a signal from anywhere across the planet's surface, no matter what they're looking at it. It's a work in progress; unfortunately, we've now lost signal of the first couple of equipment pieces we dropped. And I doubt they'll survive in the heat for long enough, either.

I had to speak to Chris Sabah as he questioned my frequent use of the transmat to access the ship for the recording of this log. It is not his place or his right to question me, and I think he should be very careful. I may allocate him to working on the heat shield at the top of the ship for the next couple of days. He'll feel right as rain after that, I'm sure. I must admit that it's taken longer to receive rescue than I'd initially hoped, but I have a feeling in my gut that we'll get out of this before too long—the ISA is unlikely to have missed our contact methods or to delay in trying to rescue us. The planet must just not be chartered everywhere, which may have caused the delay. I hold out hope and remain faithful in the ISA's ability to find us.

MDL32591217.1452.1/Yavelda's 4th entry

The ship is on the trucks, the trucks are moving it around the planet to stay in the dusk, and we are all working every moment of every waking cycle just trying to keep everyone alive. We've largely given up on being able to restore the ship enough to escape that way, so we're not growing biofuel for now, just food. We have growing stations set up along the outer edge of the underside of the ship, with lighting and mirrors rigged up carefully to work together. Many of the plants are nonetheless struggling without real sunlight. Luckily, we had many botanists and farmers on board, and they are capable, so I'm hopeful they can keep the food resources going. Dr. Goldberg is overseeing that effort, so I only need to be involved for the mechanical needs. Dr. Goldberg has wisely barred anyone from going near these food stations—including supervisors—unless they are on the work details.

None of the comms equipment seems to be getting a signal through the considerable solar interference here. We've attempted messages from the ship itself and have even left equipment out behind us, hoping it might send a signal in the full dark, but I'm certain it can't operate in the intense cold of night any more than it can in the full sun. We'll be able to check in a few cycles, but we'll probably only be salvaging whatever equipment survived. I'm also working with the supervisors to send an ultra-amplified message from the ship in a few cycles, when our astrophysicists say we should be most closely orbitally aligned for the signal to match up with ISA receivers. This will spend a lot of our power reserves, unfortunately, and we've had to further restrict everyone's access to extras, including even entry to the ship for sleep. We've slung hammocks up from the bottom of the ship for adults and older children. Younger children and nursing mothers are all on the same cycle now and must all enter the ship for sleep at the same time. We've set up caregivers to always remain in the ship as well, so the outside caregivers can sleep while the children are in the ship and vice-versa.

The ship's water systems and plumbing are still operational, though we've had to get very creative about waste, as we can't just let the ship fill up with it. So, we're dragging a very large hose behind us, trailing into the dark. We also had to set up a creative latrine system dragging near the end of the hose for the people outside to use. There are only two latrine stations, and there's always a line to use them, so we'll have to set up more when we can. It's dangerous since it's so near the planet's full dark–it'll take only one slip for a person to die in this process, and so it's only a matter of time. (I'm continuing to work on the problem.) We've set up a similar system for non-compostable trash, on the other side of the ship. We're like a giant slug, leaving two disgusting slime trails behind us. But at least the trails will freeze and then burn, so we're hopeful they won't cause disease as we re-encounter them every planetary turn.

Operations Supervisor Trystan's operations log, entry 404

Our rotations began 35 days ago. I can only imagine the laughter back in the officer's mess back home. Every day now feels almost the same: we rise, check the outside of the ship, and a team leaves communication antenna out to collect signals from every direction of this darned planet, but we never gather any meaningful data. No sign of rescue yet. Engineers come in from the trucks, they go out, they come back, they go out. The layout of our situation would seem almost funny to the outside observer. I don't find it particularly amusing.

I must be frank: I am starting to feel undermined in my position onboard this ship. Not only has Dr. Goldberg reinstated Sabah into his old officer's post without checking with me—in fact, I also didn't even know it was going to happen beforehand—which is exactly the sort of thing, according to ISA deep space emergency protocols 161.4.1, that should have been run past me. Krylov and her team have also started collecting data from the communication antenna to collate into some kind of diary, maybe with the opportunity to send off a large amount of data at once. I haven't been consulted on this either—what'll be said, how it'll be worded, what data will be left out, anything. Why should I expect anything less at this point?

We're starting to approach our first full rotation of the planet now, which seems promising in terms of a data-collection perspective, but less so from an immediate-rescue perspective. I sat down to oversee our weekly fuel checks, talked to our other surviving officers, read for some time, took lunch, and then went out with the engineers, some of whom are putting up extra reflective material on the outside of the ship. I then returned inside and spoke to Krylov and Goldberg again, before playing some stupid card game with some of the kids onboard.

On the positive side of it, our food and water cycle systems seem to be working fine, and everyone is relatively happy because of that. I suppose I must tip my hat to Krylov and her team for managing it effectively. My stash of extra food has, so far, gone unfound by any nosey parkers. Let's hope it stays that way. Anyway, I best get off before Sabah asks why I'm using the transmat to record a short and essential Operations log.

The ISA will give me a medal for putting up with all of this.

MDL3260.0121.1433.1/Yavelda's 5th entry

Food stores are going faster than food is growing. We've set up additional growing stations, and the death rate is balancing it some as well, since we haven't gone a single cycle set without at least one death. We've lost eight children. Three cycles ago, one of my best engineers threw himself into the cold. We've had to add corpses to our trash-side slime trail.

The comms equipment we recovered proved not only inoperable but also probably unrepairable. We spent the energy to send the super-signal out, but frankly, I think the ISA is just ignoring this problem until it solves itself. Which, given our death rate and depleting reserves, won't be long.

There is so much more to document, but this log is the very lowest of my priorities.

Operations Supervisor Trystan's operations log, Entry 431

The primary update today has to be the discovery of a probe. This is not an ISA probe, but one from Terrastorm, a small, private terraforming company, who perhaps own a couple of moons in a couple of systems not far from this one and have by chance a probe running not too far from this system. The plan is to send a message out continually with our current location and situation. Krylov insists we not include information about our role and purpose for the ISA, but I'm sure that won't matter. It would be bold indeed for this Terrastorm company to question anything that the ISA would do or any decisions up until this point. This is our chance.

The first thing we did today was to meet as a set of team leaders, to arrange a safe point for the rescue crew to meet us at a safe location. All across the planet, there are 'safe stays' which I've mapped out, little nooks and crannies where there is enough shade that realistically we could stay for some time. Our problem is, most of them are not large enough to host the entire crew, ship and all our other accompaniments. I did suggest we leave some people, but unfortunately that was too much for the likes of Goldberg and Sabah. I know it's harsh, but that's the realistic lens you need to look at situations like this through.

My aggravation with the other team leaders aboard the ship continues. Today, Krylov ran the meeting, making decisions about how we will program our radio parts. This is not her ultimate call to make, its mine, as she should know, and as everyone listening to this will know as well. Goldberg suggested that we should put together a strategic plan to work out who will get evacuated in what order, under the slim chance that Terraform does not have rescuing capacities to take all of us at once.

Sabah also made an argument for taking parts of the ship. Parts of the ship? What a fool.

Maybe this log; it's useful that it absolutely doesn't fall into the wrong hands. But other than that, I can't think of any reason why we'd need parts of the ship. Situations like these remind me why I decided to demote him all those weeks ago.

Anyway, I shan't get too down in the dumps with this situation. We'll be safe soon, and I'll be rewarded for the leadership I've shown through these tough times.

MDL3260.0205.1429.1/Yavelda's 6th entry

No answers from ISA; definitely no rescue.

But we found a probe! It's from Terrastorm, not the damned ISA, so maybe if we play our cards right, we can get them to pick us up. I keep telling Trystan why we can't let them know we're ISA—no private company would want to get tangled up in the rat's nest of political scrutiny and paperwork that would follow our rescue. (Maybe saying that will cost me my job someday–and if I survive long enough to be canned, I'll be happy enough!) But Trystan really doesn't seem to understand what I'm telling him, despite being exactly the kind of trash who would never rescue someone if it meant the slightest inconvenience to himself. He's ISA to the core, so I guess, like him, the ISA can do no wrong. I'm trying to keep him out of the plan as much as possible, but he keeps butting in. He's miserable despite having one of the easiest jobs in this place, and he wants us all to be miserable with him. Well, those of us he sees some value in—the rest, he'd just as soon abandon to their deaths. He'd probably put me at the top of that list, really, except for needing me to survive.

Crew morale is up a bit, thanks to the probe, but everyone is hanging on by mere threads. I've tried to train some of the civilians to do crew work, but it's hard to spare the time to teach when it's so much faster to keep doing the work we, and the work just piles up more. The settlers all seem pretty shell-shocked, too, so I've only found a handful to try training.

MDL3260.0207.1449.1/Yavelda's 7th entry

We're going to die.

Terrastorm refused to pick us up for a variety of reasons that sounded very much like flimsy excuses. The recording they sent back was… off. Off, like someone messed with it. I'm looking into it instead of sleeping this cycle.

I'd like to have done that during my shift, which just ended, but one of the damn trucks stopped in its tracks earlier. The other trucks were still going, of course, and by the time they got the radio alert and stopped, one corner of the ship had slipped off the dead truck. There was not enough time to repair that truck before the dark caught us. I spent my entire shift working that problem—we had to proceed with the corner unsupported, while we got another truck out of the ship (a damned difficult feat) and aligned it under the corner, just letting it scrape into place. Definitely not ideal; the corner sustained damage, including the food-growing station near it, as did the top of the truck. But we're all still ahead of the dark, if barely. I sped us up for one cycle to try to move away from the edge of the dark more, but of course that means we're burning more resources.

Why am I working myself to the bone to buy us another day? I guess I can't believe they're all just going to leave us here, despite every sign that this is so.

Operations Supervisor Trystan's operations log, Entry 433

The rescue failed, and I am certainly disappointed. The controls of the probe stated that they couldn't possibly be seen to be helping an ISA terraforming project, given the current political climate. Talk about a way to play with innocent people's lives!

Just this morning over breakfast, I spoke to a young girl who wanted to pilot ships. She showed me a delightful drawing of some space fighter ship, with rockets on the back and a set of laser cannons on the front. I of course told her peace between separate solar systems was the best way for technology to advance and our people to be happy.

Terrastorm also stated that they couldn't pick us up due to our current situation—none of their rescue craft are designed for a planet of such heat, as they predominantly deal with terraforming small, cold exo-planets. Certainly, an oversight on their organizations' part; you'd never deal with such crap from the ISA. Luckily, I managed to omit my mention of the ISA when Krylov and Goldberg played back the message earlier; otherwise, I'd probably be in a lot of hot water. Not that they can really do much to me—I'm still their boss. And anyway, how could I have known that the divisions between Terrastorm and the ISA would really be that serious?

Krylov wants to lead an investigation, but the human bison is unlikely to find much. To be honest, I think I've covered my own back fairly well. She definitely thinks that she's more popular aboard this ship than she really is. Even if she can turn people against me, I have things I can use to undermine her and her position. After all, if she felt that strongly about the circumstances under which we crashed, she could have stepped in and actually done something, but did she? No. I wonder what the rest of the crew and the remainder of the senior officers will think of that when they hear it.

Anyway, I'm going to retire for this evening—as comfortably as I can, at least. While I'm not losing sleep about the results of Krylov's investigation (you wouldn't send a bull in if you were looking for a needle in a haystack, would you?), I must admit it's the first time that I've felt slightly uncomfortable in my position aboard this ship.

Let's see what tomorrow brings, or hopefully, doesn't bring.

MDL3260.0210.1403.1/Yavelda's 8th entry

Trystan is out. I easily found his dirty little secret in the recordings—he *told* them we were ISA, despite the leadership group all agreeing it was a bad idea. Again, he decided he knew best and went around everyone else. That, combined with his meddling that led to us being on this forsaken planet in the first place, was too much. I wasn't expecting them to exile him— ironically in one of the shady spots he mapped out himself—but everyone was convinced if he stayed, he would find some way to ruin any further chances of survival. It's a harsh punishment and no doubt he'll die miserably out there. But I can hardly feel any sympathy, given how many other people have died from his arrogant idiocy.

But… what further chances of survival? With ISA and Terrastorm both ignoring us, the chances of encountering anyone else are very nearly zero.

But I and my crew will carry on. I've got a small new team to help with minor repairs. One of these, Jayme, was well suited to electronics work, so he's dedicated entirely to radio now. He's using every spare part from scrapped systems, amplifying, repeating, and sending in all directions. We have to try, even with no real hope. When I start to doubt the point of it all, I go look at the children's ward. They look terrible, honestly, so scared and hungry, but they're alive. These ones are still alive, and if they don't make it, it won't be because I stopped trying.

Karl Trystan's personal diary - day 1 – recorded on his own personal digital recording device.

Dear Diary,

Today was a terrible day. I was forced off the ship by the other team leaders and no one—no one!—stepped in to fight my corner. Yavelda revealed through her 'digging' that I'd told Terrastorm that we were ISA, something which obviously I'd been told not to do. To further that, she decided to reveal it was my decisions with the fuel lines that had led to us crashing in the first place.

Not quite how I saw it at the time, obviously. But that's it; I've lost my position and my literal place aboard the ship. I'm forced to go it alone.

Obviously, the demotion is a pain. These people, they don't understand how to run a ship, run a crew, not like I do. I wonder how long they'll survive without me, and how quickly they'll start to regret having forced me out.

One small mistake, and then suddenly I'm vilified? Forced into 'exile' as if we live on medieval Earth? I was allowed the 'luxury' of one suit and a limited supply of food to allow me to get to one of the 'safe stay' areas, but that was it. I must admit that I have no real plan now beyond getting to the safe stay area I picked out, but at least it's very close to where the ship will pass by again, so there will be further chances.

For now, I must go it alone, with nothing but the food, suit, and skills I have to get by. I will access the radio parts left across the planet, where I can, when I can, and try to keep myself updated. I'm certain a rescue attempt will be made again before long, and I intend to be on that rescue ship when it lives.

I'm not out of the game yet; I'm stronger than that.

Yours truly,

Karl

MDL3260.0217.1403.1/Yavelda's 9th entry

We've settled into what seems like a relatively survivable routine. More of the settlers have figured out how to make a life in the shadow of the ever-moving ship, sometimes in hammock systems, sometimes walking. Many people are eager to help as much as possible, which, while little enough, is something. My crew is still overworked, but we can at least get enough sleep and enough calories to keep going.

We still walk the razor edge of survival, of course, with food growing, but not at the ideal rate. We did come across an extra store of rations when we searched that bastard Trystan's room, which burned up the one last ounce of sympathy I'd had for him. He saw those hungry children every day!

We pass by him every planetary rotation, of course. He can only survive in the shaded spot he walked to, which is all too near our track. A few of the settlers are making trouble about his exile—not that they liked him, exactly, but they think the leaders were wrong to exile anyone for any reason. They say we're tyrants. And I guess we are since we have no time for democratic decision-making. I've started carrying a stun gun, just in case.

Jayme continues his efforts. One problem is that he's using every bit of technology he can for sending signals, but our listening apparatus is still the same old tech we had, so we won't know if anyone hears us—and someone would have to be really close to hear us. Hope is in thin supply.

Karl's 9th entry - recorded on his own personal digital recording device.

Today I saw a ship approaching this planet. I flagged it down, but it ignored me. I don't know what to think anymore. I sit here, and I feel like I'm losing my mind. I have my regrets, but I know that when I had to make the tough decisions, I made the right calls. No one, not ever, is going to tell me otherwise.

I've not had something to eat for three days now. But I keep moving. I do what I need to. I tried my hardest to attempt to sneak back onto the remainder of the Ark, but it didn't happen. Unfortunately, that scumbag Krylov saw me—and fired a stun-gun at me! Not much longer after that, I saw the same ship leaving this planet, and the Ark sat abandoned. A shadow of what it once was, so that rescue ship must have taken the ship apart, removing the trucks it stood on, a lot of the rations and personal items—even my old supervisor log recordings, for god's sake. That'll come back to bite me, possibly. I didn't know anyone else was going to listen to those.

This might mean that I'm completely alone on this planet. With the rations and life-support suit that I managed to take with me from the Ark, I think that I could last maybe another week, and perhaps in that time, someone else could come and rescue me, too. I'll need to go over the remaining radio equipment aboard the Ark. I don't think I'm quite out of the game yet.

I'm going to keep it short and sweet, as I know everything that I have with me is fleeting, and I need to conserve what energy that I have for the days ahead.

Signing off,

Karl

MDL3260.0219.1411.1 Yavelda's 10th entry

A ship answered us.

I can hardly believe it.

It's an unregistered freighter, but I don't care. I offered them every bit of the tech they could haul away, so long as they haul us away, too. I don't care where they drop us off, either, as long as it has cities. They agreed. We insisted on everyone being picked up first—several trips in their shuttles—and my crew will help them disassemble everything else when all the other settlers are safe in the freighter.

It's obviously dangerous to put ourselves at these likely smugglers' mercies, but nothing is riskier than staying here. I've armed the entire maintenance crew. Hope is finally kindled, however.

Epilogue

Karl Trystan fell on the rock. The ship disappeared into the distance, and as the harsh sun bore down upon his skin, he reached out, trying to grasp the ship, as if it were only one foot away from him. As Karl tried to swallow, he tasted nothing at all. Not even the lack of taste. Just nothing.

Slowly, Karl lowered his arm and brought it back down to his side. The bright orange light of the rescue ship became smaller, and smaller, driving away from him in a direct line across the twilight sky, almost taunting him by how visible it was and how much less visible it was becoming.

He looked at his digital recording device and used a monumental amount of effort bring it up towards his face. "Karl Trystan's personal di…" He began, but swiftly stopped, and tears welled up. Not like this. Slowly, he placed a hand on each knee, and then stood up, taking all of his remaining strength, all his remaining calories, to do so. He groaned as he stood up and began to set one foot in front of the other, moving forward painfully slowly under the unbearable heat.

First his left, and then his right. Then his left again. Step by step, inch by inch, Karl Trystan moved forward across the surface of Knittel 16, leaving his digital recorder buried in the sound. He didn't need it anymore really—it was just a distraction. He could see the Ark, with shadow falling underneath it. If we could reach that before the sun came out in full, then perhaps, he could be ok for just a little longer. As he groaned and struggled towards it, he started feel a little hope, as if, if just reached that shadow, then all his problems could be solved.

Then, suddenly, his foot hit a rock, and Karl Trystan fell forward, unable to stop himself, smacking the ground hard. It took him a moment, but he recovered, and started to press up off the ground, trying to get back up. He bent his arms to right angles, and pressed as hard as he could, but he still could not get up. After a moment, he let go and faceplanted the sand again. Slowly, he looked up and took in the sky, one last time. The ship disappeared in amongst the stars in the sky.

It's gone. Damn that Krylov—and all the others!

Karl's eyes filled with sand, as cold began to set in around him, and he let go of everything he was holding onto, holding on to all his ambition, all his plans, all his ego, and he lay their limp. He took a breath, his lungs filling with sand which pierced his lungs like tiny daggers. Karl lay there, motionless, until he breathed no more.

THE END

Timezones

By Alex O'Neill

Date: 3575

Location: The Great Trundler

Chapter One

Slowly, The Great Trundler barrelled through the emptiness of deep space. It was a long, small, concrete-grey space trawler, with small repairs to the hull here and there, some welded, some with tape. Brightly coloured jet flames blasted out from various small ports, mostly around the back of the ship. At the end of the ship's long nose nestled a cramped, rusty cockpit, around which five the ship's occupants sat.

Within that cockpit, a faint sound came from one of the cockpit's computer screens. Hattie, the ships navigation officer and chief beer-drinker, was the first to notice it. She was a well-muscled woman, with short brown hair, a small, tight mouth, and a scar underneath her left eye. She leaned over, squinting to look at the tiny navigation section of the screen, and saw a blip on their radar.

"Boss," she said, turning towards T, the ship's captain. "We got something here."

"Something?" T asked from the chair to her left, raised up slightly above hers. He was a modest man, with a still-brown beard on his chin but only a few sparse grey hairs on his head. He turned his long, hawkish nose and sharp eyes toward her.

"Well, it is an object. Large, asteroid size, Ten kilometres large. But readings say it is… metal."

"So, not an asteroid then," Nic, the science officer, chimed in. She was a tall woman with cold eyes in a pretty face, sporting a leather jacket with various bits of tit and tatter attached.

"… No," T stated slowly, looking between the two women. "Must be a large ship or a space station."

"There's nothing recorded as being in this area," Bot, the co-pilot, reported. Bot, a small, humanoid robot, was initially silver but was now rusted to a dark grey brown. Hattie looked at Bot and then up at T.

"I think we should back off," she said. "Who knows who that station could belong to?"

"I mean," Nic stated, "It might not belong to anyone. It could be abandoned. It could be a score. It could a floating bank drifting in space, for all we know."

"That's unlikely," T responded.

"Or it could be full of armed guards," Trig chipped in. Trig, the ship's main pilot, was a ginger-haired lanky man with a face too large for his head. He, like the other four, never told the others his real name "Could be some secret military training station, full of hard bastards armed to the absolute teeth."

"It's worth just leaving well alone," Hattie stated. "We've got a job—that cargo ship with the radiation leak we're supposed to hit is only another few hours' travel."

"T, I'm looking at the scanners now. There've been no radio signals from that ship in weeks, and it's just drifting. We could be zipping past the score of the century." Nic stated.

"Trig is right," Hattie insisted. "It could be death trap."

T pondered. He sat, hand on fist, breathed in through his nose, and then out through his mouth. He paused for what felt like an eternity and then looked between Nic and Hattie.

"Ok, let's go in," he finally stated.

"Let's make this quick, then," Hattie muttered. "No messing around."

"Trig," T ordered. "Bring us in, lad."

As the ship powered across the sky, they could determine that it was a space station, shaped like a donut. The huge vessel reflected the thin light of the far-off star in that system, appearing almost like some ebony monster rather than a man-made construct.

"Look at this," Trig gawped. "It's vast—it must have multiple control decks. Look! Those windows, they are huge, but they're blackened out. You can see out, but not in."

"Clearly the owners wanted to remain undisturbed, Trig," Nic said. "Unfortunately, we won't be obliging their request today."

"Let's not speculate," Hattie growled. "It could be anything. It could be there for any reason."

"Ooo," Nic responded, waiving her hands around. "Someone's touchy. God forbid you actually let something interesting happen for once, Hattie."

Hattie blushed.

"I just don't like going off-mission. I've been off mission before, and it never ends well."

"Well, that would have been different," Nic stated.

"Oh?" Hattie asked.

"You never had me there before," Nic smiled, but Hattie did not return it.

"Cut the chatter, we're making the approach," T overcut them. "Bot, do you think you'd be able to access this space stations docking panel?"

"Yes. It does seem to be an older model, perhaps this is one of the delivery hangars, but I have the protocols," Bot answered. He then inserted his right hand in a perfectly shaped space in front of him, in The Great Trundler's control board. After a moment, a beam of light came out from the front of The Trundler and connected with a panel to the left of the closed docking station door.

Slowly, the door lifted, and T smiled.

"Not bad, Bot."

The Great Trundler moved forward into the ship's docking hangar, the lights slowly blinking on as they landed. The Trundler touched down smoothly, engines and jets whirring and hissing as it lowered.

"Let's see what's what," T stated, and unclipped his seatbelt, standing up and heading out of the cockpit. Nic and Trig quickly followed suite, and Bot turned to Hattie.

"Time to get out, ma'am," Bot stated bluntly. "It seems we have a new mission now."

Hattie sighed in response but stood and followed the others out of the cockpit. Once the five of them were out in the hangar, they got a greater appreciation of where they were. The hangar was huge, twenty times larger than The Great Trundler. Nic and Hattie stepped forward to the nearest door, followed by T. Hattie grabbed the handle and tried to force the door open. It did not budge.

"It's locked," she called out.

"Hold on," Nic said, and grabbed the door handle, too, and both women pushed against the door with all their weight. It still did not budge.

"No, it's definitely locked," Nic agreed. Hattie stared at her, unsmiling.

"Bot," T said. "There is an info panel over there, looks deactivated. Any chance you could reactivate it?"

"Will do," Bot said and strode off to work on the panel. Trig went with him, holding pieces of the info panel as Bot changed a few of the wires on the inside.

T stroked his chin. He sighed.

"Everything ok?" Hattie asked.

"This station… it gives me a weird feeling" he admitted.

"Me, too."

"I can't help thinking… what happened here?"

"There's something off about this place, no lights, no detectable radio signals, nothing."

"Same!" Nic cut in. "But I also get the feeling that we're going to find a huge haul here!"

"I wouldn't be so sure," Hattie snapped back.

"Info panel online!" Bot stated from across the room.

"Well," T said, nodding at him. "Looks like we're about to find out."

***

Location: Naples, Italia, Earth

Date: 57AD

"Again," stated the Roman Optio.

A young man, Aetius, who might have been just twelve, swung at him again, arcing down with his large wooden sword. The larger, more experienced man stepped aside quickly, and the wooden sword hit the ground with a resounding *thunk*!

"You missed," the Optio stated, grabbing the young man by the scruff of his vest and thrusting him backwards, nearly pushing him over. But Aetius stayed on his feet.

"Try again," the Optio ordered, his face showing no empathy.

Aetius gritted his teeth and tightened his grip on the wooden sword. He looked up and down at the Optio. He was large, larger than most men of their time, with balding ginger hair, broad shoulders, and a robust torso. He wore not much more than Aetius, just a straw shirt, simple trousers, and a bracelet. He held his sword in his left hand, which Aetius figured could leave his right side open if Aetius misdirected him.

Aetius tried exactly that. First, he stepped towards the Optio, leaning in towards the man's left. As Aetius had predicted, he thrust his sword towards the younger man, so Aetius changed his weight onto his other foot, and leaned towards the Optio's right hip. The Optio, however, spun on one foot and grabbed Aetius by the wrist, and squeezed with force, causing Aetius to drop the sword. The Optio now had Aetius, weapon-less, in a vice-like grip.

"You have no weapon now, and you've left your entire torso open to me to cut open however I please," the Optio stated.

"You cheated. You moved too fast for me to know what to do!" Aetius complained.

"Too fast?" the Optio scoffed. "The enemy will not wait for you to decide where to put their sword. They'll have already killed you. They won't—"

"Brullus, that's enough!" came a loud, commanding voice. Aetius recognized the voice and spun on the spot. It came from his father, and Optio's commander, Centurion Camelius Eclectus. Optio Brullus turned, too, and took in the sight of the Centurion. He was also well muscled, but not as tall as Brullus. He had thick brown hair, with warm eyes and a small mouth.

"I appreciate the service that you do for my household," Camelius stated, "but that is enough training for one morning." He moved forward, putting both hands on his son's shoulders.

"Of course," Optio Brullus agreed, nodded, and moved away. As soon as he'd cleared the courtyard, Camelius felt his son's shoulders relax a little.

"Father, how long must this go on?" Aetius asked.

"Until you can fight I as well can," Camelius replied, turning his son around and giving him with a short smile.

"And what if I never get as good as you?" Aetius asked innocently.

"Then I suppose we'll just keep going," Camelius responded. "And Brullus will have lifelong employment as our household sword trainer."

"Father, where have you been?" Aetis asked, keen to change the subject.

"I've been away, patrolling the perimeter with some of my guard," Camelius responded, before seeming to think about what needed to say next. After a pause, he followed with "There's something coming. I can sense it. Enemies, but I don't know to what allegiance yet. I don't think we will stay here much longer."

"Are you worried?" Aetius asked.

Camelius paused again, gave another short smile, then stood up to his full height, and ruffled Aetius's hair.

"I need to think," the older man stated. "I'll be in the plains just beyond the town… tell your two brothers I'm back, and that I'll see them this evening."

Camelius turned swiftly from the courtyard in one direction, and Aetius turned to leave in the other.

Centurion Camelius Eclectus walked slowly across the grassy plain, the long strands whipping at his knees. He had walked for far longer than he first intended, into the early hours of darkness. He peered out into the night sky.

What he saw wasn't possible. A huge bright light appeared in the sky, lower than any star or comet he had ever seen. A huge trail of fading light followed behind it, seeming totally out of place within the night sky, which slowly faded out. He squinted, looked around—he was completely alone in the field—and then looked back. The star had gone, but it had seemed so bright, and so close. Surely it was a sign from Zeus. He had to tell the rest of the town as soon as he could. He felt that this comet, for some reason, could mean something for the entire Roman empire.

***

Location: Horninsdalvatn Lake, Norway, Earth

Date: 923AD

Ragnaretta Northbrook was the niece of the fiercest Viking Chief, Harald of Stargald, in their part of Norway. Only a small girl, she already prided herself on being the finest child warrior in their clan, able to lead grown men and women to battle.

She was on the outskirts of her clan's central encampment, which occupied the small open land between the dark pine woodland to the camp's east and the deep blue tidal lake to the camp's west. As the sun fell over the horizon, Ragnaretta was taking her customary early evening walk around the edge of the lake, her fellow clan members just in view, busy by their encampments. Her nearest family members were just in view, two men that Ragnaretta relied upon often for guidance.

Ragnaretta was in fact under the careful watch of her uncle, Harald, their most capable warrior, and his father, Ragnarald, who had now retired from fighting. Between the two of them, they now ran the clan like a tight wooden battleship. They were the Stargard clan, strong, tenacious, and loyal. Their encampment was large—there were hundreds of them—and it was made of many great warriors as well as other skilled members of their clan, cooks, smiths, butchers, hunters, gatherers, and leaders.

However, despite their strength, their life was constantly under threat. Every couple of nights, something that wasn't welcome would visit their encampment, and unfortunately, it struck fear into every man, woman, and child.

"Dragon!" came a yell, and there it was. It appeared to emerge out of the setting sun itself, a great winged dragon, with gem-purple eyes, a whipped tail, teeth the size of carving knives, and a burning hide, as if it was made from pure starlight, formed, slightly nearer than the lake's horizon.

Ragnaretta's head pricked up like a t as the monster appeared over the lake in front of her; she ran back to the camp as fast as her small legs would carry her. Within moments, she was by Harald's side, and he moved to protect her.

"It's never here this early in the evening," Harald said. "This beast is getting braver and braver."

Nearby a large, broad-shouldered man with a brown beard threw a tomahawk axe at the dragon, but it seemed to simply disappear into the Dragon's hide. The Dragon roared loudly, rearing its head up high, but then levelled it and stared at them intently. It began to walk over the water of the lake towards them. Every able-bodied person readied themselves to fight this creature, but, as it approached the bank, it dissipated. Its flaming body melting into hundreds or thousands of tiny orange dots.

And then, like that, it was gone.

"Same as ever," Harald said. He turned and nodded to the other weapon-wielding Vikings, and they sheathed their respective weapons. The large Viking sighed and turned away to walk towards the tents. Before long, the other warriors followed suit.

As the adults began to move off, Ragnaretta hung back, uncertain of whether she should follow. Something told her that she shouldn't. A sound, barely audible, came from the other side of the lake. A high-pitched repeating sound, like a squeak, almost a beeping noise. It was coming from almost exactly behind where the dragon had been. For a moment, she peered into the distance, on edge, almost expecting the dragon to reappear whilst she was alone.

"Let's go," came a stern voice.

She turned to see Ragnarald stood behind her, waiting for her to join him.

"Grandad," she said, "can you hear that noise?"

"There is no noise," he responded.

And he was right. When she turned to look out over the lake again, the noise had definitely gone.

"Let's go" Ragnarald said again, and Ragnaretta took his hand before the two of them walked away from the lakeside together.

***

Location: Philadelphia, USA, Earth

Date: 1928

The Grey Lagoon Jazz Bar was one of the classiest speakeasies in all of Philadelphia. Managed by the firm but kind Jonathon Adams, a balding man in his fifties, helped by his wife Marissa and his half-brother, Steven. Tonight was a Thursday, and like usual, the bar was busy, perhaps not as busy as it would be on a weekend, but still busy enough. Tonight, like most Thursdays, Jonathon drank alongside his customers. A plump bald man, and a slim woman with jet-black hair sauntered past him, both of them smiling and chatting. Ronald and Jane, two of their regulars. Ronald worked in estate management; Jane had trained as a nurse. Steven, Jonathon, and Marissa knew every regular that came through their doors. They had to—all it would take is one mole to speak to the police and their entire operation would be thrown in the bin.

From across the small bar, Jonathon could see Marissa up on the balcony, speaking to one of the city mayor's assistants, a sharp man with warm eyes called Daniel. The pair of them saw Jonathon at the same time, and they smiled and waved. Jonathon waved back and turned to see his house-band, The Soul Brothers, stood waiting for his cue. Jonathon gave them a smile and nod, and the lead singer, a tall black man with broad shoulders and long arms, picked up the microphone. The rest of the band quickly followed suite, and Jonathon picked his whiskey up from the bar.

Helped by The Soul Brothers' upbeat but calming tunes, the customers of the Grey Lagoon soon got chatting, and mass merriment could be heard across the room. Before long, Dan, and another one of the mayor's men, a red-faced young advisor called Nick, had hunted Jonathon down and began to talk at him about their business partnership plan for the next two years. Jonathon smiled and nodded curtly, used to this kind of idle talk that meant very little, as Nick and Dan went on and on. He made eyes with Marissa, who was now stood behind them, and rolled his eyes at her without either of the other men noticing.

Just as Jonathon began to relax and let their words simply wash over him (as he came in with the occasional 'mmm' or 'sure'), the sound of a commotion came into the background noise of the bar. Conversations stuttered out to hear what sounded like a fight coming from the next room, the larger bar and floor area.

"Cut the music!" Marissa ordered, and, mid-word, the singer stopped singing. The doors to the larger room burst open and Steven burst into the room, sweat pouring over him. He almost fell headfirst into the bar, were it not for Jonathon and Nick's quick reactions, catching him under both arms. They stood him back up, and Jonathon stepped forward, brushing his younger brother down.

"What the hell is happening in there?" he hissed. "A fight?"

"No, worse" Steven responded.

"Police!?"

"Worse still. Listen, you oughtta see it for yourself."

Marissa and Jonathon followed Steven into the larger bar and gambling floor. This room was darker, with almost orange lighting and a carpeted red floor. It was at least twice the size of the staged bar room, and it looked almost empty.

Around the side of the room stood all of their guests, terrified and unmoving from the *thing* in the middle of the room. And that thing in the middle of the room was unlike anything that anyone had seen before. It floated in the air, like an airplane; however, it was not moving like any airplane. It just hung, stationary. It was circular, too, with no wings. A set of small metal rods stuck out of the top, and a large white circle emitted light near the top of its body. It turned to face them, emitting a loud constant hum. Marissa was the first to approach.

"Hello," she said.

"It came in through the front door," Steven whispered to them. "Off the street."

"We mean you no harm," Marissa added.

"Be careful," Jonathon told her. The thing's eye kept focused on her as she approached.

"I think… it's alive," she said, holding her hand out towards the thing. Swiftly, the thing produced a small metal rod from its side, which nearly reached her hand. Like lightning, Jonathon rushed between them and grabbed Marissa and pushed her back.

"THREAT DETECTED," the thing stated in an inhuman voice, and shot Jonathon with a laser, blasting him into a hundred little pieces. Marissa screamed, staring at the place where her husband had been stood, until Steven grabbed her by the hand, pulling her away. As mass panic broke out in the gambling room, they ducked back into the staged bar room. Steven, tears in his eyes, looked at Marissa, who was now inconsolable.

"What the goddamn hell is that thing?!" he yelled to no one in particular. Whatever the hell it is, it was incredibly dangerous. No one had that kind of technology—not the Japanese, not the Russians, nobody in Europe.

***

4250AD

"HELLO," stated the info-panel in a chirpy, robot voice "I am info-panel 319, located in delivery hangar 3".

"It's on," T stated, approaching it quickly, Hattie and Nic close behind. Trig walked up behind them, keeping some distance away.

"Ok," Hattie piped up. "Request for information—identification of space station and purpose?"

"Thank you for your question," the info-panel sung. "You are on board the third Imagination Station. The Imagination Stations were designed by Rogan Miller in the year 4237 and created by the Hause Organisation in 4245 following his designs."

Hattie looked quizzically at T, her eyebrow raised, and he raised his eyebrow back.

"Their purpose was to provide the paying customer with a holiday experience beyond their everyday lives," the info panel continued.

"And where is the paying customer you speak of now?" Nic asked. She turned to T and Hattie and indicated money with her fingers.

"Thank you for your question," the info-panel said again. "I'm afraid this station has been in a staff-induced lockdown since the end of 4249 due to an outbreak of Optovirus. All customers have been forced to remain in their specific sections of the station."

"Ok, what about the staff?" Hattie said, "There's no one around the hangar."

"Thank you for your question. I'm afraid all the staff have been killed by the Optovirus. The ship is now set to run off standby power, and the customers are kept to their specific sections for now, living off recycled food. All Imagination Stations are built to allow their customers to remain onboard for as long as they wish."

"Or as long as they're able to pay for," Nic cut in.

"That is correct," the info-panel replied.

"Ask what the sections are," Trig whispered closely into Hattie's ear. Hattie turned, frowned at him, and then turned back to the info-panel and relayed his question.

"Thank you for your question. Each section of an Imagination Station is dedicated to a different 'imagination sphere,' a place where you can choose to live your life however you desire, outside of the norms of modern society."

"Sounds like a place to go on holiday," Nic said "Who are the customers?"

"Thank you for your question. It is the Hause Organization's personal friends and family who were allowed to stay for this new Imagination Station's maiden voyage. I hope this information has been useful to you."

"Ok," Hattie said. "Thank you for your help." She took a step back, and turned to T, whose brow was deeply troughed.

"So," she asked, "what's the plan?"

"We have a load of people in lockdown," T stated slowly. "seven and a half thousand, in fact. I think the best course of action is to lift the lockdown and free these people. They're sat there, no hope. It's not going to easier to locate and get to the control desk. This is a big ship—a very big ship. A ship in a state of lockdown, and a set of 'sections' where there could be God knows what."

"Weapons," Trig stated.

"Well, possibly weapons" T stated "But this is a place where people go on holiday, so maybe that's unlikely. There is quite likely to be security."

"All the staff are dead, it said," Nic responded.

"Correct," T replied. "But there could be robots still."

Trig shivered at this, and Hattie rolled her eyes.

"There could be electrical security systems, lasers, turrets, heated floors. We ought to have our wits about us, and probably split into teams, each with our own specific target, to cover more ground."

"This is a lot, T," Hattie responded. "We could just leave right now and report this finding to some relevant authority and get back on with the job we were doing."

T opened his mouth to respond, but Nic cut him off "Think of the opportunities here. Even if we can't get to the control decks, then surely the 'friends and families of the Hause Organisation' have some riches we could take with us? A ton of riches if we were honest about it?"

"That's not what we're going to do here" T responded, "That's not what we do, Nic, and you know it."

"We steal from the rich… everyone onboard has got to be richer than rich to be here," Nic argued.

"And think about the money we could earn honestly from rescuing these folks instead," T retorted. "Nic, I need you with me on this. These folks are richer than rich, so I'll make sure you get paid handsomely. If you're with me."

With that, Nic fell quiet.

"Here's what's going to happen; Bot and I are going to get to the central communications station and try get in contact with the Hause Organisation to let them know what's happened here. Nic, I need you to get to the power-control station, at the rear of the ship, start to reroute power to the engines. Do you think you'll be able to do that?"

"Shouldn't be too different from the stations I grew up working on," she responded. "Will I able to get help if needed?"

"Good. Yes, of course," T responded, and handed out a set of communicators for each person to put into their ear. "Trig and Hattie, I need to you to get to the main command deck. If the lockdown was issued from anywhere, it's going to be there. You'll need to be extra-careful. That's the furthest from here, and likely the most secure of all three. The lockdown will allow us to move in the staff-only areas, but we won't be able to access the sections until the lockdown is lifted. Any problems, any issues, we use the communicators, and we help each other. We get in, we do what we need to do, and we get back out. Can't be doing with any authorities from the Hause Organisation working out who we are. At least not yet – we need time to think of a cover story, and that's not a priority. Any questions?"

"The virus?" Trig asked.

There was a pause, and they all looked at T.

"That virus," Nic answered for him, "is fast spreading and fast to die."

"Still," T stated. "Switch your breathing filters on."

Each of them touched the comms link in their ear, which created a bubble face mask over their mouths and noses.

"See you on the other side," T said, the sound of his voice distorted by the breathing filter.

Around an hour later, Hattie and Trig found themselves crouching and walking down a tight passageway, a series of silver metal pipes to either side of them.

Trig panted and sweated up in front, his tall frame bent double as they continued to waddle along. Less contorted, Hattie followed closely behind.

"Trig," she said, looking forward at the pilot, "why are you scared of robots?"

"I don't know what you mean," Trig replied nonchalantly.

"Don't be silly," Hattie said. "You wouldn't speak to the info panel. And you made a funny noise when T mentioned that there might be some onboard, as security."

"I suppose," Trig said "you can't reason with them. They don't have feelings like us."

"You trust Bot," Hattie responded. "You must trust him a lot, since I've never been on a job with one of you and not the other."

"Bot's not the same. Bot's one of the team."

"He's no different, really. He's maybe got some low-level personality programming, and had his morality chip tampered with, but deep down he's a factory line pilot robot."

"You have to ruin everything," Trig grumbled. "Do you know what they call you when you're not around?"

"No."

"Horrid Hattie."

Hattie sighed, "You made that up."

"Maybe," Trig said. "You are a grumpy sod, though."

"Someone has to be a realist in this line of work, and I decided early on that it was going to be me."

"It doesn't always have to be you," Trig responded. "I think I'm gonna spend some time away after we do this job. Spend time with me mum and my dad. You could do the same."

"I don't have a mum and dad, Trig," Hattie said, as they carried on walking. "They died when I was little. I was raised by my aunt."

"And your aunt?" Trig asked.

"She's dead, too. Met with a nasty end, but that was an occupational hazard."

"What did she do?"

"She did this, too. Piracy. Introduced me to it at the age of eight, and I've been in it ever since."

The rest of the way they hunch-walked in silence.

After some time, Hattie and Trig found a small passageway blocked by a fallen piece of debris. It was a huge panel made of metal, which had fallen and swung off its metal hinges.

"Hattie to Bot," she said down the radio. "We have a blocked passage… can you track our location?"

"Bot to Hattie," came a quick response. "I have located you."

"Our forward route is blocked. Is that the only viable way to our destination?"

"That is correct, unless you and Trig are willing to backtrack for over five hundred meters."

Hattie grimaced at this idea, and Trig shook his head, mouthing the words 'nah-uh.' Hattie took a deep breath in through her mouth, and paused for a short time before she gave a response "we'll have to go back then, I guess, unless…" she paused again, and began to pull away at the wiring in the wall "All of these wires are attached to another removable panel, behind the wall. And if I can pull them out—what's through here, Bot?"

"I would proceed with caution," Bot's voice came in over the radio. "We're looking at one of those secured guest sections."

"I mean," Hattie muttered, as she and Trig began to lift the second panel out of the wall, and lowered it slowly onto the group, "let's just be careful. It can't be any harder than what's in here. There's a third panel—I think that's the outside of the other side of the wall. Trig, do you have your burn torch on you?"

"I never go anywhere without it," he stated proudly, and bounded forward into the hole in the wall to get to work.

"Ok, thanks Bot, looks like we'll be through here in no time at all," Hattie confirmed. "Let's see what the customers onboard this ship have been up to for the last few months."

***

Ragnaretta was walking wistfully through the tall grass just outside of her campsite, just before the high trees. Everything was normal as the sun dropped behind the horizon, the cold Nordic wind blowing slowly through her hair, the crickets chirping in the background, and just enough heat from the autumn sun to keep them content.

Then, from nowhere, she heard a hiss, getting louder and louder. Quickly, she gathered up her axe and approached a nearby tree, which seemed to be making the hiss. She placed her hand upon its bark and then snatched it away in pain. It was burning hot. How could that be? Clutching her burnt palm, she shook her hand vigorously, trying to take away the pain. Then the thudding began. First it was quiet, and then it got louder and louder. It was coming from the tree.

Ragnaretta took a step back and took in a deep breath. The side of the tree nearest to her had begun to shake. Still, the repetitive thudding continued, getting ever louder.

Ragnaretta took up her axe in her good hand and readied herself into a fighting position. She gritted her teeth and growled; whilst she was small, she was fearsome and scarred from early battles.

Then, suddenly, the nearest side of tree broke open and fell to the ground by her feet. Inside the tree were two adults—a man and a woman—wearing the strangest clothes Ragnaretta had ever seen. The man wielded an axe that emitted flame.

"Outsider!" Ragnaretta called out. She needed to get the attention of the clan as quickly as possible.

"Wow!" exclaimed the woman, as she stepped out of the tree towards her, "It's ok. I'm not going to hurt you."

The woman's voice was oddly distorted, and then she lifted something off her face, like an invisible helmet, and she continued talking. "You're ok now, you can…" the woman paused as she stared at Ragnaretta, "you can put the axe down."

The woman turned to the man and motioned to him. Quickly, the man put his flaming axe away.

"It's ok," the woman said, her hand reached out. Still, Ragnaretta said nothing in response to her. Slowly, the woman approached, crouching slightly so that her eyes were level with Ragnaretta's.

"My name's Hattie," she said.

"And mine's Trig," the man added.

"We're here to help," Hattie said.

Chapter Two

T and Bot continued to head down the large, wide-open walkway.

"So," T said, panting to keep up with Bot's large, elongated mechanical strides. "Looks like we should be in one of these customer sections, according to the info-panel's map."

"This one, among others, is designated with a 'CFR' marking," Bot stated.

"Which might explain why we were able to wander straight in," T responded. "I wonder what CFR stands for?"

"Scanning…" Bot responded. "Closed for Refurbishment."

"But what does that mean?" T asked, as he put a sequence of numbers into the nearest control panel, to get them out of their current hangar. As he moved his hand away, suddenly the lights to the control room flicked off and a loud voice rang out.

"CAUTION. TESTING ENVIRONMENT NOW IN PROGRESS.' THE HAUSE ORGANISATION TAKES NO RESPONSIBILITY FOR ANY INJURIES THAT MAY BE PROCURED DURING THE TESTING SEQUENCE," and then the lights flicked back on, and T and Bot turned to each other.

"What the hell was that?" T asked, wide-eyed.

Suddenly they heard an almighty hiss, like nothing they'd ever heard before. They turned around to see what had emitted the noise, where they saw… an Allosaurus, a huge predatory therapod dinosaur.

"Christ!" T exclaimed and fell backwards as the Allosaurus lunged at him, knocking Bot off his feet. Bot steadily stood himself back up, and brushed himself down as T started to run for the far wall of the large room that they were in. The Allosaurus gave chase, its enormous legs allowing it reach double the speed that T could run. T turned and looked back at the massive creature, each of its steps giving an enormous *thud* noise. T continued to run, his heart in his throat, and his clothes drenched in his sweat. But he didn't have time even to tire; he was too scared. He could feel the saliva, the heat, the hunger of the creature at his back, but he was not going to let himself be dinosaur breakfast if he could help it. Suddenly, he tripped, and smacked his head, landing on the ground hard. He turned over and saw the huge jaws of the dinosaur hang above him for what felt like eternity. And then they began to get closer.

Bot stood and watched as the enormous creature chased his boss around the room, following him from one corner to another, before turning to the control panel, pulling one large lever, and then, as suddenly as it'd appeared, the Allosaurus disappeared.

From across the room, T, still lying on the floor, soaked in sweat and white as a sheet, turned to Bot.

He lay there open-mouthed for a while.

"What was that?" he eventually exclaimed.

"It was a hologram," Bot stated.

"I can see that!" T responded, his panic turning to anger now.

"I had my theories when we first arrived onboard this ship when I hacked that info-panel. Now my suspicions are confirmed," Bot explained.

T stood up and brushed himself down, taking in a few deep breaths, before returning to his usual calm demeanour.

"Bot," he stated, looking at the robot in its eyes. "I'm your Captain. If you have knowledge about a job, or a particular situation, then you need to tell me. I have to make the decisions here."

"Sorry, sir," Bot responded. "You must understand that this is no ordinary job. Also, I did need a guinea pig for my theory."

"I don't think that was a good enough reason," T said, "to launch a dinosaur hologram at me. You said you had theories when we accessed the Info Panel?"

"I had heard rumours whilst working on another job of something similar to this. Powerful imagination spheres, recreating other worlds, other places through a mixture of holograms, costumes, sights, smells, even the composition of the air is altered to make a slightly different atmospheric makeup."

"Right," T responded. "And this is what we're dealing with here?"

"It would seem so," Bot stated.

"Why would anyone want to make an Allosaurus hologram?" T wondered.

"Many people claim they could live a more authentic life in the past," Bot responded.

"I think these people might not have read many history books," T muttered. "The past never sounded very nice to me."

"These are the friends and family of the Hause Corporation," Bot responded. "There may be an element of more money than sense."

"Very true," T said. "Now let's get to that control room. It's not too far now."

Bot managed to open the door into the next room, and the two of them stepped on through.

***

Nic continued to clamber through the small, narrow passageway. This ship seemed to have fallen into disrepair. *Several hundred uncareful previous owners*, she thought. This Haus Organisation are almost certainly about the show, and not much about the finer aspects of the daily maintenance of this station. Mistake number one. As Nic was alone with her thoughts, she mulled over this mission—maybe there were good reasons for them to save these people—maybe they would offer them a handsome reward. Or maybe they should have driven straight past this place and gone straight to the salvage ship that they were supposed to be robbing. They'd likely have a tight window to rob that place before someone else swooped in and robbed it instead; that was always the case. Now they were here, doing what they were doing, and The Governess was almost certainly going to let them go from her employ. *She could always do one of these jobs herself,* Nic thought.

Suddenly, she turned a corner to find a large, silver door, with a control pad. *Might be a shortcut,* she thought. She opened the control pad, and swiftly nipped a couple of the wires, and like magic the door opened for her, and then she stepped inside. The sight in front of her took her breath away: a room full of houses surrounding a large villa, built from stone. There was an enormous field with men, women, and children, moving around, soaking in the sun, which was impressive even though she knew it was artificial. There were a couple of young children in togas and sandals running around and playing, whilst a woman walked past, carrying a bundle of clothes in a woven basket. Across a path from them, in the next grassy area, a dozen men in light armour moved around, sparring with one another. And at the front of them, in grander armour, stood a broad-shouldered, handsome man. Nic realized far too late that he was staring right at her.

The handsome Roman man moved swiftly towards her, not at a run, but a quick walk. Nic, feeling confident, moved towards him and put her hands up.

"Listen," she said, "Mr. Roman leader. I don't mean any harm."

"My name is Centurion Camelius Eclectus," he stated.

"My name is Nicola," she responded.

"Did you come on the fireball?" he asked before she could say anything else.

"The fireball?" Nic asked, one eyebrow raised.

"It flew overheard two nights ago" Camelius stated firmly "And shone brightly."

"Erm," Nic responded, "That could have been us, yes."

"Us?" Camelius asked.

"In my spaceship—you see, I'm from the future," Nic told him. "And you're not really you. You're probably some interplanetary funds banker with two hover cars and a swimming pool."

"I do not know what any of the words mean," Camelius responded. "I am a Centurion in Emperor Nero's army."

"Ah," Nic said. "I have a Centurion too, I guess. He's not a very good leader, though. I sometimes wish I could kill him and take his job—I'm joking."

"I still do not understand," Camelius responded.

Before Nic could say anything else, they had been joined by another Roman, this one larger and uglier.

"Optio Brullus," he stated angrily. "Sir, should we kill this outsider? She wears garb that no Roman would wear—is it Carthagian material? And look at the doorway behind her. Should we report this to the Primus Pilus?"

"There is no need to inform him yet," Camelius said. "We can solve this here ourselves."

"Thank you," Nic stated, holding her hands out. "You are clearly the intelligent one here, Centurion."

"Sire, she insulted me!" Brullus stated and quickly drew his sword. Like lightning, Nic rushed forward and unsheathed the dagger attached to his leg. Before Brullus had time to think, Nic buried the knife into his shoulder.. Camelius rushed forward, punching her hard in the nose. The force of his punch caught her off-guard, and she tripped over the step of the door back into the corridor. Suddenly she was surrounded by grey panels and wiring once again, and as Camelius stepped forward towards her, his own sword now unsheathed, she rushed up and pressed the largest button in the control panel.

Luckily, this button closed the door, slamming it closed onto Camelius's face. Once the immediate danger was gone, Nic took a moment to breathe, sitting by the doorway, staring down the corridor she had come down, into the nothingness. Nice one, Nic, started a war with the bloody Romans.

It was whilst she was staring down the corridor that she spotted something unusual, a small panel left wide open, and some others next to it that were closed. Slowly, placing a hand on each knee, Nic hauled herself up and walked up to the panel.

It had a small keypad attached to an electric mechanism. It must have faulted. Nic peered round and took in what she could see. A small locker, with small electrical devices, a wallet, a watch, and a small ruby. She pored through the wallet, and found hundreds of cards, pennies, pieces of money from all of the galaxy. Slowly, she slipped all of them into her jacket pockets.

Then, with efficiency, she pried open the next locker with the small dagger that she'd found. In it were earrings, perfume, and a necklace that she draped over herself whilst smiling. Lovely.

She swiftly moved onto the next one. Maybe this won't be such a bad haul after all. Slowly, she pried open the next semi-open locker, revealing another wallet, an Ecard for an online bank, and a silver ball about the same size as a Mango. Nic picked up the strange, silver ball, moving it around in her hand until she saw it—a nuclear weapon logo. This was a nuclear grenade. She'd read about them but never seen one in the flesh. The ISA had banned them outright in all their controlled sectors. The Haus Institute had some very dodgy rich friends indeed.

She tucked the grenade into her jacket pocket and then moved on to the next locker.

***

"You," Ragnaretta said. "You don't belong here. How did you get past the sentries?"

"We're... from a ship" Hattie explained slowly. "A ship which landed here, from the outside."

"Are you parents around?" Trig asked.

"I don't need my parents," Ragnaretta stated, perplexed that they would ask such a question. "I'm twelve now."

"Who goes there!" came a booming voice, as a large man appeared, wielding a huge sword, from the forest, behind Ragnaretta.

"Sorry, err…" Hattie.

"Harald" stated the man. Now Hattie took the man in, she was quite scared; he was large, his shoulders broad, a thick ginger beard sat on his face, he held the axe down by the ground but in just on hand, and on his head, he wore a horned helmet.

"And we are warriors of the Stargard clan,"

"I need you to understand, and this is going to sound weird…but you're not really Vikings. You're not even on Earth," Hattie tried to explain, her hands held out wide.

"I think we should probably find the others," Trig tried to whisper in her ear, but he misjudged the volume.

"Others?" Ragnaretta asked, and as if on cue, two more fully clad Viking warriors appeared from the bushes behind her.

"Who are they?" the left one asked shortly.

"Intruders," Harald said. "Strange ones, too. They seem to have appeared out of the tree."

"Who are you?" Ragnaretta asked, slowly creeping towards them. She lifted her small axe back up and held it aloft, pointing it towards Hattie.

"My name's Hattie, I said already" she responded quickly "This is Trig—we're here to help."

"From what tribe?" Harald grunted.

"We're not from a tribe."

"Not from a tribe?" Harald asked, "By Odin, where are you from?"

"If you must know—I'm from a ship of pirates. We get selected, asked to do certain jobs for a woman called The Governess. We find abandoned or skeleton-crew level ships, go in, rob them blind, and usually scrap the ship of valuable parts on the way. We're junkers, as they say! But we're not a threat!"

"A foreign tribe," Harald growled.

As Ragnaretta took another step forward, Hattie leapt forward and grabbed her, taking control of the axe, and pulling it from the girl's hand. Harald quickly swung his axe back and then forward towards Hattie. In the blink of an eye, Hattie dipped to her right, Ragnaretta still held firmly in her arms. As Harald's axe entered the space where they had both been stood, Trig parried it by swinging the now switched-off burn torch at Harald. As the two weapons collided, the axe smashed the thin body of the metal burn torch into a hundred pieces, and a large chunk spun directly into Harald's right eye, causing him to yell in sudden pain.

As Hattie took in what had just happened, Ragnaretta managed to bite into her hand, which caused her to scream and let the girl go. Ragnaretta turned to face Hattie, who, with her free hand, pulled back her fist and then punched her square in the nose. The resulting collision caused Ragnaretta to fall back, landing on her arse. Hattie, unsure of what to do next, turned to Trig, who mouthed 'what the hell' to her.

The second Viking warrior pulled a sword and swung it at Hattie, who pulled to her right, spun and then parried it with Ragnaretta's dagger as best she could. The third Viking quickly approached Trig from out of the forest and moved to grab him. Trig jumped out of the way, but in his rush, tripped over the remains of the burn torch, which now sat nearby on the floor. He turned, panicked to see the third Viking stood over him, a sword in both his hands, ready to bring it down, but Trig managed to grab a tool—an electrical grinder—blocking the sword swing. The third Viking brought the sword down hard and buried it into the rubber handle of the burn torch, so that it was now stuck. He tried to pull it from the torch, but to no avail. Trig, seizing his opportunity, stood up and shoved the torch towards the man, forcing the sword handle to thump the man hard in the throat, and then he went down.

The second Viking and Hattie continued to tussle, ducking and diving between trees, and then back out into the clearing again. As the two blades met, the Viking moved his sword down to the dagger's hilt, where he managed to give Hattie a small cut. She cried in pain and let go of the dagger by mistake. In her confusion, the second Viking managed to cut her in the hip as she tried to dodge his attack, and she clasped at her side.

"Trig!" she yelled, but her colleague stood frozen and watched.

Slowly, the second Viking backed her over the clearing towards Harald and Ragnaretta, who were both on the ground, but conscious. Hattie looked around and tried to grab Harald's enormous axe from the ground, but it slipped out of her bloodied hand, too heavy to hold when she was in such pain. As the Viking advanced towards her, she moved backwards.

As he lifted his sword, Hattie swung and grabbed the horned helmet from Harald's head, holding the horns, using it to block the blow. The Viking shattered the helmet in two, leaving Hattie with two horns in her hand. As fast as she could manage, wounds now getting to her, Hattie rammed the two horns into the Viking's earholes, and left them stuck in there, causing him to fall to the ground, writhing in pain.

"Christ!" Trig cried. "Glad you're on our side, aye?"

Trig began to laugh, nervous from the adrenaline. Hattie stood and stared at him.

"Bit weird, though, I must admit," he guffawed. "I read the Vikings didn't even have horns on their helmets. That was added years later."

Hattie walked up to Trig, limping as she went passed Ragnaretta, who had started to get back up, and looked the lanky junker pilot up and down. Trig looked back at her; his eyebrows raised high. And then, without saying a word, she punched him hard in the crotch.

***

T and Bot stepped into the next section of corridor, ducking into a lower but wider area. T moved comfortably, whilst Bot creaked forward a little more awkwardly behind him.

"Ok," T said. "Behind this next door should be the section before the central control room. Who knows what monstrosities could abide there. Prepare yourself."

The door in front of them powered open to reveal... a small marble bar room. A few people in suits and dresses stood holding glasses and drinks. A small band of men stood on a stage, playing slow, almost solemn jazz music. The man nearest to them, ruddy-faced and brown-haired, turned and took the pair of them in visually, frowning instantly.

"A goddamn metal man! An alien!" he exclaimed, and grabbed Bot, throwing him to the floor. Before anyone else could move, T pulled his breathing visor off his mouth and unsheathed his pistol, pointing wildly around the room.

"Don't try anything," he stated firmly, and the man let Bot go. Slowly, an attractive woman with brown hair stepped forward and made eyes with T.

"Please," she said. "My name's Marissa. This is The Grey Lagoon. We don't mean to hurt you. We're just scared."

"Scared?" T asked, "You've only just seen us."

"You're not the first alien we've met," she explained.

"We're not aliens, dear," T said, smiling. "What makes you think that?"

"We had… a visitor. A couple of days ago," Marissa explained. "Maybe you might be able to recognize it."

She nodded at the men nearest the bar's door, both of whom were armed with rifles, and they opened the door. She stepped on through, and T followed. Bot jumped up and over-dramatically brushed himself down, huffing at the man who had thrown him to the ground.

The three of them stepped through into the main room, where, strapped to one poker table was a small, round, metal drone.

"Bot," T said as soon as he laid eyes on it.

"Don't worry; it's restrained now," Marissa said. Bot scanned the robot, and his eyes glazed over, numbers running through his head.

"Sir," Bot said. "It's a Security Droid. Designed to do regular routine searches of the ship's staffed areas, disintegrate threats, and make regular reports to the captain. That's it."

"It must have gotten lost," T stated. "But that is good news."

"How so, sir?" Bot asked.

"Well, it means that we must be near somewhere that is a staffed area of the ship—or at least meant to be. We ought to find our way to it."

With that, he stepped forwards towards the door on the far side of the room.

"Where are you going?" Marissa asked.

"Out," T responded, pointing towards the door on the other side of the room.

"We don't go out there," she stated. "Not since the—the security robot arrived. It's been closed off."

"You don't leave?" T asked.

"No," Marissa stated. "We sleep in the basement. I wouldn't want to leave. That robot killed my husband!"

"I'm sorry to hear that," T stated sincerely. "But me and my friend, we're going out there."

"Very well," Marissa said, and watched as Bot and T walked up towards the far door and opened it, stepping out of the room. As the doors to the gambling bar closed behind them, they found themselves in a large white room with white pillars. There were control buttons built into almost every surface, and a huge holographic map of the ship lay right in the middle of the room. To one side stood several booths, with the words 'teleportation centre' written on the plastic panel above them.

"Sir," Bot stated. "I believe that we've found the central control room."

"I believe so too, Bot," T responded, eyes wide as he took in the sights.

"Plan, sir?" Bot asked. T turned to look the robot in the eyes.

"Get the teleport up and running. I'm going to look at the map and work out the most efficient way to give everyone their memory back. And then we contact the others."

***

Slowly, Nic crept down and onto the next set of stairs, stuffing a huge pink scarf from one of the ships' lockers into her coat pocket.

"T," Nic radioed. "This is Nic. Are you on the bridge?"

"Hello, Nic." responded T's familiar, level-headed voice. "We're on the control bridge. Are you in position?"

"I'm in location," Nic responded.

"I assume you've been into a chamber or two on your way?" T asked.

"I have," Nic told him. "Met a lovely bunch of Romans—well, they weren't the friendliest of folk, if I'm honest. One was really quite handsome, though."

"We can get you to the bridge," T said. "There is a working teleport system. And it seems like some sort of chip, a cognitive repressor, has been used on the guests. If we can get everyone to go to this place down ship, The Memory Bank, they will remember who they are. Might take a bit of doing to convince everyone to go there, but I suppose there's five of us, so we just divide and conquer."

"Can we hold off one second?" Nic asked. "I found something."

"Something?" She heard T ask incredulously.

"There's a huge room of lockers here," Nic said. "Customers' personal belongings, likely quite a lot of riches."

"Leave it," T stated sharply.

"But boss, this is a haul. That is what we do. We take things that don't belong to us. I shouldn't need to remind you of that," Nic responded down the radio-mic angrily.

"These people need our help," T said. "This ship is completely off track from its original position—who knows how long it will take someone else to come across this ship? Or they're hit by an asteroid? Or their food recycling system breaks down, killing them all?"

"I'm not hearing a reason not to rob them," Nic growled. "These people, have you spoken to them? They're all high and mighty, taking holidays in their 'space doughnut,' pretending they're Romans, or new age space explorers, or ancient Japanese Samurai. Some of them earn per rotation more than we would in ten jobs, twenty jobs. I highly doubt all of it through honest means either, since one of them had a nuclear grenade in their locker."

"Stand down, Nicola!" T barked. Nic had never heard him speak like that on all the jobs she'd done with him.

"That is an order," he continued, more calmly.

For a moment, neither of them said anything at all.

"I'm afraid I have to invoke Clause 97," Nic responded. "When a senior member of the haul team feels that the captain of the team's decisions are no longer in the best interests of the job that they are—"

"I know Clause 97," T said loudly. "I am removing *you* from this job."

"You're not the boss of me," Nic responded.

"I think you'll find I am," T said, and suddenly Nic looked down at her hands, feeling a tingling feeling rippling through her fingernails, and then down her fingers into her hands, and then down her hands and towards her elbows.

"Oh," Nic said, realizing what was happening "You're beaming me!" She grimaced, and closed her eyes, as the tingling feeling enveloped her entire body, spreading through her torso and legs. Nic stood very still and closed her eyes.

Then she was no longer in front of the lockers. She opened her eyes, and she found herself on the bright white and grey control deck of the Imagination Station. The room had several large pillars built of what was most likely steel, but painted to look like marble, running through the middle of it. The outside of the room was a complete juxtaposition, covered in grey panels with flashing lights, buttons and levers of many colours littered all over them.

Bot and T stood in the middle of the room, facing her. For a long time, no one said anything. Then, after several moments, T spoke.

"Nicola" he said. "We need to talk."

Chapter Three

Before Bot and T could say anything else, Nic moved towards the nearest control panel to her. Like lightning, T whipped out a small laser pistol and pointed at her, and she stopped in her tracks.

"I told you that you were done," T said.

"I don't think you should make the decisions around here anymore," Nic growled, moving around the control, whilst keeping her eyes on them both. "Your decision-making is flawed."

"I am the captain of the Great Trawler, and I am lead onboard this job," T responded. His forehead was covered in sweat, but his hand remained steady.

"Come in," came Hattie's voice over the radio. "T, Nic, Bot, anyone…"

As Bot leant over to grab the radio, Nic swiftly whipped out her own pistol and fired at Bot's hand. The laser bolt collided with Bot's right hand, blowing a hole straight through his palm. T fired back at Nic, who ducked behind the nearest pillar.

Bot still moved to grab the radio, but as he made contact with the device, so too did a loose wire in his hand, and in a moment, there was huge electrical reaction, and the robot went flying sideways across the floor. The radio was flung from his hand.

Nic saw him skid past through the corner of her eye and smiled. Never trust a robot. As Bot came to a halt as a heap on the ground, Nic heard the rapid footsteps of T coming towards her position. Nic spun on the spot, and leapt out from behind the pillar, grabbing T's gun hand with her free arm, and clubbing him in the face with her pistol. The small man fell away from her, and readied himself again, the two of them raising their pistols at the same time.

Then, for what felt like an eternity, the two of them just stood there.

"Give this up, Nic," T said. "I promise you the Governess will let this go if you cooperate with me now. I won't mention a word of it. Bot can be put down to a freak electrical accident, and the other two will be none the wiser."

For a moment, Nic said nothing at all. T began to ease up, and both of them began to lower their weapons in unison. A gentle smile began to appear on T's face.

Then, as swift as a bullet, Nic raised her pistol back up and shot T straight through the neck. He fell back, dropping his weapon and clasping at his throat. From the small, precise hole that now appeared in it, he was bleeding out. T's skin went white as a sheet as he struggled for air, rolling around on the ground as he panicked.

"You see, boss," Nic stated. "You've been out of the con came too long now. I can tell a lie a mile off."

T didn't respond, as he continued to writhe, his eyes wide with panic.

"Oh, stop that," Nic said, rolling her eyes, and whipped out the pistol again, shooting T in the face. This time, he stopped moving altogether. Nic sighed and put her pistol away, moving over towards one of the other control panels. As she made her away over, she heard a crackle and a pop coming from the radio Bot had grabbed! From the floor, the damaged but functional radio began to become more audible "Hattie to T, come in, please; we're in a difficult spot and need assistance."

"God's sake," Nic growled, and walked over to the broken radio. With one swift move, she lifted her foot, and stamped down onto the radio, destroying it completely.

***

By the time Trig was stood back upright and had recovered from the skirmish with the Vikings, Hattie had their radio in her hand and was pacing up and down.

"I can't get through to them. It might be the distance—they're probably a long way from here by now."

"Try that red button at the back," Trig said, nodding at the back of the radio. "The emergency frequency."

Hattie pressed the button hard and then spoke down the radio.

"Hattie to T, come in, please; we're in a difficult spot and need assistance."

Hattie released the button, and then the two of them stared at each other. Nothing. Hattie grimaced, and starting to head back towards the gap in tree, clutching her axe injury with one hand while she walked.

"What are you going back there for?" Trig asked.

"I'm not going further in there," Hattie responded, nodding at the forest, with the low lights of the Viking encampment in the background.

"We can't go further, though," Trig said, "That panel is lodged in the floor and wall… and the grinder's destroyed now."

"And what do you think the Vikings are going to do when we march into their camp, and they find out we beat up the four of them, including a little girl?" Hattie said.

"Well, you did," Trig said.

"Do you want another punch to the balls?" Hattie asked, her eyebrow raised. "We're going to get to the other side of the section, find some kind of emergency exit, and then get out of here. It's not a great plan, but it's the best we've got."

Trig said nothing, nodded, and followed Hattie out of the forest and towards the busy encampment. As they got nearer, the sky above them began to darken, marking some kind of dusk. As they began to be able to pick out faces on people, a small girl left the nearest tent and pointed towards them. It was Ragnaretta. She pointed towards them with one hand. In the other hand, she held the pinkie finger of another Viking warrior, an older man with white hair and a beard that nearly reached his waist. Behind them came another load of Viking men and women, all looking ready to fight.

Trig eyed Hattie, and slowly turned around to make an exit, but he found himself face-to-face with Harald, battered, bruised and now with his axe back in his hand.

"You," said Ragnaretta, "You are omens."

"Omens?" Trig asked.

"Omens of the great fire demon."

"I don't know no fire demon."

"They lie," said the older Viking warrior.

"What fire demon?" Trig asked, when suddenly a chill came over them, as if the entire sun had just been completely snuffled out. A huge orange flame appeared behind Trig, who, seeing all the panicked faces of the Vikings, turned around. Nothing could have prepared him for what came next. The flame morphed into the shape of a dragon, four, maybe five meters tall. The light from the creature lit up the area around them, reflecting from the water next to it and the trees in front of it. The silhouette of the behemoth was visible in Trig's eyes as he stood, transfixed by what he was seeing.

"What is that?" he asked, as the Vikings around him, their weapons readied, slowly began to back away from the creature.

"You idiot!" Hattie yelled, grabbing him with both shoulders "It's some kind of advanced hologram technology! There must be a projector around here, help me find it!"

The fire dragon took a sweep at the Vikings, which was met by a chorus of wows, and a couple of them fell backwards. Hattie squinted and then looked down towards the fire dragon's feet. For a moment, a sharp shot of orange light blinded her, and then it was gone.

"It's behind it," she growled. "Trig, you go left, I'm going right."

As the dragon leaned back to make another move, she swiftly ducked under the Dragon's leg and dived for the source of the light. Hattie's hands hit a large metal box, roughly two foot in either direction, hard. At the back, there was a huge, red switch. She pressed it.

And then, as quickly as it had appeared, the flame dragon disappeared in a puff of air. The Vikings looked around, shocked, and Trig, having not moved an inch, stood there open-mouthed.

"Hail!" yelled Ragnaretta suddenly. "Hattie the dragon slayer!"

The Viking warriors began to put their axes against their shields, and Hattie smiled. Slowly, she turned back towards the box as Trig came to join her, and they gave it a further inspection. It was mostly black and featureless, apart from the large dark red switch, most likely designed to disappear into the background.

"How are you holding up?" Trig asked, nodding at her injury.

"Ok," Hattie responded, staring the box up and down.

"There's a brown button," Trig stated. "Might do something."

Hattie pressed it, causing one panel of the box to fall away and reveal a small selection of labelled buttons and commands. A large blue triangular one read: "Early release. Only use in emergencies."

Hattie and Trig turned to one another, and then Trig tentatively pressed the button. Initially, nothing happened, and then, slowly, an enormous light flickered on, filling the room. All around them, huge grey walls became visible, showing the Viking encampment and forest to be clearly a mock-up, with some trees real and some others fake, made of shining plastic. In each wall, were large, blue metal double doors. This room had clearly been used as a hangar, once upon a time.

"What in—Odin!" the older Viking warrior stuttered. All of them turned to Hattie, stunned and unable to understand what was going on.

Hattie swallowed and took a deep breath.

"This may come as a shock," she said finally. "But you're not Vikings. You're not on Earth. You're guests aboard a space-station. It was shut down due to a virus, some months ago now. The year is 4250, in Earth years. My name is Hattie; this is Trig. We don't know you, and you don't know us, but we're here to help."

The older Viking warrior took a step forward towards them, his axe still in his hand. Once he was roughly two meters from them, the man lowered his axe slowly and placed it on the ground. The other Vikings all began to do the same. The older man looked at them, and for the first time, Hattie and Trig didn't see a Viking, but a modern man, lean but strong, with warm eyes and tanned skin. *Almost certainly someone's loving Grandad,* Hattie thought.

"I believe you," he stated firmly.

"We need your help, too," Hattie said. "There are other people on this ship who are stuck, like you, thinking they are people they aren't. We need to get out of here, and help them, and you, get your memories back. Then we need to make sure you get home—to your real home. Are you with me?"

"I am!" Ragnaretta yelled.

"I am," the elder man stated.

"Me, too!" came another voice, a younger adult male, and then more and more of the ex-Vikings agreed.

"Awesome," Hattie stated, smiling. "Let's do this."

***

One by one, Trig and Hattie moved through different sections from the outside, releasing each one from their section, and more and more people began to join them, moving with them, dressed in all manner of Earth-based historical garb. Trig managed to open an information panel, which displayed a holographic map of the entire Imagination Station. Hattie saw that, from where they were stood, they were only a few sections away from The Memory Bank.

In one corridor, Hattie, closely followed by Trig, called a halt with her hands, and the two of them stopped on the spot.

"We have one active section on the left," she said. "I'm going to go in there. I think you should push forward from here and just try to get to The Memory Bank."

Trig nodded in response and replied, "Yes, boss."

Following her own instructions, Hattie took a swift turn to the left and headed down the corridor, which led her up to a familiar-looking pair of blue corridors. Just as she reached out to open to door, the opposite door opened, and a large, handsome man clad in Roman armour marched past her, followed by another Roman man, this one bald and clutching his shoulder.

"You!" he exclaimed upon seeing her. "Do you know what is happening? One moment I was saddling my horse to ride with my family to Londinium, and then my son found this box. It was like no box I have ever seen. There is an enclosure around my village!"

"My name's Hattie," she stated as calmly as she could with the two Roman men watching her every move—her every breath, it felt.

"I'm Camelius Eclectus," the man stated slowly "Centurion Camelius Eclectus. This is my garrison. I want some answers."

"You're not a Roman," Hattie said, repeating what she'd said to the Vikings earlier. "We're on a spaceship, in the year 4250. And your memories—your real memories, have been replaced. I'm here to help you get them back."

Slowly, the features of Camelius's face softened, and he relaxed.

"Truth," he said slowly, "is often strange. I've seen things today that I can never explain."

The other roman, the bald one, lowered his guard, and said, "Optio Brullus?"

"My second in command," Camelius stated proudly. "One of the finest soldiers I've served with."

"Camelius and Brullus," Hattie said, looking between them "If you trust me, get your people. Come with me. I'm going to give you your old memories back. Your real memories."

Camelius and Brullus paused for a moment and then nodded and headed back into their section. A moment later, they returned, with a load more people dressed as Romans. Hattie smiled, and headed back into the main walkway, making her way towards the Memory Bank. As she headed down the corridor, a heap of Romans following, Camelius caught up with her, walking alongside her.

"Are you with the other woman?" Camelius asked. "She was dressed like you."

"Other woman?" Hattie asked.

"She said her name was Nicola. Spoke with a strange accent, not one I'd heard from across the empire," he explained.

"Yes… she's with me," Hattie confirmed, as they entered up into the enormous Memory Bank room, a dome with tapes and discs, and light-up trays covering the walls. In the middle of it sat Trig, who had a queue of people. He was deprogramming each in turn, placing a helmet on their head and quickly scanning their original memories back into their head.

"She seemed rather angry" Camelius continued "Spoke about your own centurion and how she wished to slay him. She tried to kill Optio Brullus and nearly succeeded."

"Erm," Hattie said, suddenly worried.

"Trig?" she asked, approaching her crewmate. "Any chance you'd be able to teleport me to the command deck from here? I think we should touch in with the others now."

"Yeah, sure," Trig responded. "I'm happy doing this with the costume crowd; it's very therapeutic."

Trig leant over and programmed in a command into the computer next to him. Hattie relaxed her shoulders, getting ready to make the jump, but someone grabbed her by the wrist. It was Camelius.

"Where are you going?" he asked.

"I need to see that… friend of mine, Nicola. And our… centurion."

"Allow me to come with you," Camelius requested.

Hattie looked Camelius up and down. He was a large, muscled man, clad in armour, and most importantly, carrying a sword.

"Yes," she said slowly. "I suppose that could be helpful. You have to wait a while for your memories anyway."

She gave Trig a nod, removing the teleporting band from his wrist and placing it on Camelius's, who stared at it.

"Ok, Camelius," she said. "Take a deep breath. This is going to be a very strange sensation."

Trig flicked the switch and white light surrounded them. They became weightless and frozen for a brief moment of time, and then they were gone.

***

Hattie and Camelius appeared suddenly in the Imagination Station's control room. Hattie swiftly scanned the room; two bodies on the floor, and neither of them Nicci. It was T and Bot.

"Damn," Hattie whispered more to herself than anyone else, as she headed over to T and saw his injuries. Dead. Behind her, Camelius approached Bot's immobile shell.

"This man," he said. "Is made of metal."

Hattie looked around to see what he was talking about.

"There isn't enough time to explain," she said, turning back around and closing T's eyes.

"Goodbye, boss," she said quietly, and stood back up, turning to Camelius "There's a massive bomb connected to this ship's central power control panel."

She looked over the nuclear grenade and then got on the radio to Trig.

"T is dead," she told him. "And Bot. Nic is not here anymore."

Trig swore.

"Any ideas where she could have gone?" he asked.

"Get yourself here," she said, and in a moment, Trig appeared in the comms room.

"Christ!" Trig said, his eyes wide at the sight of the nuclear grenade, the big metal ball now hooked into the marble white control deck. "Is that what I think it is?"

"It is," Hattie confirmed. "Set to blow in five minutes, too. Do you think you can disable it?"

"Possibly," Trig replied. "But I can't make any promises. Where do you think she's gone?"

"Teleported," Hattie replied. "Must have—but where?"

"There'll be a signature on this teleport station," Trig replied, moving over to the other side of the room, peering at the information panel. "From the looks of it, she teleported herself and a tonne of riches into The Trundler a few minutes ago."

Hattie hit a few switches on the main control panel, and a visual came up of the hanger where they had parked The Trundler.

"It's still there," she said. "But the engines are running. You'll have to teleport us now!"

Hattie took Camelius by the hand over to the teleport stand, as Trig stepped away.

"Get that grenade disabled, by any means necessary. If she gets away, we have no way off this ship," Hattie told Trig.

"On it," Trig replied, as he fired up the teleporter.

"Here we go again," Hattie whispered, and the light began to surround them. This time, Hattie held Camelius' hand as they began to disappear, and she closed her eyes as the light engulfed them.

When Hattie opened her eyes again, they were back onboard The Great Trundler, still parked in the hangar bay where they'd left it, thank God. They were in the cockpit, but Hattie barely had time to take that in when Nic entered the room, looking flustered. She raised her pistol at Camelius, who was nearer.

She pulled the trigger, but he quickly raised his sword, blocking the shot, which smashed the sword in an instant. During the confusion, Hattie leapt on top of Nic, and the two women went down in a pile. Like lightning, Nic pushed Hattie off, and was up back on her feet. As Hattie stood up, Nic thumped her hard in the face. As Hattie attempted to counter, Nic dove out of the way and grabbed Hattie, throwing her hard against the wall. As Nic raised her arm to shoot her, Camelius leapt up out of nowhere and thrust the remains of his sword up through her armpit.

Nic growled, and turned her outstretched arm, shooting Camelius through the shoulder. The big man yelped and fell backwards, landing with a thud on the floor. Nic aimed the pistol at his torso, but Hattie leapt on Nic again, grabbing the sword, now implanted in Nic, by the handle, and shoving it further in using as much force as she could, until Nic screamed in pain, and let go of the gun. Then Nic paused, smiled, and pulled a regular grenade from her belt, flinging it at Hattie.

Camelius leapt up and enveloped Hattie in his arms, and the two of them fell down The Trundler's open ramp and down onto the hanger floor. The grenade followed them down, rattling along until it came to a rest at Hattie's feet. The ramp to the ship began to close, and The Trundler began to take off. Hattie kicked the grenade away, past the Trundler, and it continued to roll, hitting a clamp on the hangar floor and exploding with a brief flash and *wumph*! It didn't damage The Trundler, but it also didn't kill them. Despite having failed, Hattie took a deep breath and relaxed. Both her and Camelius lay in an injured, tired clump on the hangar floor as The Great Trundler began to take off.

Hattie reached up to her earpiece.

"Bad news, Trig. She's getting away."

"Also, bad news," Trig responded. "I've detached the bomb, but it's still on a timer. She's fiddled with the safety catch—it doesn't work anymore. I don't think there's any way to turn it off now. Less than a minute until it goes."

"Damn," Hattie responded, still lying on the floor. "Can you teleport it into space?"

"I can only send it to an approved link location, and they're all on the ship," Trig responded, "I'm sorry."

"That's… not true," Hattie stated, looking up off the floor to The Great Trundler as it disappeared out of the hangar, and started to get smaller and smaller.

"What do you mean?" Trig asked over the comms.

"She's set a link up to The Trundler, hasn't she?" Hattie responded.

"Ah!" Trig said. "I get your drift, boss."

Nic crawled, slowly, to the cockpit of The Great Trundler, Camelius's sword—a damn sword!—still embedded in her, and hauled herself up on to the captain's chair. She turned and surveyed the star-filled sky in front of her and then turned back to look at the reflector mirrors, showing her the ever-shrinking Imagination Station in the background, a huge sinister metal doughnut. Nic looked at the piles of gold, silver, platinum, physical and digital credits, and mobile tech she had picked up from the friends of the Haus Corporation.

Then, slowly, she turned to the photograph of her, T and Hattie on a previous job, which hung amongst other sentimental items of her former captain in the cockpit.

"Screw you," she said, lifting her fingers in a V at the photograph. "Screw the pair of you. Trying to pretend you were anything other than what you are, look where it got you!"

She laughed from the pain of the sword embedded in her and then began to program the ship to transfer power to its FTL engine and take her to the nearest Medi-bay.

Just as she punched in coordinates for the nearest one, she witnessed a bright white flash of light and turned in her chair to see… nothing.

But a noise caught her attention, and she looked down. A large silver metal ball rolled along the cockpit floor and landed by her feet. The Nuclear Grenade. On it, a note read: 'With love from Trig and Hattie.'

In a dazed rush, Nic picked up the grenade and flipped it over to find the safety switch had been pulled completely out. The front of the grenade had a counter with bright blue LED lights.

"3"

Nic looked around, trying to find the nearest airlock. She was bleeding heavily.

"2"

Or maybe there was some material in the ship that could contain the explosion. Something from one of their hauls.

"1"

Nic sighed, and sat back down, holding the grenade to her chest.

"0"

The grenade went off.

The huge blaze of light from the nuclear grenade detonating was visible from the hanger. The burning of the flame was so bright, that even from now miles away, Hattie had to squint.

"Wow" Hattie stated, unable to look away from it, even from her awkward position lying on the floor next to Camelius. Camelius said nothing. He just remained staring, dumbfounded by the majesty of the explosion in the distance.

"Well," Trig stated over the comms. "Did we get her?"

Slowly, Hattie sat up, placing one hand on her knee and raised her hand to her earpiece again.

"Trig," she said solemnly. "It's over. We got her."

***

It was only half a day later when the rescue and evacuation crews arrived. Trig sat and deprogrammed the entire guest program of the Imagination Station, one by one. If there'd been an easier way to do it, he and Hattie didn't find it. Hattie stood and talked for some time to the people leading the evacuation program, explaining to them what happened. Bot and T's bodies were placed in statis caskets, and Trig and Hattie stood and watched as people they'd known as Viking warriors, Roman soldiers, and American Jazz fans, now milled around the various hangars as smaller transport ships from the Haus Corporation came and went. Hattie and Camelius had both had their injuries seen to by professionals, who seemed somewhat unfamiliar with having to deal with sword and axe injuries in the forty-third century.

After all had been said and done, Trig and Hattie stood by a small supply ship watching the busy scenes. As Hattie turned to leave, a man in a suit and a girl in a fine checkered dress approached them.

"Hattie," the man said.

"Camelius," she said.

"My name's Cameron," he said, and then offered a hand to the girl—Ragnaretta. "This is my daughter, Rachel."

"Oh! Oh, wow," Hattie smiled.

"We've kept our 'historical' memories,'" he explained. "I won't forget what you've done for us here today. You helped us, even though you didn't have to. I think there's not quite enough of that any day and age."

"I suppose not," Hattie responded.

"What's next?" Cameron asked her.

"I'm not too sure—I guess we all go back to living our lives as best we can," Hattie said. "This can be one of those weird stories you tell your grandchildren."

"Dad, give her the card," Rachel interrupted, nodding at Hattie.

"This," Cameron said, stepping forward and reaching into his pocket. "Is my business—it's a small family bank on the second moon of 55 Cancri in the Copernicus system. We're owned by the Haus Consideration. You said—you have no family? No prospects outside of… whatever it is that you two seem to do. And no ship. I might be able to help you get on your feet doing something else. And I will give you one of the supply ships—this one. In fact, I've already registered it to you. It won't compensate for the ship you lost, but it's a start."

"Thank you," Hattie said, with a small smile. "We can use the help."

"It was nice to meet you," Rachel said, and Cameron shook their hands.

Then, hand in hand, the two Imagination Station customers turned away, Rachel turning and waving. Both Trig and Hattie waved back.

Trig and Hattie turned to the supply ship that Cameron had allowed them to have and looked it up and down as it stood small and alone in one corner of the hanger.

"New ship," Trig said.

"Yes," Hattie responded, all business. "You know how to fly something like that?"

"No," Trig responded. "But how hard can it be?"

As the last rescue ships began to depart, Hattie and Trig clambered back into The Great Trundler 2 and began to fire up the engine. Trig looked back at the bodies of Bot and T, who lay in caskets in the corridor behind them. *They deserved better deaths than what they got*, he thought, and then he turned back to look at Hattie.

"Hattie?"

"Trig?"

"Did we do the right thing, helping these people?" he asked.

"What do you mean?" Hattie responded.

"Helping these people, these folk, did we do the right thing? They all would've died, but…"

"It's what we did," Hattie said.

"I know, but was it worth the deaths of three of our crew and the destruction of T's ship? Our ship?" Trig asked. "We could have just flown past, gone to the job, all gotten home and spent the haul on a good time."

"I don't think it matters," Hattie said "It's what we did. No speculating is going to change that now. All I know is we need to get out of here and move on."

"Where to, boss?" he asked.

"We can take both of the boys home to T's family," Hattie said. "And then we can go… wherever we like, I guess? Because I'm not going to work for The Governess anymore."

"I think I'm with you on that," Trig said. "Any ideas?"

"I don't know for certain," Hattie responded, smiling as the Trawler 2 lifted up off the ground, and began to head for the forcefield at the edge of the hangar bay "But I've heard that the 55 Cancri is quite nice around this time of year."

As they left the forcefield, Trig leaned forward and programmed in the FTL commands and then braced himself. Hattie sat back, clipped herself in, and punched the large green button in the middle of the control deck's flight-board. Within an instant, the ship disappeared off into the depths of space, leaving The Imagination Station long behind.

THE END

The Great Gamble

By Alex O'Neill

Date: 5000

Location: New Singapore, Alpha Centauri C

Chapter One

Gerion York stared across the table and flicked the compass between his fingers, allowing it to rotate smoothly between his index finger and his thumb. His eyes shifted from a vacant gaze to slowly narrow as he took in the small object in his hands.

He needed a ship. That was not debatable. The *how* getting that ship was not as clear. It would involve no shortage of charm and trickery.

He placed his head onto the table and continued to rotate the compass in his hand.

Suddenly, the door to his room swung open, and a great beast of a man walked into the room, sopping wet. Gerion lifted his head and looked at the man, taking in his height, his broad shoulders, his mane of dark grey hair, and the great grey coat, even darker than his hair.

"Still raining, Mal?" Gerion asked.

The tall man grumbled.

"It's always raining on this damn planet," he said. "Did it rain this much last time you were here?"

"Global warming," Gerion responded, without really looking up. "Gets everywhere in the end."

Gerion stood up slowly, and pressed his hands onto Mal's shoulders, taking off his coat. Mal relaxed and allowed his friend to remove the piece of clothing. Gerion took the wet coat, bundled it into his arms, and walked over to the heater in the corner of the room.

"I was happy back on Sirius-1," Mal grumbled.

"I know you were," Gerion replied, looking alive for the first time. "But that's not the point. We need a reliable and cheap ship with FTL capabilities. Are we going to find a reliable and cheap ship with FTL capabilities on the Sirius-1 deep-space docking station?"

Mal didn't reply.

"No, we aren't," Gerion stated, answering his own question. "Mal, listen, this mood you're in? You'll be more use to me if you snap out of it sooner rather than later. I need you at your best, soaking or not."

"Fair enough," Mal responded, moving over to the table to start playing with the compass Gerion had left there. "I suppose we'll be meeting your contact after dinner?"

"Yes," Gerion replied. "But not until nine. Elysia wishes for it to be dark."

"I don't like that," Mal said. "It's not what we agreed."

"I know you don't," Gerion said, getting up to stand next to his friend, who continued to fiddle with the compass "But we don't exactly have a plethora of options available to us right now."

"You understand my concern," Mal grunted, turning away from Gerion. "People who change plans are not to be trusted. Why have they changed the time? Ask yourself. You think you can trust her? Or this Stoneglow Guild?"

"I know them. I worked for them, once upon a time. But whether I can trust them is a different matter. But I trust Elysia, and that's all that matters. If she's willing to be in the room, I am," Gerion said. "She thinks she's found us a ship."

Gerion took a seat on the sofa, turning on the flat's Holovision. Mal poured a glass of water, before joining Gerion on the sofa.

"Even the holovision programs here are crap," Mal grumbled. "What's this one supposed to be?"

Man versus robot, injury edition," Gerion stated, barely taking his eyes away. "One person versus one robot, and the aim is to injure the other as much as possible without killing, or in the robot's case, destroying them."

"Bloody hell," Mal responded.

"That's somewhat tame for Centauri Holovision. You should watch Survival Island... a team of people go out to a deserted island and the last one to literally die is the winner," Gerion stated, with neither joy nor sadness at the idea of the show.

"And what's that other one that I caught you watching the other day? With the men in horned helmets?" Mal asked.

"Elite Gladiator Championship. Teams of four people kill their way to the top, Roman style. Fascinating people, the Romans. Did you know that they invented sewers?"

"Reminds me why I don't watch Holovision," Mal said.

Arran Thompson, the third member of their party, opened the door to their apartment's living quarters. He was a broad man, black of skin with a bald head that shone even in their poorly lit apartment. He had large green eyes, and a small but warm smile. He wore brown cargo trousers and a green jumper which looked several sizes too large.

"Still raining out?" he stated more than asked, looking at Mal.

"What gave it away?" Mal grumbled, and he wandered over the fridge.

"I wouldn't bother," Arran stated, holding out a hand to Mal. "Rat infestation again; had to clear out pretty much everything."

"Really?" Mal asked, turning to look at Gerion. "Could we not have somewhere a little better than this for our stay?"

"I'm cutting costs," Gerion said, still twiddling the compass and not really looking at either of his accomplices. "Plus, it's low-key. I'm not exactly Mr. Popular around these parts anymore."

Arran and Mal exchanged a look, before turning back to look at Gerion. Suddenly the blond man snapped out of his daydream and stood up with a whip of energy.

"Food!" he announced. "Let's get some."

***

The rain drizzled down on New Singapore's undercity streets. Gerion, Mal and Arran had ventured down into their neighbourhood's larger food courts, but still, it was next to deserted. The three men each bore enormous overcoats to shield themselves from the weather, each of a different colour. Mal and Arran stood together under an umbrella as Gerion returned from the street vendor. He smiled at them as he made his way over and licked his fingers.

"Katsu Chicken with noodles," he said, tucking in before he had even reached the umbrellas.

"They're well-made," Mal nodded.

"They're not, of course, made from actual chicken," Gerion said. "That would be ridiculous."

"Synthetic replication," Arran confirmed. "It was common where I grew up."

"You see, the history of food is quite interesting, when you think about it. On Obsidian 1 to 3, they maximize the yield of one genetically modified animal and then clone it thousands of times," Gerion lectured. "This practice was first used by early space colonists and then they terraformed Titan, the moon of Saturn in the original system."

"You need to get out more," Mal said.

"I know. But a little late-night reading never hurt," Gerion responded.

Arran, ignoring both of them, nodded at the food vendor. The vendor, innocent-looking, smiled back at the man.

"She's human," he stated. "You don't see much of that anymore."

Gerion stopped eating, turned, and looked at the young woman who had served them their noodles.

"I suppose not," he responded. "But while robot chefs are abundant in New Tokyo across the Shallow Sea, they're not so much here."

The three men then ate their food, standing together in a huddle as far away from the downpour as possible. Gerion received a beep on his watch.

"We should be ready to meet Elysia before too long," he said. Mal groaned.

"Do we have to go with her?" He asked.

"I trust her. She's one of my oldest friends."

"I'm your oldest friend," Mal cut in.

"Yes. And she's one of my other oldest friends."

Mal and Arran exchanged another look between them.

"And I'm saying that you've got other friends."

"Better friends," Arran chimed in. Gerion looked at Mal, and then back at Arran, and slowly raised his left eyebrow.

"We're chartering a long-distance, FTL journey. We're going to need a pilot capable of handling a less-than-robust medium-sized ship with FTL capabilities. Someone with experience, and willing to take part in a dangerous journey for less than the going rate. Is that you, Mal?"

"No," Mal grunted.

"Or you, Arran?"

"No."

"Then you see why we need her."

"She robbed you," Mal said.

"And then I shot her ear off. I guess now we're even," Gerion smiled. "Eat up, we've got places to be."

***

The three men arrived at their meet-point, further out from the central neighbourhood, a huge disused shopping mall, which may have once been fantastic in its hey-day, but now sat quiet and rusting, the shops and stalls all fit behind great corrugated metal doors. The entrance ways to the mall were open and accessible, with anyone visiting New Singapore able to wander in and visit whichever corrugated metal door that they desired. *Nothing's worth locking up when nothing here is worth any money*, Gerion thought.

Gerion walked down the white and empty walkways first, with Mal following closely behind him, and Arran took up the rear, always checking over his shoulder. Underneath their great raincoats, all three men were kitted out with laser-based weapons, tools, and knives. Outside the great mall, they could hear the pitter-patter of the rain continuing to come down.

"This is the place," Gerion stated, and as he approached one particular corrugated metal door to open it, it suddenly opened from the inside to reveal their contact, Elysia. She was a handsome woman, with large glasses, a light brown coat and black clothing underneath.

"Gentlemen," She stated, taking in the sight of a soggy Mal, Gerion and Arran. "Right on time."

"Wasn't the easiest place to find," Gerion said. "Do you really think this relocation was necessary? There was nothing wrong with the old place."

"Well, when the mall became available, Catan thought it was too good an opportunity to look past," Elysia explained, leading the other three into a dark and empty store, and closing the metal door behind them. She then opened a hatch at the back of the store that they stood in, revealing a set of steps tunnelling deep into the ground.

"Follow me," she said.

"How far does this go?" Arran asked, one eyebrow raised.

"Far enough," Elysia responded.

As they walked down into the depths of the under-mall, Gerion attempted to make some small talk.

"I see the ear's grown back," he said.

"It's fake flesh."

"That's quite expensive."

"Money's good when you work for the Stoneglow Guild."

"You work full time for these people now?"

"Work is work, Gerry, you know that more than most."

Gerion turned and looked at Mal, who exchanged the same look back with him.

"I don't know if it'll be a permanent arrangement," Elysia stated as they continued down, "but at the moment, I find them clients and occasionally disappear the odd problem client. Hush-hush, as you can imagine."

"There's money in that?"

"The Stoneglow Guild pay tons for everything. They could afford to pay their service droids if they wanted."

"I don't like robots," Gerion stated. "Call me old-fashioned. I prefer people."

"So you always tell everyone," Elysia responded. "Here we go."

They approached a second door, having reached the bottom of the stairs. Elysia leaned forward and slowly pressed a small yellow button on the front of the doors, which then caused the doors to lift up and fold into the roof, revealing a huge chamber.

"Where are we?" Mal asked.

"From my best guess, somewhere underneath the underground tram system—there's a line that used to connect to the mall we accessed through—that whole section of the system has been disused for years."

"That's exactly where we are," Elysia responded. "I've managed to arrange what you asked for: a meeting with Catan the Cold."

The huge chamber was shaped like an enormous brown egg, with long metal beams reaching up towards its top point. Around the bottom of the chamber were huge banks of theatre seats, between each set were tunnels that disappeared off somewhere else, much like the one that they had come through. And in the middle of the chamber was a metal ring full of people standing.

As Elysia approached this small throng of people, one emerged, standing tall above the rest. The tallest man, they had ever seen, with bulbous eyes, a large grin on his face, and using huge walking sticks that probably doubled as stilts for a normal-sized person. Ever since mutations had become legal, people of power, particularly crime lords, had decided that the best thing they could do was to mutate themselves to look as terrifying as possible. The end result, at least for Catan, was a man who sort of looked like a giant slug with a face and legs.

"Catan," Gerion said, nodding.

"Gerion," the other man growled, as the mass of people parted for him.

"It's been some time," Gerion stated.

"Yes," Catan agreed. "And Mallador Shan and Arran Thompson. What a bunch of arseholes."

Slowly, Catan approached them, his enormous frame towering over even Mal, who was a very large man. Catan eyed the three of them up, and Gerion caught the other two's uncomfortable looks.

"I heard that you had a potential ship for me," Gerion said.

"Ahhhhh," Catan said, snapping suddenly to look at Gerion and only Gerion "That I do."

Catan fumbled in his trouser pocket, leaning on his walking canes, before pulling out a small digital device. He slammed his fingers into the device, a hologram of a ship, with a sleek silver hull, a pointed stern, a set of large thrusters on the rear. Along both sides it appeared to be fitted with rotatable laser canons, and large raisable sails on the top to slow the ship down upon atmosphere entry.

"The New Excalibur," Catan stated, looking at her. "Isn't she a beauty?"

"That would be exactly what I'm looking for," Gerion stated.

"She could be all yours for ten million New Singaporean Dollars. A crew supplied, too. You would just need officers, which you seem to have brought with you. You're not going to find a deal better than that on his side of Alexandria. Let's say it came to me under…unconventional circumstances."

"Ah."

"If you don't have the funds immediately, I could perhaps… give you a set of time to acquire it? Say, six months."

Damn, Gerion thought, *it'd take six years to find that amount of money*. Catan, seeing the apprehension on his face, smiled, and then started to laugh. It was an ugly laugh.

"Erm," Gerion stated, looking between Catan and then Arran, then Mal, then Elysia and then back to Catan. "Would you take an offer?"

"I'm afraid not," Catan stated.

"Then perhaps we should go. Sorry to have wasted your time, Mr. Cold."

"Hold up," Catan said, and pressed a button on his digital device, causing all the tunnels running out of the chamber to immediately slam shut. Catan began to step towards Gerion, who had turned his back on Catan. Catan only stopped when he was less than a foot behind Gerion, who turned to look up to the bigger man.

"You see," Catan stated, "I think you have a lot of balls to come back here, after what you've done. And I know you work for my competitors now. Letting you buy this ship… would show weakness. On the other hand, it would get its real owners off my back."

"Exactly. I wouldn't find a ship as good as this as cheap anywhere else," Gerion stated.

"I know," Catan grinned, his awful teeth almost touching Gerion's face. "Well, well, well. This is quite funny."

"We won't tell anyone," Gerion swallowed. "We can just… move on, pretend this never happened."

"I can't see that happening," Catan stated. "Men… at arms!"

All around them, large guards around the room ready to fire their laser weapons. Gerion turned and looked at Mal and swallowed.

"You've ruined this," Arran exclaimed. Mal simply shook his head. As Gerion turned and looked at Mal, he caught a glimpse of the sword under Mal's robe and flung his hands up in the air.

"Stop!" he exclaimed.

There was an almighty pause, and then Catan waived his hand for his guards lowered their laser weapons.

"I'll get you the money," Gerion stated.

"How?" Catan asked. "I'm going to need some insurance."

"I… am going to enter Elite Gladiator Championship next month. The prize money is more than enough to afford that ship."

There was another almighty pause, before Catan roared with laughter, and his followers—even the robots—joined in.

"You?!" he exclaimed between guffaws. "You make me laugh, Mr. York."

"Yes, me, and my team"

"Ooo," Catan emitted, lifting his hand to wipe a tear from his eye. "This is fantastic. I always bet on the Elite Gladiator Championship. Sometimes, I enter a team, or two, or three. This month, I will have a more personal investment. If you win, you get the money, and I suppose, if you lose, you die, which will be mightily satisfying for me to watch."

"I suppose it will be," Gerion stated, feigning a smiled.

"Very well," Catan the Cold nodded. "I have considered this, and I find it… amusing. You have one month, Mr. Gerion York. Win that competition and the ship's yours. Lose, and you die in there. Either that, or I'll just kill you for being a nuisance."

The enormous man walked away into the crowd, and the laughter died down. Gerion looked down to find Elysia grabbing his sleeve.

"Time to go," she said. "Before you say anything else moronic."

***

"What on Alpha Centauri C were you thinking?" Mal exclaimed, shoving Gerion against the wall. The large shaggy man, usually calm in demeanour, was as red as a tomato. They were stood outside the corrugated door entrance to Catan's base.

"We should do this away from the door," Elysia stated.

Arran, who had somehow kept his cool, paced up and down.

"How much money do you get for winning 'Elite Gladiator Championship'?" he asked.

"Forty million dollars," Gerion said from the position where Mal had him shoved up against the wall.

"That's only if your whole team survives," Mal growled.

"And the catch is?" Arran followed up.

"The whole aim is to kill as many opponents as you can. The team that racks up the most kills in total, wins their hearts and then works their way up, fighting one-on-one with other teams of four until the grand finale, where the whole team has to work together to fight the other final team," Elysia said.

"This is barbaric," Arran stated.

"This is Alpha Centauri C," Gerion cut in, and Mal let go of him.

"Did you have any team members in mind for this mad venture?" Mal asked.

"I'm looking at them," Gerion stated.

Three blank faces stared back at him. Their jaws nearly scrapped the ground. Arran was the first to speak.

"I'm in," he said. "I need those ten million dollars, damn it."

There was a long pause, before Elysia slowly lowered her electric prod.

"You're an idiot—a total idiot—but so do I," she added. "Catan knows I've started working for other people, including you. And he's threatened me with the rack. I need to get out, get away. Last week, he electrocuted one of the tobacco runners for being an hour late. An hour!"

There was a longer pause, before Mal slowly backed away from Gerion, and looked the man up and down.

"If I die for this ship, and for you, I'll find you in the afterlife and wring your bloody neck," he stated.

Gerion swallowed nervously and then pushed himself back off from the wall.

"Grand," he stated. "We have an accord. I know this is not perfect, but you're three of the finest fighters I know. We need to register for the competition and find some extra arms. Don't worry, I've got this all-in hand."

Gerion smiled at the three people standing in front of him, none of whom smiled back, and turned away. Reluctantly, Arran followed him, and then Mal.

"Damn it," muttered Elysia "In for a penny. Anything that gets me out of working for Catan the Cold anymore."

Chapter Two

TUESDAY

Arran and Elysia stood together as the lift rose up into the higher quarters of the city's Media Towers. They rose up, along the outside of one the oval towards, the lift raising up and along the curve of the outside of the building. The sun rose out high, above the sky, Arran lifted his hand up above his face. Elysia put on a pair of sunglasses and smiled.

"First time in the Centauri system?" she asked.

"Yes," Arran responded slowly. "It takes a bit of getting used to."

"I suppose," Elysia said. "But you are taking it well."

Arran took a deep breath in through his mouth, and out through his mouth.

"I grew up orbiting one giant sun, rather than three not-so-giant ones," Arran stated.

"Betelgeuse," Elysia stated "And how was that? Probably very different to here?"

"It wasn't too bad," Arran responded, his eyes squinting. "I remember...I remember bits. Life was simpler. There were no vast cities like this one, only small settlements. People lived simply, worked simply. Things got done, but there was never much rush. After my planet was officially terraformed, I didn't even see anyone from the ISA until I left to go travelling. Very different to the Centauri system?"

"Very," Elysia responded. "I can't imagine what that's like. I've never left the Centauri system. We're not all lucky enough to go travelling across the stars. Plus, there's plenty here for a woman to do. It's a big old world."

"Mm," Arran agreed. "That is true."

"Floor 94," came the autotuned voice attached to the lift, and both bronze metal doors pinged open. 'Please have a lovely day."

Arran and Elysia stepped forward and stepped out into the huge room. It had a musty green floor, huge class windows all around, and a huge reception desk, with escalators running up behind it. Sat at the desk were a panel of androids, each one with a small digital clock placed in front of them, reading 'COMPLAINTS' 'APPOINTMENTS' 'STAFF INQUIRIES' and 'OTHER.' Sheepishly, Arran and Elysia approached the appointments android, a friendly looking gentleman with a cheap ginger afro wig and a smart shirt. Clearly the staff and dressed these robots to look as friendly and as inviting as was possible.

"Hello," said Arran, as the robot looked up at them.

"We've got an appointment in ten minutes to meet a Mrs. Carlisle?"

"AH. ALLOW ME TO CHECK IN WITH HER. SHE HAS BEEN RUNNING A LITTLE BEHIND DUE TO APPOINTMENTS WITH OTHER CUSTOMERS LAST TIME SHE UPDATED ME," the robot stated.

The robot's hand drifted to a buzzer on the table in front of it, and it smoothly pressed the button down.

"HEAD UPSTAIRS," It stated through a motionless, lipless mouth. "JENNY CARLISLE WILL BE WITH YOU IN ONE MOMENT."

Arran and Elysia smiled, nodded at the robot, and left the desk, heading up to the nearest escalator. Once they arrived at the top, they were met swiftly by a tall, thin woman with curly brown hair. Her lips were pursed, and she held a clipboard tightly under one arm.

"You must be …Arran Thompson and Elysia Lorch."

"That's correct," Arran stated.

"Representing a Mr. Gerion York?" she asked.

"Correct," Arran said.

"Come to my office," she replied.

Elysia stared out of the huge glass panel window to her right. Sticking out in a ridgeline were Media Towers, leading from the tower where they sat all the way into the city's enormous commercial centre, surrounded by all the main amenities, the World Museum, the central ground transport station, and the city's central hospital. The day began to calm, with great clouds passing in front of a couple of suns. Huge hovercars and buses passed in and out of the towers, blasting out into the Continent. It was very rare that she ever found herself out this way, in this part of the city.

Arran sat to her left and was holding most of the conversation with Mrs. Carlisle.

"I must say," Mrs. Carlisle began, her voice nasal but not unfriendly, her finger wandering over the written document on the table in front of them. "We were a little unsure of your application to the show. Now, we get all sorts of bizarre applications to be part of the program. We have to make decisions on marketability, popularity, and likelihood of endurance. I was intrigued to find that you haven't, from what I understand, come from any kind of fighting background, any of you?"

"No, I wouldn't say so."

"And you're receiving no kind of sponsor, any formal training, or backing?"

"Only informal," Arran stated. "We have our own internal weapons supply, and the application was self-funded. We're not after a fighting contract."

"What's in the competition for you then?" Mrs. Carlisle stated.

"We need money, and fast. This seemed like a practical way to obtain it" Arran replied.

"There are easier ways to make money," Mrs. Carlisle said, her eyebrow raised.

"Depends on your skill set," Arran stated.

"I suppose," Mrs. Carlisle replied. "You don't have any backing fighters? We'd recommend on top of your four primary combatants, at least four more in case any of your team… die during the competition. It's in your best interests, Mr. Thompson."

"We don't need anyone else," Elysia stated, cutting into the conversation suddenly.

"Of course," Mrs. Carlisle replied. "It was merely a suggestion. You understand that use of projectile weapons will give your team a points disadvantage to begin with?"

"Yes, of course," Elysia responded. "We intend on using no projectile weapons.".

Mrs. Carlisle paused, mouthed "interesting" and then ticked a certain box on the paper in front of her.

"What's the verdict, then?" Elysia asked.

"This application has been accepted by the organizers of Elite Gladiator Championship, to compete in next week's tournament," Mrs. Carlisle stated firmly. Arran smiled gently.

"This is great news," he said, as Mrs. Carlisle handed him a document and a pen over the table.

"One of our representatives will meet you at the end of the week to give you further instructions. All we need now," Mrs. Carlisle stated, "is for you to consent to our terms and conditions."

Arran dragged the document over to their side of the table, and slowly unravelled it, revealing page after page, and his eyebrow raised slowly.

"I'm glad we came this early in the day," he stated, smiling.

***

"They got it," Gerion stated, catching up with Mal as they headed down the steps.

"Huh?" the big man asked, an eyebrow raised.

"Elysia and Arran," he clarified. "We're signed onto the show"

"That's good," Mal responded.

Mal stood on a concrete path, looking over a huge beach, with boats and ships passing in and out, some old, some new, and impossible to even tell. The beach was long, flat, and covered in yellow sand. It was relatively quiet, with the odd family or even lone child playing out amongst the shallow pools of water. The Northern Port, the city's main port for crossing to the larger New Tokyo. Next to them stood a row of large shops, larger each than anything they'd seen in the Undercity, with nice names too. The suns bore down up on them, and Mal covered his eyes with his huge muscular arm.

"I'd rather it was raining if I'm honest," the big man growled.

"They got it," Gerion said. "We've got it."

"They aren't going to be any use to us if we've got no weapons," Mal replied.

"Luckily," Gerion said, "It's just about time to open up."

and with that, the metal door nearest to them lifted open to reveal a small, muscled man with brown hair. As soon as the man caught sight of Gerion, he smiled.

"Gerion York!" he exclaimed, and the two men embraced. Mal looked slightly taken aback as Gerion turned and waved his hand at him.

"Louis Foreman," Gerion stated. "This is my oldest friend, Mallador Shan."

Louis stepped forward from behind his stall and shook Mal's hand enthusiastically.

"Mal, this is my friend Louis," Gerion stated.

"I've heard the stories about you," Louis beamed.

"You have?" Mal asked.

"Of course," Louis stated, "I owe Gerion my life."

At this, Gerion, turned, smiled, and shrugged at Mal.

"Couldn't this guy have put us up for a few days while we were in the city?" he asked.

"Low-key," Gerion mouthed. "Anyway, Louis's got a young family, I highly doubt he would have liked three big ugly men sleeping in his warehouse."

"What's brought you back here?" Louis asked.

"I'm glad you asked," Gerion stated, beaming from ear to ear, and Mal rolled his eyes. "I'm planning something back. Really big. I need a ship. And to get that ship, I need money. Money I no longer have. I'm entering myself and my team into Elite Gladiator Championship."

"That's very brave," Louis stated.

"It is," Gerion acknowledged. "We'd like to borrow some weapons if that's possible. And maybe use your training space."

"That would be… fine. Let's discuss it over some coffee; come inside," Louis stated, and laid out a little plaque on the shop's work desk which read "ring for service."

Gerion smiled at Mal. "Come on."

"Anyway, where are you holing up at the moment?" Louis asked.

"We're doing fine. Old family house in the commercial centre," Gerion responded, and Mal had to bite his tongue. "All the essential services really, android servants, the rest."

"That's lovely," Louis stated as they headed in, followed by Gerion, and followed in turn by Mal.

That night, Gerion and Mal had dinner with Louis and his family. The room was well-light, small, and warm. Bronze vintage-style lights hung in every corner, with Louis sitting at one head of the table, his wife Helena sat immediately to his left, and then his children Robbie, April and May sat on one side, with Gerion and Mal next to Helena. Mal smiled slowly, as he tucked into some steamed cauliflower.

"First decent food we've had in weeks," he whispered to Gerion.

Gerion leant back over to him and whispered, "Shut up."

Mal grumbled, and shuffled in his chair, accidentally kicking Robbie in the shin in the process. Mal's eyes briefly met the wide-eyed teenager's and mumbled an apology.

Gerion turned to the twin girls, April and May, and pulled a funny face at both of them, holding a pair of cauliflowers over his eyes. They both started giggling.

"So, Gerion," Louis stated. "Helena and I were talking in the kitchen earlier."

"Yes?" Gerion asked, his fork paused in front of his face.

"You said you were planning something big?" the weaponsmith asked.

"I am," Gerion stated. "I'm putting together a ship, and a crew."

"For a job?" Louis asked.

"Mm," Gerion said. "Well, to a degree. It's actually more… more of a quest if you will?"

"Like something from a fantasy?" Helena asked, a grin on her face.

"I'm going to look for aliens," Gerion stated, completely straight-faced. Helena and Louis both started laughing but then stopped when they realized that Gerion was not laughing at them.

"Seriously?" Helena asked.

"Seriously," Gerion stated "I've lost you, I know, but try to stay with me. I've spent the last few months looking at anomalies—that's jargon for weird things. Call it a sabbatical. Specifically, the ISA and every university on Proxima Centauri B's records for UPAS, or Unresolved Potential Alien Sightings."

"That's amazing!" Helena stated. "Do you think you'll find anything?"

"Yes," Gerion said.

"No," Mal said simultaneously, and Gerion elbowed the bigger man sharply under the table.

"Well, I say: good luck to you!" Louis exclaimed "You know, the moment that I met you, I always thought you were special."

"Ha-ha, thanks," Gerion chortled. "I think I've met a few people who'd disagree with you on that one."

"Well, none of them are here," Louis stated.

"Thank you," Gerion responded. "How's life been for you? When did you move to the Northern quarter of the city?"

"Oh, about six months ago. Trade has really been a lot better since we moved," Louis said. "Customers are much nicer, too—a lot of tourists."

"That's fantastic," Gerion smiled. The talk soon devolved into such riveting topics such as North Port footfall, the best Alexandrian cheeses, and the correct method of measuring the width of a curved scimitar sword. The children retired to bed before long, then Robbie, before only the four adults remained, and they talked for much longer, late in the night. Gerion and Mal slept over on the Foreman's' sofas and returned to their apartment in the city centre early in the morning, as the sun rose over the horizon.

FRIDAY

"Again," Mal ordered, and Gerion came at him, metal sword in hand. Mal raised his staff again, and stepped forward, swinging the staff up over his head, which Gerion stepped into and blocked using his own weapon. He then pushed the staff away and spun on the spot, trying to move around Mal. Fast as lightning, Mal grabbed Gerion by the shirt collar and threw him away, across the workshop floor. Arran stood at one corner of the workshop, leaning on one of the walls. A slight smile crept up the side of his mouth. Robbie Foreman stood in the other corner, and when he noticed Arran's smirk, he dropped it.

Gerion rolled along the floor, and then as he came to halt, sat up.

"You're quick," Mal stated. "But predictable. If you fight someone for more than a few minutes at a time, they're going to be able to tell exactly what you plan to do next."

"There's a way around that," Gerion stated, jumping up onto his feet in one single move.

"Defeat them in the first couple of minutes," Mal looked at Arran, and both men rolled their eyes.

"I don't think you seem to have grasped the seriousness of this competition. People train all year round, they might have physical enhancements, projectile weapons, armour. Which are all things that we don't have?

"But we are a team," Gerion said. "We all know each other and trust each other."

"That's not true," Mal said under his breath.

"Arran," Gerion said. "Let's give it a go."

Arran stood up from the corner of the wall, kicked his wooden staff up into his arms, and Gerion did the same. Arran stepped forward and started to circle around Gerion. Gerion did the same. Arran came in first, thrusting the far end of his staff towards Gerion. Gerion quickly stepped towards the other man with his sword, which Arran swiftly knocked away. Arran came in again, this time Gerion took a step back, smacking the wooden stuff up and stepping forward to try and jab. Arran was too fast, lifting his staff up and towards Gerion, who spun quickly and knocked the staff away. Then, with one arm, Gerion pushed Arran's staff arm away, and brought the sword in with his other arm, levelling the tip with Arran's chest.

"That'd be fight over, I reckon," he beamed, and he and Arran shook hands.

"Not bad," Mal said. "I suppose your two-minute logic worked that time. It's Elysia that I'm more concerned about. I've not seen her fight yet."

"She'll be fine," Gerion stated.

As if on cue, Louis Foreman entered the workshop, followed by Elysia.

"Elysia Lorch is here," he said. "Along with a stranger."

Coming in from behind Elysia was a small man in a dark suit, with a 'Media Towers' lanyard around his neck.

"Gerion," Elysia said, "this is Representative Green. He's here to give us the lowdown on Monday."

"And inspect your facilities," the man, Green, stated, and squinted around the room at the weapons around the room.

Gerion stared at the man, who then spoke again.

"I believe you're… self-funding?" he asked.

"That's correct," Gerion nodded.

"And it's just yourself, and the three people in this room?" Green asked.

"That's also correct," Gerion responded.

"Hmm," Green took a deep breath, rubbed his left eye, and then as his arm fell away and he looked at all of them.

"Very well. You will need to meet me at Entrance 3 to the Pine in Media Towers. 9 a.m. on Monday. You will be required to bring all your support staff and all of your weapons with you on the first day. You are placed in Heat B and will be expected to fight on the first day."

"Ok," Gerion stated.

Green smiled a fake smile, nodded, and gave Gerion a paper with a barcode on it. He then turned and started to leave.

Just as he got to the door, he turned and looked back at them.

"I'll be honest," he said, "that I'm surprised they let you on the show. They absolutely wouldn't let an unknown team in over regulars usually. But the corporation don't expect you to win. In fact, they expect you all to die. They do expect you to put on a good show, though, and that is what's get bums on seats."

Gerion swallowed.

"I see. Glad to see they have so much faith."

"Best of luck," Green stated, and then was out of the door and out of their lives.

MONDAY

Finally, the day had come, and Gerion and co jumped off the train, and walked up to the arena. Representative Green met them, and ushered them through a series of rooms, leading from the back entrance of the Pine, the first of the row of Media Towers. There was some press milling around, which Green waved to some large, rotund androids to shoot away. The group of five walked in silence, until they arrived at a small doorway.

"Careful," Green stated, "it's quite a low doorway," and he ducked on through, followed by Gerion, and then Arran and then Elysia. Mal, taking up the rear, had missed Green's warning, and smacked his forehead as he walked on through.

"Damn," he growled, as the centre of the door collided with the centre of his forehead. As he looked up, he found himself at the edge of a huge workshop, separated out into sections, with Media Towers staff, human and android moving in and out of various teams of contestants.

There were huge weapons, swords, stuff, guns, chainsaws, bows, crossbows, axes, maces, flails, and flamethrowers being tested and sparred with all over the shop.

"You're in Heat B," Green stated. "So you'll receive a call at around 11 a.m., if Heat A runs to time".

He then nodded at them and then disappeared off to begin talking to another new arrival.

"Well," Gerion said, clapping his hands together, and turning to the rest of them. "Looks like this is it. We did it!"

"Now for the hard part," Mal responded.

"I suppose," Gerion said.

"Well, well, well," came a voice, and Gerion turned to find the familiar face of Catan the Cold leering at him. The man's face was held open in a gigantic, animated smile, which he held so long that a drape of drool dropped out onto the ground below them.

"Gerion York," he said slowly.

"Catan the Cold," Gerion responded.

"You're brave doing this," Catan growled. "Braver than I had you pegged for, really."

"I'm full of surprises," Gerion retorted.

"I'm sure you are," Catan stated. "So am I."

A team of people seemed to appear next to him, all well-armoured, strong, and muscular. There were three strong men, and in the middle of them, a very muscular woman.

"Alice and the brothers," Catan stated. "My own team, entered in competition every month."

The one Gerion could only assume was Alice stepped forward and shook his hand.

"Alice," she stated. "Team leader. These are my brothers."

She removed her vice-like grip of Gerion's hand as quickly as she had applied it and pointed over his shoulder.

"Heat B," she said. "You're in with the Children of Arcadia. They're last month's runners up. Very formidable. Good luck."

Then she stood back in line with her brothers.

Catan looked between the four of them and smiled slowly.

"Best of luck," he growled, and then turned slowly away, and walked away on his canes, Alice and the brothers following closely behind.

Without saying a word, Gerion turned, and the others turned to watch him.

"Where do you think you are going?" Mal asked aggressively.

"I need to think," he responded, without stopping or turning to look at them.

***

Gerion sat alone in their dedicated area, watching the results from Heat A flash on and off the screen. Alice and The Brothers romped into first place, beating out The Flamers, a team of madmen with electrical flame weapons, all of whom died very quickly once Alice had destroyed their kit with EMPs. The other teams within the group, The Barbaric Ones and the Champions of New Jurong both failed to get much of a reaction out of the live audience, being brawlers more than refined fighters, both fairing badly against

Alice and The Brothers' well-practiced moves and deadly arsenal of weapons.

Maybe the competition won't be quite as stiff as everyone thinks, Gerion thought. Half of these teams fighting like this was the result of a drunken bet.

A firm hand was placed on his shoulder, which he instantly knew was Mal.

"It's time," Mal stated.

"Who are we fighting first?" Gerion asked, standing up from the plastic box he was sat on.

"A team called Believers in the New Light," Mal stated. "They've been entered by a religious fanatical cult. Seem to use hand-held or unarmed. No projectiles, from their profile."

"Ok, ok. Let's see," Gerion moved over to the middle of their section, where Arran and Elysia seemed deep in discussion.

"I think we're up," he said. "We need to suggest someone to go in for the first fight."

"You," the other three said together as one.

A thousand thoughts rushed through Gerion's head, but he eventually decided to respond with, "Ok. That's fine."

He leant over and grabbed his weapon, a metal cutlass, and a broad metal shield. He took a deep breath in through his nose, closed his eyes, breathed out through his mouth, and opened his eyes again.

"Best of luck," Arran said.

"Give 'em hell," Elysia added.

"Don't die," Mal finished.

***

Gerion stepped out into the arena, a huge silver circular room, hundreds of meters running with stalls running up and down the wooden walls of each side, some boxes hanging above the arena with VIP viewing stations, all manners of people sat in the crowds, watching, chanting. Made to resemble an ancient Roman Colosseum, Gerion noted, but they've tried too hard. It's too clean. Too detailed. Like a theme park.

Gerion slowly took a step forward.

A huge, booming voice came over the Tanoy, drowning out the sound of even the crowd.

"Gerion York from the Combitatus Questors," it stated, "against Brother Joseph from the Believers in the New Light."

Gerion stopped, and looked around for a moment, but couldn't see anything. Apart from him, the arena was empty. He drew swords and slowly started to move forward among the pillars within the arena, creeping forward foot-by-foot.

Suddenly a blur of brown and white appeared behind the pillar to Gerion's left. Gerion dived backwards, nearly taking himself off balance, but then gained composure and spun away.

He took in his adversary; Brother Joseph—a large man, broad-shouldered, and bald. The man attacked again. He was quick, Gerion realized.

Gerion raised his sword and parried the man's weapon, which he looked at fully for the first time. A mace—a metal stick with a spiked ball on the end. Classic weapon of the Byzantine Empire, Gerion noted.

Quick as lightning, the man recovered and swung again, Gerion this time pushing the weapon away with a swing of his sword. Gerion readied himself, countered, and made a quick thrust at Brother Joseph, who swiftly stepped out the way of the weapon, causing Gerion to move off balance, and he fell forward, landing in the sand. He scrambled quickly to his feet as Brother Joseph approached him, and as Brother Joseph leapt and him, Gerion swiftly side- stepped and pushed him away with both hands. His sword was lost on the other side of Brother Joseph.

Brother Joseph. caught his balance and swung again, this time Gerion stepped backwards out of the way, and the man's mace got caught in one of the stone pillars, which stood behind where Gerion had been only moments before. The metal mace sunk into the pillar, where it remained lodged. Brother Joseph looked wide-eyed, as he tried to pull the weapon from out of the pillar, and he turned to Gerion, who smiled, and brought down his sword straight into the man's left shoulder.

Brother Joseph screamed, making an audible sound for the first time.

"I'm not going to kill you," Gerion whispered and pulled the sword back out from the man's shoulder. "But I have beat you."

Brother Joseph fell backwards, letting go of the mace, and clasped at his left arm with his right, falling to the ground.

"Victory for Gerion York," stated the voice over the Tanoy. Gerion smiled slowly, and turned to look around the arena, heads no larger than pins jostling up and down in excitement and applause.

Quickly, doors lifted from either side of the arena, and before he knew it, Gerion was surrounded by staff, both people and androids, two of whom carried Brother Joseph away on a stretcher.

"He needs to get a hospital," Gerion said, "if he's to compete in the next round."

A large woman wearing a staff uniform turned to him.

"His team can treat his wounds," she stated. "But no one leaves the arena until the competition ends."

"That's barbaric," Gerion replied.

"That's the competition," she responded. "You should have read the small print."

***

Gerion sat alone again in the waiting area, with fighters coming and going, in and out. It was all a blur of noise to him. Mal stood in the other corner of the waiting area, talking avidly with Arran. Both men faced away from him.

The door to their area lifted up and Elysia stepped inside. Arran and Mal turned to face immediately, and slowly, Gerion looked up.

"We're through," Elysia stated, grabbing a towel to wipe blood off her sword, and turned to face Gerion. "That means the easy stuff is over. We're going up against the Children of Arcadia, Gerion, you know, the tough guys."

Gerion didn't respond to this.

"Get up," Mal growled, and picked Gerion up on his feet "Been a little while since you've had to kill people, isn't? What were you expecting? Draw of first blood? Those people would tap out at the first bruise. This isn't that kind of game."

Gerion placed both hands of Mal's chest, and shoved him away, the two men fell apart and Gerion fell backwards.

"You got me into this mess of a competition," Mal said. "So I'm going to get us, including you, out of it. Focus up. Elysia, what do you know?"

"The Children of Arcadia. Strong team. Originally acrobats, they hail from Centauri C, they use sharps, mainly swords and knives. No projectiles, at least from what I know. They're very aggressive and very fast."

"Ok," Mal said. "Projectiles, then. Keep our distance, try and get a clear shot. If they get us close, then we resort to projectiles. Remember, they're going to try and intimidate us—just remember, they're one person, we're each one person."

"Right," Arran responded.

"Got it," Elysia added.

The three of them turned to Gerion. Elysia raised her right eyebrow at him, in a way that made him respond, "Got it."

"Arran," Mal stated, "I want you to go in first."

Arran looked between the others "I can do that."

He leant over, and picked up his staff, and mid-sized sharp weapon. He attached a couple of detachable explosives to his feet, before nodding at Mal and Gerion.

"Best of luck," Elysia stated, and the two exchanged a look, before Arran turned away to get himself in the zone.

***

Gerion looked up again once Mal had returned from his fight. The big man was covered in bright red blood, covering his face, hands clothes, weapons, the lot. His face was covered in a permanent scowl.

"We're through," he growled "my fighter submitted, leading to a defeat."

"Just you left," Elysia stated, turning to look at Gerion. "All you have to do is not die."

Gerion placed his hands on his knees, took a deep breath in, and stood up.

"Brilliant," he stated and picked up his sword.

"Give 'em hell," Elysia exclaimed, as Gerion began to walk away from her and towards the exit to there are. As he passed Mal, the big man placed a firm hand on his shoulder.

"If you die in there, I'll kill you," he whispered.

Gerion pushed Mal's hand away. Arran stood by the door, as Gerion approached it. Arran simply smiled and nodded and patted Gerion on the shoulder.

Gerion ducked and stepped out through the door without turning to look at the other three.

Once he was out in the arena, Gerion once again felt a little more like himself. *Come on then,* he thought.

"Gerion York from the Combitatus Questors," came the familiar arena announcement voice, "against Alex Tremon from the Children of Arcadia."

The wind within the once-still arena had picked up, and he felt the slightest chills run down his neck. Slowly he moved forward, blaster in one hand and sword in the other.

"Gerion York," came a voice, deep, but not unnaturally so, and Gerion stopped. He had no idea from which direction it had come.

"I know who you are," the voice said again. "The last child of the York Crime Family. I thought you'd have changed your name."

Gerion said nothing in response, and began to move forward again, one foot at a time. Then, the voice came again.

"I suppose you thought you were being honourable, embarking on this quest."

Gerion continued to creep forward. The voice seemed to come from beside him, but also behind him. He felt the crunch of sand deep within his ear. In one swift motion, Gerion unsheathed his sword and held it in both hands, ready to attach.

"I've read all about you," the voice stated. "Your little… quest. You truly think you're something special, don't you?"

Gerion said nothing, turning on the spot to take in his immediate surroundings. Nothing.

"You can't truly believe you'd succeed? You'll lead your followers to their deaths," as the voice lingered on that last word, Gerion turned and swung, his sword clashing against another. As both swords fell away, Gerion had his chance to take in his attacker for the first time; another blonde man, medium build, with intense eyes, and a huge scar running across the middle of his face.

"You're ugly," Gerion stated, and the man snarled, swinging again, which this time Gerion blocked, and the two men swung again, Alex beginning to push Gerion backwards. Alex swung at Gerion and missed, giving Gerion to thump him hard in the face. Alex swung his sword up in retaliation, and caught the inside of Gerion's sword hand, causing him to yell out in pain, and let go of his sword, dropping it on the ground. In retaliation, Gerion slapped a mini jetpack onto Alex's shoulder, sending him flying backwards away from him.

As Alex picked himself back up, Gerion looked down at his bleeding hand, and muttered under his breath. Slowly, but surely, he picked his sword up with his non-dominant-hand and moved forward towards his foe.

Alex Tremon stood for a moment, before pulling a laser shield out in one hand, and a blaster in the other, and began to grin, revealing a mouth full of crooked and broken teeth.

Quickly, Gerion unloaded an explosive with his bleeding hand and lobbed it at Alex, the device falling short. Still, it was going to do what Gerion needed it to do.

The grenade went up, lifting the arena sand into the air, and for a moment, Alex lost all sight of Gerion. Suddenly a sword slammed into Alex's laser shield, corrupting it. Gerion grabbed Alex's laser blaster, and Alex growled, firing the blaster straight through Gerion's hand, creating a hole right through the middle of it.

Gerion screamed but kept hold of the gun with every ounce of motivation that he had left. He swung down towards the blaster, but Alex caught his hand, and the two men stood there, locked together.

"You'll never succeed in your quest," Alex stated. "You're just some spoilt rich-boy. You don't know what real hardship is, real sacrifice. I fought hard to be the leader of the Children of Arcadia."

Then he headbutted Gerion hard in the nose, and the two men fell apart. Alex ran at Gerion before he had chance to recover, and pushed him over, causing him to get flailing head over heal into the sand.

Gerion was down. Alex sent a hard kick right into his genitals, and then another. *Get up,* Gerion thought.

"Stay down, idiot," Alex stated. "Surrender, and I'll let you leave this place. Keep fighting, and it'll be over."

Gerion sighed, face down in the sand. *Get up,* he thought.

"I know of your quest," Alex continued, and he kicked Gerion again "Word travels fast in New Singapore."

How can he know? Gerion thought, closing his eyes and grimacing with the pain.

"You'll fail," Alex said. "Just like you always have."

Gerion opened his eyes again and saw a glint of reflection poking out of the sand at him. It was Alex's sword from earlier, with his bloodied hand, Gerion reached out, as lightning, grabbed the sword, and swung it hard into Alex's ankle. The other man screamed in pain.

Grimacing, Gerion drove the sword hard through the man's ankle, and Alex Tremon fell to the floor. Seizing the opportunity, Gerion leapt upon on top of him. Grabbing the gun from nearby, Gerion slammed the nozzle down onto the man's head, bruising him badly.

"You're wrong," Gerion growled, "and now you'll fail."

He turned the gun around, shooting Alex Tremon at point blank range, killing him.

Slowly, Gerion looked down at his bloodied hand, and fell off Alex's dead body. Slowly, as blood continued to appear from his hand, Gerion faded away.

Chapter Three

Gerion awoke to find Mallador Shan stood over him. His friend was surrounded by the familiar lights of the waiting area. Gerion slowly looked down at his left hand – he had a huge hole in the middle of his hand that had been sown shut, like a horrific doughnut. He squirmed and wriggled in the position where he lay, until he sat upright.

"How long have I been out?" Gerion asked, as he blinked himself into awareness.

"Three rounds," Mal replied. "We're in the final next."

"Bloody hell," Gerion responded, as he sat up. "What… what's the game plan?"

"We're up against Catan's team," Elysia said. "Alice and the brothers."

"They're a family team," Mal stated.

"As the name would suggest," Gerion responded.

"Yes," Mal nodded. "Which means they were raised together, trained together, possibly all their lives, if they're under the employment of Catan the Cold."

"Yes," Gerion stated, getting up slowly, staggering at first, but then coming to fully. "I doubt that this is their only means of income, fighting on TV."

"Regardless," Mal stated. "They're big, they're strong and they're mean."

"We're going to have to fight as a cohesive unit better than they can," Elysia added. "I've never seen these guys before."

"But we're all tired and injured—one of us pretty severely," Arran stated from the side of the area.

"And they don't seem to have a scratch on them," Elysia stated.

"Gerion," Mal said, in a way that made the man's head swing straight towards him. "We're going to need a plan."

"That's your department… you're a soldier."

"It was," Mal responded and turned to him. "But not anymore. We need to be working as a team here."

"Hmm," Gerion pondered and looked to see that everyone in the room was looking directly at him. Their eyes stared so sharply that they could have cut his skin, as no one blinked.

And then slowly, Gerion smiled.

"I've got a plan," he stated. "You just need have a little faith."

"FIVE MINUTES UNTIL OUR GRAND FINAL," boomed the Tanoy, as Arran and Elysia stood arming themselves, as Gerion walked past, over to where Mal stood, fixing wrist armour.

"You going to be, ok?" Mal asked, nodding at Gerion's bloodied hand. Between them, they'd bandaged up his hand relatively well, Elysia using a staple device to tie the wound back up together.

"Oh, yeah, that," Gerion said, as if he'd seen the injury for the first time. "It should be fine. I need to talk to you about something, and just you."

Mal's eyes darted over towards Arran and Elysia, who stood chatting amicably, comparing their weapons. Gerion then placed his good hand on Mal's waist and slowly pushed the bigger man back away from the other two, Mal allowing him too.

"The last guy I fought," Gerion stated, "Alex Tremon. He knew what our quest… the Combitatus Quest… he knew what it was. He told me. And there's no way he could possibly have known."

"Right…" Mal responded.

"Only the four people in this room know about that," Gerion followed up.

"You're saying that there's a potential spy? But why?"

"Half the criminals in this city hold some sort of grudge against me. Any one of them would want to sabotage some grand plan of mine."

"That makes sense," Mal agreed.

"You think it's …?" he asked, nodding in Elysia's direction.

"That would make sense," Gerion whispered in response, "but before this job, I'd not seen Arran in years, and he's been living in this city all that time, when I've been back and forth"

"I don't think it was Arran. He's the most straightlaced of this whole group," Mal stated.

"Exactly," Gerion responded, placing a hand on Mal's chest. "That'd be the perfect cover. That guy knows the legalities of this competition, the quest, and the political layout of this city. Turns up on time, always has the right currency."

"That's just who he is," Mal stated. "When was the last contact you had with Elysia before this job?"

"Some months ago," Gerion responded firmly.

"She works for Catan the Cold" Mal stated.

"I know," Gerion responded. "But she doesn't like him. She's said that to all of us. He doesn't know she's coming on the quest."

"TWO MINUTES UNTIL OUR GRAND FINAL," came the booming voice on the Tanoy

"We can't talk about this now," Mal whispered, "we have a championship to win."

"Damn right," Gerion responded "This'll have to wait for now."

***

Gerion was the first to step out into the arena, and turned slowly on his position, holding his good hand aloft to give the crowd a wave. He held his cutlass in his good hand, with a bag strapped Mal followed closely behind him, holding a laser cannon in one hand, and a large metal staff in the other. Arran joined swiftly on the other side of him, holding wooden stuff in both hands. Beyond him, Elysia formed rank, holding a blaster pistol in each hand, and holstering a pair of knives in her belt. From across the arena, they could see them: Alice and The Brothers. Their four opponents looked armed to the teeth.

Even from the way off, Gerion could see that Alice, the largest of them, was giving a leering smile. The brother furthest to their right let out a huge burst of fire from his firearm. A flamethrower.

"I'll take the flamethrower," Elysia stated. "I've got the distance weapons."

"I'll take that big ugly bugger," Mal growled, nodding at Alice.

"I'll take the other two brothers," Arran added, brandishing his double wooden staffs.

"Spread out," Gerion ordered, and the three of them began to move apart as they headed forward across the arena.

Gerion looked down at the tools he had pulled out of his backpack. This is going to have to be quick.

Elysia was the first to approach Alice and the brothers, using her jet pack to blast over towards them. The nearest brother to her, the one brandishing the flamethrower, fired a blast towards her, which she dodged effectively, cartwheeling in the air away from the blast. The first brother fired towards her again, and she blasted herself upwards, avoiding it again. The man growled and started to pursue her across the arena. Alice turned to the second and third brothers and nodded.

"Take the laser swords," she said. "I'll deal with this oaf."

She nodded at Mal, who was making his way across the arena towards her. Brandishing a huge white and blue electric cannon, she fired towards Mal, who ducked swiftly behind a nearby pillar. The huge blue swirl that the cannon fired sored past him and right past Gerion, smacking into the stone wall behind him, which then promptly exploded.

Gerion hid his head from debris and covered his ears. Slowly, he looked up to see the hole made by the blast.

"Damn," he whispered to himself, looking at the hole in the wall behind him. "Mal, we need to take that thing out."

"Working on it as fast as I can," Mal replied over the intercom.

"I'll try and draw her fire," Elysia replied and passed above where Mal was hiding firing off her dual laser pistols at Alice, who then turned to look at her. Alice nodded at the first brother, who then promptly took off into the air with his own jet boots, giving pursuit to Elysia.

Gerion gritted his teeth and went back to work.

The remaining two brothers squared up, large razer-covered laser swords in each hand were Arran appeared from behind a nearby pillar. He brought his staff quickly against the second brother's laser sword, which cut the wooden weapon in half, and the far end fell to the floor, away from him.

"Damn," Arran whispered to himself and quickly dived out of the way of the third brother's swing. Standing back up quickly, Arran backed up, keeping one eye on the brothers to each side of him. Swiftly, he threw the remaining part of his staff at the nearest brother, turned his back, and ran.

"Gerion!" he exclaimed. "I'm coming towards you."

"I need more time!" Gerion yelled back.

"Mal!" Elysia cut in. "I'm going to fly by again!"

As she exclaimed this, Alice fired her cannon again, blasting the pillar Mal was hiding behind, cracking it in half. As Elysia flew past, the falling pillar cracked the back of her jetpack, causing her to go flying into the ground. She lay there for a brief moment, before Mal grabbed her and pulled her behind the pillar.

"We need to make a move to Gerion, too," he said. "We can't play this game for much longer."

"Ok," Elysia nodded. "My pack is damaged; we're going to have to run for it."

Mal nodded, and the pair of them started to move quickly across the arena. Both Alice and the first brother started to move in towards them, as Elysia lay down covering fire with her dual pistols. Mal grabbed her and swiftly pulled her behind another pillar, narrowly avoiding a blast from Alice's electro cannon.

The two of them held each other close as the first brother closed in on them, blasting this pillar with the full strength of his flamethrower.

"Bloody hell," Mal growled, the heat getting ever-more intense as the man walked closer to the pillar.

Then they heard a thump as one of Alice's electro cannon balls smacked into the base of the pillar, but a crack through the width of it. Then the first brother let off his flamethrower again.

"I've got an idea," Elysia stated. "Do you trust me?"

"I've got not choice," Mal responded.

"In three, shove the pillar away from us," Elysia stated, and then took a deep breath and nodded up at Mal. "Three!"

They shouldered the pillar above the crack together, and it went toppling over towards the first brother. Mal and Elysia turned and ran as fast as their legs could carry them towards the side of the arena where Gerion was still working.

"Damn!" he exclaimed and quickly engaged his jet boots to take him out of the way of the falling pillar, which crashed down next to him. The first brother's jet-boots spiralled out of control and sent him flying into the sand. Alice walked over to him and gave him a hand up.

"Let's get these idiots," she stated, without the slightest modicum of emotion.

The second and third brothers pursued Arran, as he ducked and dodged between the arenas, blocks and cagers littered across the arena floor. He clipped his shoulder on a nearby block of concrete, and the second brother used this opening to swing for him. Arran just avoiding this, dropping his shoulder back, so the brother's laser sword hit the ground where there had been milliseconds before. Using the opening, Arran swung as hard as he could at the man, thumping him across the jaw. The second brother fell headfirst backwards into the third brother, and both men stumbled over each other.

Arran ran into them, and grabbed the third brother from behind, pulling him away. Like lightning, Arran pulled a small metal dagger from his belt and held it to the third brother's throat.

"Leave it!" Arran exclaimed firmly. "Walk away now, or I'll kill him."

"Kill him," the second brother growled, as he raised his laser sword towards Arran's face, "and I'll kill you."

"Is my life really worth your brother's?" Arran asked. "Walk away."

"Is your life really worth this competition?" The second brother retorted. "Let him go."

"I'll kill him," Arran said.

"I believe you," the second brother replied.

Calm as anything, the third brother brought his laser sword back and clipped the edge of Arran's ankle, causing him to yelp out in pain, and the two men fell apart, the brother pushing the metal dagger away into the sand.

"Game's up," the second brother stated, and Arran spun on the spot, turning and running towards Gerion, his ankle now seething in pain from the burn it'd gained from the laser sword. The two brothers quickly gave pursuit, but Arran didn't let up, outrunning them even with the burn. Gerion, once a dot in the distance, became larger and larger as Arran put every foot forward, trying to build distance from the two brothers. As Gerion's features became distinguishable, Arran was joined by Elysia and Mal, who were also running towards Gerion. Alice and the brothers were all giving chase, beginning to close the gap with them, weapons aloft. Gerion stood in front of them, perfectly still. A huge, mounted gun stood in front of him.

"Ok," Gerion stated. "3… 2… 1… Duck!".

The other three dropped to the floor, and the Gerion's weapon launched an enormous blast, which hit Alice and her brothers, stopping them in their tracks. Slowly, but surely, the weapons they held in their hands depowered, the laser swords stopped moving, and the lights in the flamethrower and electro cannon faded out.

"EMP weapon," Gerion smiled, clapping his hands together. "Thank you for standing together, I only had the one shot."

"Damn," Alice whispered, as she shook her Electro cannon. "He's killed it."

"You see," Gerion said, walking up to Mal, Elysia and Arran, and giving them each a hand up in turn. "That's my secret. I make everyone believe that I'm not a threat. Right up until the last moment."

With the last word, Elysia passed Gerion a small, round, metal device. Gerion swung his arm back and threw the device hard at their opponents. It bounced off Alice's head and landed in the middle of the four siblings. And then it engulfed them in an enormous grey circle, and they were gone, reduced to dust.

The four of them stood staring at the space where Alice and her brothers had been stood.

"Jesus Christ," Gerion said after some time. "That was an incineration grenade. I thought we were just going to blind them."

***

Elysia, Mal and Gerion stood in the entry bay to the Elite Gladiator Championship press room, people pushing past here and there to speak to someone somewhere, but the three of them had managed to find a cordoned off area to themselves. Coming down from a nearby flight of stairs to the offices above, Arran gave them a smile and wave.

"It's all here," he stated, smiling and bringing over the cash reward from the fight. "They kept their word."

"Fantastic," Mal said, and nodded towards Gerion. "We can get your hand mended, and we can get that ship?"

"Sounds good," Arran chipped in before anyone else could respond. "But there is something that still doesn't add up."

"Oh yeah?" Gerion asked.

"The thi-one Alice's brothers, he knew about the quest, the Combitatus Quest," Arran explained.

"But… only we know about that." Elysia asked.

"So did the Steve from the Children of Arcadia," Gerion stated grimly. His eyes moved between the other three.

"Both teams are funded by Catan the Cold," Elysia stated slowly. "He'd have any reason to sabotage you. I can think of a hundred."

"So… he'd want to know as much as he could about the quest?" Arran asked.

"But… how?" Elysia asked.

"Only the four of us know," Mal growled, looking between the other three.

"We've all come close to giving our lives for one another, and for the quest. It can't possibly be any of us," Gerion stated, nodding at Mal in order for him to calm down.

Arran took a deep breath.

"Is there anyone else that might know?" he asked.

Gerion's eyes met Mal's.

"Louis Foreman!" They exclaimed together.

"Louis is the spy?" Elysia exclaimed, an eyebrow raised. "The guy from the weapons shop?"

"No," Gerion stated firmly. "Someone must have gotten the information from him!"

"So, join me here outside the Media Towers where we're about to be joined by local legend, ex-conman Gerion York," a ginger-afro-owning reporter stated to the cameraman, and beyond him the crowd of Elite Championship fans.

"York is a one-time graduate off the University of New Singapore," the reporter continued, "and his team the Combitatus Questors, have romped home to a victory at this month's Elite Championship, the first ever self-funded team to have ever done so. We've got word that they're about to join us outside the main arena, and here we are—oof!"

Gerion sent the reporter flying, and as his cameraman turned to see what was happening, Mal smacked into him hard, knocking him to the ground. As they all ran past, the reporter stood back up and fumbled to pick up his microphone. A series of hovercars were passing slowly past the edge of the crowd, and Gerion grabbed the driver of the nearest one, pulling him from the vehicle, and throwing him to the ground. Mal jumped into the passenger seat, closely followed by the other two who leapt into the back seats.

Gerion leaned over and put the vehicle into turbo-boost mode, turning the car's propulsion engines down towards the ground, and took off, the hovercar blasting quickly up into the sky. The crowd watched as the vehicle got ever smaller, blasting off quickly away from the scene.

"Well," the reporter said, dusting himself down and smiling once again at the camera, "It would appear someone's keen to spend their winnings."

***

Gerion and Mal Prize opened the door to Louis Foreman's weaponsmith shop and found a horrendous scene. Catan the Cold stood in the middle of the warehouse, a gun to Louis' head. Catan's people stood all around, holding all of the Foreman family hostage.

"Let them go," Gerion said. "They've got nothing to do with any of my actions."

"Oh, Gerion," Catan smiled. "Do you really think I could let you go with everything you know? I've kept my distance, sure, but all this time, I've known where you are, what you're doing, who you talk to, where you have a poo, the whole shebang really."

"Let them go," Gerion repeated.

"Give me the money," Catan growled, and grabbed Louis Foreman by the neck, pushing the smaller man forward. He kept moving until Louis and Gerion were nearly face-to-face. Catan looked down at Gerion, and began to smile, revealing a huge row of yellow, mishappen teeth.

"Catan," Gerion said, "go to the dentist."

Gerion swiftly took a step sideways, revealing Mal with the EMP cannon strapped to his chest.

"That was cold," Mal stated, and fired an EMP at Catan, knocking the huge man flying. Everything that happened next took over seconds but felt like a lifetime to Gerion. Catan's guards, their weapons now knocked out by the EMP, downed their guns, and grabbed their shortrange weapons. Elysia turned to the nearest guard to her and punched them square in the nose. Arran pulled a blaster from his bag and moved quickly to start laying down fire, across the room, and Mal downed the EMP, and ran towards the remainder of the Foreman family, tackling a man to his ground.

Catan, although fazed from the weapon, recovered quickly, and stood back up on his enormous crutches, still brandishing his knife. Gerion leapt up onto him, brandishing his cutlass, but Catan grabbed him with both wrists, and held him aloft like a toy. He's too strong.

"You are irritating, little prick," Catan stated.

In a moment, Louis Foreman was by his side, and pulled a small device from Gerion's belt buckle, which fast as lightning, he slapped onto Catan's neck.

"What the f—" Catan muttered as the device light up, sending blue lightning to surge across his skin. The enormous man dropped to the floor, letting Gerion go, who landed on Louis, the two men falling to the floor in a heap. Slowly, they recovered as Catan began to writhe on the floor.

"Oh," Gerion said, wide-eyed. "So that was the electrocution grenade."

"Make," Catan whispered, trying to pull the device from his neck.

"It," he gurgled, and then he tried to grab one of his canes, again failing.

"Stop."

Gerion planted his foot down on Catan, and brandished his cutlass, holding it close to the big man's neck.

"You promised me a ship worth ten million New Singaporean dollars," Gerion said angrily. "And a crew to go with it."

"Mercy," Catan squealed, as Gerion pressed down harder with his weapon, beginning to cut his neck.

"Promise me!" Gerion shouted. The rest of the room had stopped fighting and stood watching the stand-off between their leaders.

"I promise!" Catan squealed. "Stand down! For god's sake, stand down."

Gerion smiled, and very slowly released the pressure of his cutlass. He stepped off the big man and turned to the room.

"You heard him," Gerion smiled. "Stand down."

"A ship worthy of The Combitatus Quest," Catan muttered, trying to catch his breath as he fumbled his way towards being fully stood up. "And a crew."

Gerion turned, looked Catan up and down, and then turned back to the others.

"Exactly," Gerion smiled. "And to know you've kept your word, there is now a small electronic grenade injected in your neck."

"Wh-what?" Catan asked. Gerion held up his cutlass and smiled.

"Oh," he said, "this is not a sword. Well, it is, but it's also—you guessed it—a giant syringe. Any funny business, and the micro-grenade in your neck explodes, are we clear?"

***

"So," Elsyia smiled, joining Gerion as he stood on the edge of the shipyard, nodding at the huge steel doors into the nearest hangar. "It's behind those doors?"

"So," Gerion replied, not turning to look at her, "this is it."

Arran joined on the other side of Gerion.

"The paperwork's complete; it's all in your name, Gerion," he stated, matter-of-factly.

"Let's get a look, then," growled a voice behind them, as Mal walked up to stand on the far side of Arran. The four of them stepped forward into the hangar arena, and the huge doors gently drifted open.

Then they saw it. The most beautiful ship Gerion had seen in all its space-faring years, silver dart of a ship, streamlines as imaginable, covered head to toe in a beautiful bronze-coloured finish. Four large propulsion engines sat perched in the back of the ship. Enormous viewing window sheets made up part of a small, smooth cockpit dome. Outside of the ship stood a team of mis-matched looking hangar crewmen, clearly tired and overworked.

"The New Excalibur," Gerion said.

"That's the most beautiful ship I've ever seen," Arran added.

"That's impressive," Elysia added.

"Bugger me," Mal stated.

A skinny man in a boiler suit approached. He had several teeth missing.

"Hullo," he stated, nodding at Elysia, "You must be… err… Gerion York. I'm the first deckhand, Tom."

"I'm Gerion," Gerion stated, offering to shake his hand. Tom just stared at his outstretched hand. A few other men and women that Gerion had assumed were hangar staff started to approach.

"I must admit, err, this is my first space voyage," the man stated.

"Mine, too," agreed a large woman agreed behind him. "I was a butcher by trade."

"I fixed service robots," stated a tall man, his boiler suit too small, only reaching just below his knees and elbows.

"But, err, thank you for asking for us" Tom said.

"You've never been spaceship deck staff before?" Arran asked.

"I've never been on a spaceship," Tom responded. "I've actually never left New Singapore, to be honest."

Gerion turned and looked at the other three, his left eyebrow raised.

"It would appear we've got a crew of homeless and unemployed people for our deep-space voyage," he said.

"I think I've worked it," Elysia stated "We asked for the best ship that that money could buy. And a crew to accompany it. But we didn't say the crew had to be any good. Just people Catan could find at short notice."

"The less experienced, the better, it would seem," Mal added.

Gerion sighed, turned around, and took in the mismatched group of people, old and young, all with a slight look of desperation in their eyes. They were going to have their work cut out between the four of them, he realized. He looked down at the cutlass with the trigger for the micro-grenade in Catan's neck. Then his hand hovered, and then very slowly, he moved it away again.

Then he took a deep breath and accepted it for what it was. *Oh Catan*, he thought, *you arsehole*.

THE END

...but Gerion York and his new crew
will return for future adventures.

Appendix: Timeline of the Persolus Race Universe

2029: The human race lands on Mars for the first time, by a group of Russian scientists.

2030 to 2034: International tensions stemming from a number of problems, including ownership of areas of land on the Earths moon and Mars. The rate of carbon emissions increases due to an avid technological race (Space Race 2), leading to climate change becoming even more noticeable across the globe.

2036: The first Edens are created by European scientists to mitigate the effects of climate change. They are a success, and other nations begin to develop their own, which begin to cool the planet, relieving some of the international tensions.

2040: The Integrated Space Agency is created, following the 45th UN Climate Change Conference. After the successful implementation of the Edens to mitigate the climate crisis, they are then used as prototype terraforming technology.

2048: Terraforming of the Moon begins, as the first planetary terraforming project.

2065: Terraforming of the Moon is completed after 17 years.

2079: Terraforming of Mars begins.

2085: *The Woman who climbed Olympus Mons* – three teams of professional climbers set out to be the first to summit the tallest mountain in the solar system.

2090: Terraforming of Mars is completed after 11 years.

2152: The first lightspeed engine is created. This allows the human race to start traveling beyond its own solar system.

2226: The Edens are set up for commercial use, becoming the property of the ISA, and sent throughout the galaxy for terraforming purposes.

2450: *The Man in the Mountain* – A young overambitious German scientist gambles with his own sanity and life while trying to create the world's first Time Machine.

2599/2600: Most of the Milky Way is explored, tens of planets have been effectively terraformed, and many more are in development. The ISA begins to divvy up into smaller sub factions, in order to conquer different sections of the galaxy. Around this time a Second Dark Age begins, as the human race spreads amongst the stars. Not much knowledge is gained, and societal systems do not advance much in this time.

2900: The human race begins to pull out of the Second Dark Age, as the ISA builds a central empire based on Earth, and working outward, introduces communication and transport systems between different planetary systems and factions.

2949: The first successful FTL speed engine is created, allowing the human race to travel thousands of times the speed of light. This allows them to travel out of the Milky Way galaxy pretty quickly.

2949: Omniscience – A deep space engineer and her crewmates get more than they bargained for when testing a prototype FTL engine.

3259: *Nomads of the Light* – A group of settlers have to adapt to survive or die when their long-haul spaceship crash lands on the wrong planet, throwing societal roles out of the window.

3462: The human race starts to reach the nearest edge of the Virgo Supercluster. The ISA begins to settle humans on planets millions of light-years from Earth, with all appropriate planets within the Milky Way almost all terraformed.

3575: *Timezones* – A rag tag group of raiders have a tough moral decision when they come across a long-lost space station in a very peculiar situation.

3600: The human race is now out amongst the stars, and "sub-species" of human have begun to develop through genetic experimentation.

3999: The ISA makes an announcement that the human race may be alone in the universe and that alien life might not exist.

5000: *The Great Gamble* – An ex-conman and his allies attempt to deft all the odds in a gladiator competition in order to win an impressive spaceship from his ex-employer.

Acknowledgements

Much like the first book, there has been a team of people who have helped make this book a reality, to whom I must say thank you very much.

This includes alpha readers B. S. Waymire, Josh Whittle and Andrew P. McGregor, and beta readers Michael Tye and Chloe M. Brown for the feedback with my early drafts. Cover artist Amasja Koolen for that awesome front cover. M. M. Dixon for your fantastic idea for Nomads of the Light and final copy-edit. Andrea Mattevi for formatting the cover just ahead of release.

Thank you to all the friends, acquaintances and strangers who have bought Volume One online and at comic-cons, and kept the project afloat and kept my hopes high.

And, lastly, to my mother and father for their support and encouragement throughout the project.

About the Authors

Alex O'Neill (Writer)

Alex was born on the coast of North Yorkshire, United Kingdom, where he spent his time daydreaming, often to the behest of his teachers. He now writes these daydreams down and sometimes gets paid for it. He loves all things science-fiction and fantasy, and occasionally dabbles in horror and detective fiction. His favourite authors include Sir Terry Pratchett, Susanna Clarke, Michael Crichton, Anthony Horowitz, Sir Arthur Conan Doyle, J.R.R. Tolkien and George R.R. Martin.

You can find out more about the Persolus Race project at www.thepersolusrace.com, and more about Alex at www.facebook.com/alexoneilltheauthor/

M.M. Dixon (Co-writer and editor)

M.M Dixon is a writer and editor living in northern Virginia, USA, with her husband, young son, and two dogs. She writes mostly sci-fi/fantasy, mostly short stories, which she sometimes posts at mmdixonauthor.com. She spends any extra time enjoying other peoples' creations, hoping they will stretch her brain in new ways. Favourite authors include James S.A. Corey, Lois McMaster Bujold, Robert Jordan, and Melissa McPhail.

The Persolus Race will return soon…

The Persolus Race
The Interstellar Investigators

By Alex O'Neill

In this new anthology, follow the cases of Specialist Detectives John Morris and Emily Machen on a race across the galaxy. The eccentric but experienced and practical Morris finds himself partnered with the intelligent and kind-hearted but timid Machen as they investigate the murders of the rich and important all over the galaxy. Little do they know this series of cases will uncover a vicious secret that could bring the human race to the very brink. Along the way, Morris and Machen will make valiant allies, face intimidating villains and reveal deep personal truths that could end their partnership for good.

Coming soon